Reborn

Reborn

By T.M. Parris

A Clarke and Fairchild Thriller

Copyright © 2020 T.M. Parris

All rights reserved.

ISBN-13: 9798536362716

This is a work of fiction. Names, characters, businesses, events and incidents are either the products of the author's imagination or treated as fictitious with no factual basis. Any resemblance to actual persons, living or dead, or actual events is either hypothetical and entirely imaginative, or coincidental.

The Clarke and Fairchild series of novels is written in British English

Chapter 1

The Hong Kong Famous Central Golden Palace Restaurant was having a slow night. Apart from Rose Clarke herself, sitting on her own in front of a warm orange juice, its only customers were a group of five or six men in suits at the back, and one man, a Westerner, also sitting on his own. It was early evening in one of Asia's most densely populated cities, where people routinely ate out three times a day and only returned to their undersized homes to sleep. Workers were emerging hungry, with money in their pockets. Central district, packed with banks, offices, shops, was handy for the metro, the harbour, the bars. Outside in the darkening street, people passed by in front of the window, living at the frenetic Hong Kong pace of life, but they didn't choose to step into the Palace. The Palace was operating at a different speed entirely.

Elaborate low-hung chandeliers, faded red-gold tasselled curtains and white linen tablecloths pock-marked with cigarette burns gave the place an aura of faded glory. Muffled murmurs of conversation and an occasional distant kitchen pan-clashing disturbed its stagnant quietness. Every now and then a single elderly waiter would carry a tray to the table at the back, leaving in his wake a smell of sweet-and-sour seafood and stir-fried pak choi. The only other member of staff was a thickset young guy, muscles bulging under a black polo shirt, seated at a small table next to an archway into a back room.

The man sitting on his own seemed content with a drink from the bar, something long and clear with ice. Rose contemplated him. His clothes were casual but expensive, a suit the colour of flint and a white open-necked shirt. His brown hair was wavy and slightly too long, perhaps to convey that he was something of a rebel or just too busy to bother with these things. He wasn't on his phone or on a device or reading a book or newspaper. He was just sitting and waiting. Rose had entered shortly after he did, and saw that having taken the Westerner's drink order, the waiter had said something to the stocky man at the back, who had briefly disappeared into the back room before resuming his post. Rose played at perusing the menu for a while. Then she got up and approached the Westerner, whose name she happened to know already was John Fairchild.

"Bit of a find, this place, isn't it?" She leaned on the empty chair to address him. He looked up at her with vaguely enquiring eyes. "Nice bit of peace and quiet. Mind if I join you?"

"I don't have much time, actually."

"Me neither. Just a bite between meetings. Business never stops here, does it? Are you British?" He watched her sit. "Sorry. Didn't introduce myself. I'm Linda Duffy." (Entrepreneur, hence the short skirt and blouse get-up. Specialised in premium food import and export worldwide including Asia and Africa. All fabricated.)

"John Fairchild," he said eventually. (Entrepreneur, owner of a global network of diverse businesses. Specialised in information, the extraction and sale of. All, according to his MI6 file, real).

"So, you must be based here, to know about a place like this, off the beaten track."

"No, I'm not, actually." He had a trace of a public school accent, which was about right. His file said he hadn't been back in the UK since graduating almost twenty years ago. Her presence at his table had changed the atmosphere in the restaurant. The man in the polo shirt at the back was staring at her. The waiter was washing glasses at the bar, but glanced over frequently.

"I don't like to seem rude," said Fairchild, "but my food's arriving in a moment and I really don't have time to—"

"You didn't order any food." He looked at her with steady eyes, the same colour as his suit. She lowered her voice. "You're not here to eat and neither am I. We both know what this place is. It's Darcy Tang's place. You've asked to see her, haven't you? You've got business with the Wong Kai."

The eyes moved off her for a moment while he took a leisurely sip of his drink. "I can assure you," he said, "that I did order some food. The scallops are very good here. I recommend them."

Rose hadn't stopped watching him. "You certainly sound British. What line of work are you in out here? It's always good to compare notes about how to – well – get things done. If you know what I mean." Fairchild's mouth curved into an amused smile. A promising development. Rose reached for the menu. "The scallops, you said? Maybe I'll give them a try."

His eyes shifted. Behind her, the man in the bulging polo shirt was coming over. He said something to Fairchild over the top of her head, in abrupt Cantonese. Fairchild said a word or two back, also in Cantonese. His aptitude for languages was well documented in his file. Polo Shirt's expression turned to distaste. He turned directly to Rose and fired off a round of staccato, while Fairchild sat back and took another sip of his drink.

"Sorry. I don't speak Cantonese," said Rose politely. He tried again and she mimed incomprehension. The waiter had given up glass-washing and stood watching. A couple of men from the other group were also looking their way.

Polo Shirt switched to English. "You. Leave." He pointed at the door.

"Why? I'm a customer, the same as him." She nodded at Fairchild, who was looking beyond her, bemused.

Another torrent of Cantonese, at higher volume now, accompanied the same gesture.

"Sorry," said Rose, keeping her tone even. "You haven't persuaded me. In fact, I'd like to order the scallops, please." She pointed at the menu. The waiter glanced nervously towards the back room. Polo Shirt lost patience. He stepped forward, gripped Rose's arm and yanked her up by the elbow.

"Hey! You can't do this! Let go of me!" Ignoring her shouts, he yanked her arm uncomfortably up her back and shoved her towards the door. She resisted, pushing back with her heels, but his bulky frame continued to propel her in front of him. As he reached for the door handle she looked back to see John Fairchild calmly watching the scene, drink in hand.

It had taken her a long time to get to have a conversation with John Fairchild, and she wasn't going to let her target simply click his fingers and have her removed from his presence. It was a desperate act, but the situation called for it. She felt Polo Shirt's grip on her arm weaken as he went to open the door. She kicked back, twisted and punched, then, as he yelped in pain, planted the heel of her shoe directly in his groin and followed up with her fist to bring him to the floor.

As he lay groaning, she turned to Fairchild, who was still holding his drink, and straightened her skirt. "What on earth did you say to him?" she asked. Before he had a chance to respond, the groaning had escalated into an animal scream and Polo Shirt had sat up, cheeks red with rage and a gun gripped in both hands. He aimed it at her. She ducked sideways and a bullet tore past her, puncturing the cheap wooden panelling of the bar. She dived behind a table and pushed it over in front of her for cover, launching a cascade of shattering crockery. The table vibrated as a bullet crunched straight into the top of it, splitting the wood. Polo Shirt shouted in frustration. A third bullet shattered glass above their heads. A chandelier slumped and hung lopsided, fastened to the ceiling by a single wire. Fairchild said something in Cantonese in a low, calm voice. This was followed by a short silence. Rose risked peering around the side of the table. The nephew was sitting aiming the gun at the table, breathing heavily, beads of sweat on his forehead. Fairchild was standing, hands out in a gesture of pacification. He said something else. This was followed by a silence, longer this time.

Something moved in front of her. A splintering crash filled the room as the chandelier made contact with the floor and beads of glass shot out in all directions. Rose ducked back. Polo Shirt gave a shout and fired again, burying two bullets in the tabletop.

She didn't see what happened next. Polo Shirt cried out incoherently. Fairchild started speaking again, more authoritatively this time. She risked another look. Fairchild was standing over Polo Shirt, holding the gun. The Chinese guy shouted angrily. Fairchild took several steps back. Polo Shirt got to his feet. Fairchild raised the gun and pointed it at him, still talking. But whatever he was saying, Polo Shirt wasn't listening. Eyes on the gun, he dived straight at him. The gun went off. Polo Shirt screamed and fell to his knees, clutching his arm.

Fairchild, still pointing the gun, wasn't looking at Polo Shirt any more. He was looking behind Rose where a short, neatly turned-out woman in a wool suit and a pearl necklace stood in the archway absorbing the scene with an expression of utter shock.

Polo Shirt carried on screaming. Voices started up from the men at the other table, a low muttering quickly escalating into indignation. Chairs were pushed back. Fairchild put the gun on the table. Two strides and he was out of the door. Rose followed him before anyone had a chance to stop her. By the time she got onto the street he was halfway down it. She broke into a run to catch him up. When she did, he was walking so fast she had to jog to keep up with him.

"What happened in there?" she said. "One minute the guy had his arm on me, the next—"

"What happened in there," he said, his lips thin, "is that because of you, I shot Darcy Tang's nephew in front of Darcy Tang herself." He stepped into the road. Rose was about to do the same but a scooter applied the horn and swerved, missing her by a millisecond. On the other side she had to run to catch up with him again.

"That was Darcy Tang's nephew? I didn't realise."

"Next time, do your research properly before you decide who to pick a fight with."

"I didn't pick a fight. He was trying to throw me out after whatever it was you said to him. What did you say, by the way?"

Instead of replying, Fairchild pulled a mobile phone out of his pocket and speed-dialled a number. His pace didn't slow. He was heading downhill through Central's grid of streets, towards the harbour. Passers-by stared at them and stepped off the narrow pavements to get out of their way. Even after dark it was hot enough for Rose to be sweating all over.

"I need a pick-up." Fairchild was speaking on the phone. "Now. Yes, now!" He listened briefly. "OK." He hung up and broke into a run. In low-heeled sandals, Rose's feet were rubbing badly, but she wasn't going to lose John Fairchild now. She'd been on his tail for months. A police car siren whooped.

"So they call the police even when a gangster gets shot," she called to him as they both gathered pace.

"If it's the Wong Kai. Don't you know how influential they are?"

"You shot him in the arm. He's not going to die from it."

"Oh, well, that's okay then. I'm sure Aunty Darcy will be fine about it."

"Well, you didn't need to intervene like that anyway. I can look after myself."

He slowed down for a second to look round at her. "You're joking. I shot him because he was going for me. Because of you!"

"He must have thought we were together."

"Oh, I told him we weren't, believe me."

"Well, whatever you said, it obviously didn't work."

They reached the harbourside expressway. Ignoring pedestrian walkways, Fairchild jumped straight in, dodging four lanes of fast-moving traffic. He was at the central reservation by the time Rose even stepped into the road. A blaring truck, lights blazing, bore down on her. She leaped back, feeling hot air rush up from its wheels. She got her breath back and weaved through to the other side, a symphony of horns accompanying her. Fairchild was a distant figure racing eastwards alongside the hoardings lining the expressway. She accelerated. Almost out of sight, he slowed and disappeared through a gap. She counted eight seconds before she reached the same gap.

Through the hoardings, her eyes took a moment to adjust. Dark mounds of rubble towered above and monstrous plant loomed silently on either side, like giant creatures frozen in time. The building site stretched into the distance, beyond which lay the harbour, and above that Kowloon, a mass of shimmering glass high-rises. Another immense land reclamation project.

Ahead, Fairchild was a dark shadow tracking over the uneven ground. She set off after him as he moved quickly seawards along a dirt road flanked by vast piles of rocks, debris and machinery. It was hardly the best surface for her current footwear. She sank sideways into a pothole and her ankle twisted, making her stagger. She had to slow down and pay more attention to the ground in front of her. But she was losing him.

The rumbling of traffic receded and she could hear her own harsh breathing. Dust hung in the air and coated her skin. She smelled oil and diesel. She glanced behind: nobody. A police siren sounded again, fainter. She could see better now in the ambient light from the city, and upped her pace. By a stack of huge horizontal metal pilings, the road bent sharply round towards the water. Turning the corner she saw Fairchild, standing, on the phone listening. He had his back to her and turned as she approached.

"Okay," he said into the phone and hung up. Behind him lay jumbled piles of metal sheeting; the end of the road. She slowed as she approached him. "If you've got an exit," she said, "I'd be terribly grateful if I could tag along."

He appraised her for a moment. "Why would I help you? You're the reason I'm having to run in the first place."

"I'm in as much trouble as you are. And I can help."

He turned away and set off, dodging between rubble and strewn metal ware. Rose followed. The police sirens, she realised, were not getting fainter. They were getting louder. Someone on the expressway must have called them in. She tried again.

"If we're in the same predicament we should stick together. I've got a few contacts, places we can lie low."

"Absolutely not!" called Fairchild from some way in front.

"Why not?"

He stopped suddenly and turned back to her. "You're not a businesswoman. You're a spook. I can tell a mile off. Whatever you want with the Wong Kai, it's not my concern."

She improvised. "I don't want anything with the Wong Kai. My business is with you."

He stared at her. "And what do you want with me?"

"Let me come with you and I'll tell you."

His hesitation was real, though slight, before he turned and started running again. At the water's edge a flat-decked transporter ship was moored, half loaded with rocks. Fairchild hauled himself up on its thick mooring rope and climbed onto the deck. His footsteps rang out on the iron as he ran across the deck and jumped down onto another ship moored to it on the other side. Rose heard two sounds at the same time, one of them tyres spurting on dry dirt, a police car on site and approaching. The other was a distant moaning coming over the water from Wan Chai. A beacon of light from out at sea directed itself at her, growing and illuminating the swell in front of it while the moaning intensified. Some kind of motor launch was coming straight at them.

She ran to the water's edge and grasped the same rope Fairchild had used. Her shoes slid against the slimy hemp. The whine of the launch dropped abruptly and its tenor changed as the boat swung round, nearing them. Its wash slammed against the moored boats. The ship rocked and Rose lost her foothold, clinging to the rope with just her damp hands. She made a new effort to grip with her feet and gained enough traction to pull herself up, getting a higher handhold on the rope. It was enough to pull herself over the bow and ease her body onto the metal deck.

The sky filled with flashing lights. Tyres skidded on grit. Shouting and footsteps followed as the police arrived. The rope yanked in her hand: they were already climbing on board. She scrambled to her feet, crossed the deck and jumped down onto the deck of the other ship, steadying herself as the ships moved and ground together. On the other side she looked down. The speed boat had drawn alongside, a long sleek affair driven by a chunky Westerner in sunglasses and patterned shirt. Fairchild was already aboard, leaning forward and saying something to the driver.

"Hey!" she shouted down. They both looked up. "Sure there's no chance of a lift?" She could read the body language below her. The driver looked across at Fairchild, who said something short back to him. The driver yanked the gear, the engine roared into life and the boat reared to take off. Boots pounded the metal deck of the first ship. As the launch gathered speed, Rose took a single backward glance then steadied herself, filled her lungs, and dived into the water.

Chapter 2

Alastair opened the door of his flat. Rose stood and watched him take in her soggy dress, her wild hair and her bare feet.

"So how did it go, then?" he asked, stepping aside to let her in.

"Very funny. Got any of that pinot left?" Rose made a trail of wet footsteps over Alastair's parquet flooring, and perched on the edge of an armchair.

"I didn't realise you were planning a swim," Alastair called from the kitchen where he was pouring her wine, bless him.

"I wasn't. Things went slightly wrong."

"Really?" No trace of irony, just exactly the right amount of sympathy and interest.

"You were right that he was staking out that Famous Golden Palace place. That's what he was doing in Central district yesterday. So today he went in there and I followed him in. Started chatting, was all ready with my Linda Duffy cover story. Ambitious entrepreneur, wanting to use the Wong Kai to cut some corners getting into the Chinese market. But then—"

"But then?" Alastair handed her a generously filled glass and a towel, and sat down in the armchair opposite.

"Well, to cut a long story short, there was a bit of unpleasantness."

"Unpleasantness?"

Rose dried herself down and gave him an account of the events leading up to her jumping off the boat.

"That's *harbour* water?" Alastair took a horrified look at his flooring.

"Sorry. Police everywhere. I didn't really want to get arrested."

"I guess."

"I had to stay out of sight until they'd gone. Mostly submerged."

He was still looking at the wet floor. Alastair had always been house-proud. Even in their fleapit university shared house, his room had always been uncluttered and genuinely clean, with an impressive array of artwork on the walls, even if they were only prints. Dear Alastair. From their student days, it was Alastair that Rose had gone to if she needed to rant about an essay, or politics, or a boy. He was always the same; gentle and supportive, whatever the mess, whatever the time or day, ready with Earl Grey tea, cinnamon toast and a sympathetic ear. Rose had often wondered if he had a soft spot for her, but if he did, he never acted on it. Eventually she came to the conclusion that he was just one of life's great listeners and that he made everyone feel special in some way or another. With his slight build and his oh-so-young-looking face and disarming smile, his agents loved him and would take all kinds of risks for him.

"So, after months of being on his tail, I speak to him for five minutes, chase him down the road and lose him. After pissing him off, of course. Oh, and my cover is blown already."

"Really?"

"Really. He knows I'm a spook. Was a spook."

"The defensive moves were a bit of a giveaway, maybe."

"Yeah, well, it was that or lose him altogether. Which is what happened in the end anyway. I'm back to square one, Alastair." She took a large slug of wine.

Alastair frowned. "And what exactly is it that you're trying to achieve? From what little you've told me so far, you've signed up to some kind of single-handed global manhunt. I mean, of course you'll come closer to pulling it off than anyone else."

She smiled at his compliment. In training she had excelled. She was meant for great things, she was told at the time. Her performance on her first stint, in North Africa, had given her career some real kudos. Unfortunately, it all derailed on her last posting to Croatia. "I'm really not supposed to be telling you any of this, Alastair. That was one of the conditions. I'm out, after the Zagreb thing. I'm working strictly alone, only talking to Walter. He was pretty insistent on that."

"Yes, well," said Alastair. "You know you can trust me to keep my mouth shut. How many years have we known each other?"

"I just don't want to land you in trouble," she said.

"Don't worry about it. So who is Walter, anyway?"

"Well, he didn't really explain his role. But he's been in the Service since the seventies. Which puts him in the same vintage as Marcus Salisbury, for example."

"Our new boss? That's interesting. But this Walter guy is clearly not at his level."

"Or anything close, by the sound of it. Maybe he's fallen out of favour but knows too much to be got rid of. There's a few of those around."

"And how exactly did all this come about? How soon was it after…?"

"After I got the boot? Very soon. A few days."

"Hmmm." He sat back in his armchair.

"I got back to London from Zagreb. Lied to my family and everyone else about why I was back. Kicked around at home for a few days. Walter showed up at the front door. Came over as a bit antiquated at first, but he knew his stuff. We can salvage the situation, he said. You're uniquely placed to help out with a little job. Not really on the books, as such. It could get you back in. Well, I wasn't going to say no. Never get kicked out, Alastair. Normality is grim. It took me less than a week to realise that."

Alastair gave a regretful smile. He felt it too, she knew, the addictive nature of their work, how the secrecy, the artifice and the risks involved opened a door to a different world, from whose viewpoint life outside became shallow and meaningless. "So, this little job. What is it, exactly?" he asked.

"Approach Fairchild and get him face to face with Walter somehow. Walter has some questions to ask him."

"About what?"

Rose looked at him steadily for a few moments. "Well, all right then. Because I trust you and we go back a long way. There's an internal investigation going on, apparently. Someone in the service is selling secrets, details of operations and identities."

Alastair was looking sceptical. "And they know this how?"

"Operations going wrong."

"Operations go wrong anyway. It's easy to blame leaks. That's happened before. Then everyone starts chasing their tails, when in fact it was just incompetence or bad luck."

"Three ops were compromised, I'm told. Three in a row. And Fairchild wasn't far from any of them. Selling secrets is his line. His other business interests are generally for show, or for income. He's an information mercenary. He acquires and sells information for money."

"To whom?"

"Anyone who will pay."

"Lovely. They're sure it's him?"

"Some people are. Walter's job is to find out if he's involved and, if so, who his contacts are within MI6. My job is to get Fairchild to Walter, so that Walter can extract this information."

"Extract the information how?"

"That's down to Walter. My job is to get them in a room together somehow. Walter takes it from there. The problem is that Fairchild moves around the world constantly and seems to speak dozens of languages. He knows people in every corner of the globe and can just disappear when he wants. The local operations can't keep up with him. I can move around quickly, but my problem is that I end up in places where I've never worked before and don't speak the language. Walter can sometimes help by liaising with the local station, but it seems to depend where. Actually, I think it depends on whether he can ask someone he trusts for a favour without having to explain what it's for."

"That sounds tricky."

"Yes. This is happening in parallel with the internal investigation into the leaks. I'm outside of the organisation, having been sacked, so I'm ideally placed to take this on as a freelance venture, if you will. But I've been expressly forbidden to talk about it to anyone in the service."

"It won't go any further. You know that."

"I trust you. But you do understand why I'm nervous."

"Honestly, though, it does sound like you're being asked to do the impossible."

"From Walter's point of view he doesn't have a lot of other options. He's passing me stuff when he can. But it's so limited. To give you an example, Alastair, Walter messages me to say Fairchild landed in Oslo twenty-four hours earlier. I jump on a flight and spend two days in Norway trying to track him down. Then Walter messages me again to say Fairchild's already left and is now in South Africa. So I get a flight to Johannesburg. I'm there for a month trying to find him. No trace. The next thing he's flying here from Zurich."

"That's ridiculous. They need to find a way of drawing him in instead of someone following him around like that."

"He's not easily drawn, apparently. Anyway, you can see why I looked you up when I got here. I wasn't sure if I should, mind."

"Well, I'm glad you did. Otherwise you'd never have known where he was staying, or tailed him to Central district."

"And I'd never have been able to spend five minutes trying to persuade him I'm a businesswoman just like him, before screwing up the whole thing and losing him again."

"Did Walter set up your cover?"

"No, Alastair, he couldn't even do that. It would have involved too many people internally, he said. That's why it's so flimsy. I've got a website, some fake business cards, that's about it. So it wasn't the end of the world when I blew my cover in the restaurant. If Fairchild's as good as Walter says he is and did any research at all, he'd realise Linda Duffy didn't exist within a few minutes. Linda Duffy was just for a first approach. Given Fairchild's familiarity with clandestine services, it was inevitable he'd see through it."

"You think Fairchild was always going to find out you're MI6?"

"Hopefully not every fine detail, but in general terms, yes. Which is why it was critical that I'm a former officer, not a current one. Limits the risk, you see. To the service."

"And how are they going to handle that when you've achieved your mission and they give you your job back?"

"I've been assured that's not a problem."

"Really?"

"Really. I know, Alastair. But this is the only chance I'm going to get to be back in, isn't it? However unlikely it sounds, I've got to give it a try. I'd never forgive myself otherwise. I'm just not ready for an ordinary life. This is what I want to do. And I'm good at it. I know I am. Zagreb was just horribly unlucky, that's all."

Alastair was refilling her glass. "Yeah, I heard something about what happened there. Not the detail though."

Rose sighed. "My agent was the wife of a far right terrorist. One evening she calls me out of the blue. Shows up knocked about something terrible. This charmer of a guy had started suspecting her. I give her some money and try to help her get away. Which she does. He goes underground as well and that's the end of that. Next thing that happens is Sandhill."

She drank some wine and watched Alastair's eyes widen. The Sandhill mosque attack was only a few months ago. Homemade improvised devices smuggled into three different mosques all went off at the same time. Ten people were killed. Ten British citizens.

"That was them?"

"Yep. That was them. And we should have known about it."

"How? Once he suspected, that was it. You can't keep people in place for ever."

"It was the next day, Alastair. The morning after we met. One more day and we'd have known. Anyway, they blamed me."

"You looked after your agent. Not everyone would have done."

Rose swilled her glass, picturing the look of dread she'd so often seen in Tihana's face the years they'd known each other. He's not a nice man, Tihana sometimes said. She was never more specific. Rose's job was to engender trust. Sometimes people opened up about all kinds of things, took your interest in them as personal. But of course it was all self-interest. Rose didn't want Tihana to leave her husband. Tihana was saving lives. Rose wanted her in place. Tihana never said anything, Rose had told herself a thousand times. But some questions Rose had never asked, and there was a reason for that. When finally it was over and Rose gave her cash to get away, it was guilt money; that was the truth. But that wasn't something she'd ever articulated.

"They had to make an example of someone," she said. "I was the obvious person. They put me on a plane home."

"And then this Walter shows up."

"Yes. This Walter shows up. And since then I've travelled halfway round the world chasing some charmer of a guy. Then the minute I finally get to move in on him, it all goes pear-shaped and he legs it."

"What did you say about the guy who was driving the boat?" Alastair was staring at his glass thoughtfully.

"Chunky guy. White. Dark hair, gelled back. Colourful shirt. He was wearing sunglasses."

"Sunglasses? At night?"

"Yep."

"Hmmm. Well, it's a long shot, but it sounds a bit like Zack."

"And Zack is?"

"CIA or military intelligence, he seems to waver between the two. It's worth checking that out. You could go down to Lan Kwai Fong tonight, even, just to take a look at him. You'd recognise him?"

"Sure. But when I last saw him he was zooming off into the South China Sea in a motor boat."

"Hong Kong's small. He could have dropped Fairchild off on the mainland or one of the islands and come back. He's probably standing in Lan Kwai Fong with a cocktail in his hand right now."

"What makes you so sure he's in Lan Kwai Fong?"

Alastair shrugged. "It's a Friday."

"He's that predictable?"

"Zack has a particular approach to his role, whatever that might be exactly. It involves a lot of drinking, a lot of networking with expats, and a lot of women."

"Oh, great. A throwback to the good old days. So much for not doing things like that any more."

"It doesn't seem to do him any harm. You can walk there from here."

"Yes, well, I think I need to slip into something else first. Which means going back to my hotel, unless you've got anything I could borrow?"

They both smiled. "If it's him, you can say hi from me, if it'll help."

Rose shook her head. "No, Alastair. I'm not bringing you into this. I shouldn't even be here. Linda Duffy needs to do this on her own." She stood up, suddenly full of resolve. "Thanks for the wine. And everything. As ever."

They air kissed. "Careful now," said Alastair. "No more run-ins with armed gangsters. Or police."

"I'll be fine," said Rose, much more cheerfully than she felt.

Her salt-encrusted clothes rubbed uncomfortably on the walk back to her hotel. Talking to Alastair had made her realise how much she wanted back in. Find Fairchild, Walter had said. Get Fairchild in a room with me, and I can get you your job back. She wasn't even sure she believed him, but it was the only hope she had. However far-fetched, if she still had a chance of catching up with him, she'd take it.

Chapter 3

It is dangerous to talk to strangers. Especially foreigners. I have been in trouble for that before. But this stranger I have seen is a monk, just like us, except that he is a pilgrim who has travelled to our monastery from far away. I feel great pride seeing so many people come to Tibet and pass through my home. The world is big, but people tread a finite number of paths. Even Shigatse, our small town so high in the mountains, attracts people from all over the world.

He is a tall man, this monk I am watching. He bends towards the shrine, his eyes on the gold buddhas but seeing other things, I think, things from long ago. His face is motionless and the dark crowds move past him in their clockwise shuffle round the chapel. His robe is so very long, but it is light grey, not burgundy like ours. His face is worn and his nose is large and hooked. His cheekbones are high and his eyes sunken. He is still and serious. I can feel that he has seen terrible things in his life.

He doesn't see me. I am sitting on the dusty floor with my back against the wall between the shrines. It is a good place to watch the pilgrims as they file past. Even if the Rinpoche comes into the chapel, he will not see me down here behind the legs of all the pilgrims. He is responsible for the whole monastery, but he is particularly harsh on me. I sometimes think he forgets that I am an adult now. I am no longer six years old.

As if reading my thoughts, the Rinpoche enters. He is in his full abbot's regalia and strides through the centre of the hall with two of the senior lamas on either side of him. I slink down and watch the top of his headdress bobbing past towards the doorway over the heads of the visitors. I am glad he has passed by. He would not approve of what I am doing.

I watch the tall monk reach into his leather satchel and pull out a few small coins. I love coins. But not because of their value. Coins are pieces of the world, tiny souvenirs marked with their provenance. I love their weight and brightness as they rain down softly onto the thick velvet of the shrines. The Rinpoche used to pick up a handful and I would have to tell him where each was from. He would explain to me the symbols and what they mean. I became familiar with many countries this way and he told me about them and what has happened there. He taught me a few words of some of the languages. At first I thought it was all a game, but the time must have come when I realised it had a purpose. How did the Rinpoche have such knowledge? The education of a Tibetan monk rarely strays beyond the intricacies of Buddhist philosophy. He must have learned in secret, through hidden books and furtive whispers. Whispered histories, in Tibet, are the only true kind.

The monk scatters his coins over the shrine. In the yellow lamplight I see that two fingers are missing from his left hand. Inside me I feel a vibration, as if a bell is slowly ringing. What am I reminded of? Is it something in my own past, or in my previous pasts? This happens more and more now, and sometimes I cannot tell the two apart.

He shuffles on, his head and shoulders rising above the crowd around him. Most people here are my fellow countrymen, dark-eyed and dark-clothed, with bitter-smelling yak butter in plastic bags in their hands ready to be scooped out and spooned into the candle vats. They look worn and numbed by all the gold and brilliance. I know that look. Part of it is exhaustion, these people who live off the land that is so dry and hard and demands so much. Many of them have walked here from home, some stopping to kneel and prostrate themselves at every step. But also it is pure acceptance of what they are presented with. They have unquestioning minds. Even before the Rinpoche told me, I think I always knew that I was different.

The tall monk has stopped at the next shrine, staring again as if trying to absorb as much meaning as possible. I stand up and reach out for his coins. I watched carefully when he threw them to see where they landed. The coin I pick up has a double-headed eagle on it. The script is Cyrillic. My heart leaps. The monk is carrying Russian coins. The monk must surely be from Russia. It is what I was hoping for.

I cross the chapel and wait by the door, hovering in a shadowy corner. Never do anything to make people notice you, the Rinpoche says to me. But I know the Russian is important. I whisper a mantra to calm myself, and try to empty my mind. Eventually the Russian completes the circuit of the shrines and passes me, pacing slowly, looking down at the ground. He is a man who has a lot to think about.

At the doorway he stands at the top of the steps, dazed in the brilliant sunlight. The courtyard in front of him is packed with people and awash with colour. I feel a sudden burst of joy at seeing my burgundy brothers in the crowd with their shaved heads and smiling faces, and the red painted columns and the decorated awnings in which we here at Tashilunpo monastery take such pride. But over their heads I see the army checkpoint at the main gate, Chinese soldiers facing in and out. Watching us, always watching.

The Russian does not join the crowd. He holds himself like he is solitary, self-contained, private. At the bottom of the steps he takes a narrow passageway away from the courtyard. I follow as he finds a path, turning left and right, not seeming to have a plan other than to be here. I look around myself often. The Chinese are adept at persuading people to be their eyes and ears, even here in the heart of the monastery. This should be a holy place but we have to lower our thoughts and mistrust each other just to survive.

He stops suddenly by the open door leading into the walled garden. I think he is called by the beauty of the trees loaded with pale papery green leaves, as I have been so many times. He stoops to peer in through the stone doorway. And as he steps inside, silhouetted against the sun, I hear a humming and have an overwhelming feeling of rightness, that this is what should happen, here and now. I step forward to follow him.

Something makes me look round. At the end of the passageway I see a flash of crimson. Then it is gone. I stop. I should turn around now. I should be a good little monk like they want us to be. I should do what they expect, the Rinpoche says, for my own protection. But I cannot do what the Rinpoche says for my whole life. I listen but can hear nothing. I pass through the doorway.

The Russian is resting his maimed hand on the rough trunk of a tree and staring up into its canopy. I see peace on his face. Often my brothers are in this garden to practise debating, but now it is empty except for myself and the stranger. The thin sunlight warms my head and I hear no sound. It is a perfect moment. I was right to do this, to have faith, to follow my instincts. I will be safe.

I take a step forward. The monk looks round, fear on his face. But his fear dissipates into curiosity when he sees me. I want him to know who I really am. I want to reach out and lay my hands on his head in blessing, to calm his spirit. But we have so little time. So I hurry to muster the words of Russian I know.

"My name is Jinpa," I say. The monk's eyes widen. "You are from Russia, I think? I would like to talk to you. I have a friend. His name is John Fairchild."

He stares at me with wonder on his face. My head fills with all the questions I want to ask. But he frowns and looks over my shoulder. I turn to see what he sees and my heart is suddenly cold. Once again no one is there, but the door to the garden swings slowly on its hinges. Someone was watching us.

Chapter 4

Here's what you were supposed to notice about Zack. American. Loud shirt. Loud voice. Built like the side of a house. Ridiculous mirrored shades. A drink always in his hand. A bar-stool bore, suckering attractive women with his verbal tentacles and compelling them to listen to his dreary entendre-laden patter.

Here's what Rose noticed about Zack, after half an hour observing from a distant street corner in Lan Kwai Fong. Zack stood in a raised spot that gave him a good view of everyone coming and going. No one could tell if he was actually looking at the women who desperately wanted to get away, or over their shoulders. He waved his drink around but didn't drink from it a lot. And he was built like the side of a house. He looked like he knew how to handle himself, in the same way that a three-metre-thick concrete wall did.

It was definitely the same guy who was driving the boat. Rose watched him above the shoulders of the three young girls he seemed to be trying to impress. The girls were probably high school age, small and shapely in immaculate tight dresses that exposed generous areas of bare brown flesh. They giggled self-consciously as Zack applied his charm indiscriminately, directing a loose grin at any of them who responded. He raised his voice above the noise of a dozen animated conversations around them.

"I'm a soldier. Yes! That's right. US Army! What? Guns? Do I have a gun? Sure! Want to see it? Come back to my room and I'll show you."

The bar on the corner blasted out nineties music through its open doors, and was doing a roaring trade in extravagantly coloured cocktails. Its inside space was tiny and crowds spilled out, filling the narrow street entirely so that the only way through was to shuffle and squeeze. Similar bars lined the other streets, rendering the whole quadrant a noisy mass of socialisers, happily shouting at each other in a fug of sweat and aftershave and beer. The crowd comprised an eclectic mix of races, ages, styles and dress codes, from shorts and T-shirts to sophisticated partying gear. Foreigners, traders, teenagers, dealers, hostesses, it seemed that whoever you were you'd pass through Lan Kwai Fong at some point. It was a great way of keeping an eye on who was where and who was talking to whom.

"Where am I from? Ohio. O-H-I-O. That's it, Ohio! Have you been there? Don't. Stay here. It's much better. Hey! Want to see my tattoo?"

Rose edged her way into the bar through the crowds. She had a long wait to be served but positioned herself so that she could watch Zack and his audience. The back of Zack's head moved about and the three girls stared at it with fixed expressions. How often life involved women standing around listening to men talking authoritative rubbish, or talking about themselves. It was depressingly common a sight, even as part of an act.

Eventually she emerged from the bar with a pink fruit-stuffed cocktail in each hand, which smelled of grapefruit and tasted like something she'd drunk at the age of fifteen that had made her sick. She fought her way through the hot red-faced throng.

"Hey, Zack! Got you a drink. Here!"

Rose saw a moment's puzzlement on Zack's face before he hesitantly returned the greeting. She pushed the drink into his hand and continued in the same tone.

"Long time no see! So, how are things out east? I bet you're surprised to see me!"

The girls made use of the break in the one-sided conversation and scuttled away into the crowd. "Hey! No need to go, girls!" Zack took a step after them but they didn't turn back. He turned to Rose, not best pleased. "Do we know each other?"

"I know you. I wouldn't worry about the girls. You weren't getting anywhere with them anyway."

"Sure I was. The one in the middle?"

"And they've probably got school tomorrow."

"Oh, I see. So you're the moral police, are you? Don't tell me, my wife sent you."

"I'm not from Ohio."

"Yeah, I realise that." He was looking at her. At the hotel she'd put on a dark blue dress, comfortable but still dressy, and tied her hair back. She could only read his face from the eyebrows and mouth. Early to mid forties, probably, if that hair colour was real. His brows were furrowed right now. "So where did we meet?"

"Earlier today. Well, almost. I was hoping to go on a boat trip with you. And John Fairchild."

His expression became opaque. "Oh, I see."

"I was wondering why you were so keen to get Fairchild out of there. He wasn't working for you, by any chance? When he approached Darcy Tang?"

"Darcy who?" Zack sucked on the straw of the cocktail she'd given him.

"Darcy Tang. Heads up the Wong Kai. Quite a major force in the economy of Hong Kong, and mainland China. So I've heard."

"Is that right?" Said in a tone of uninterested politeness. Rose wished he'd take his sunglasses off.

"Yes, that's right. Plenty of reasons why the US might have an interest in them. Clandestine ones, of course."

Horizontal lines marked Zack's forehead as he assumed an expression of innocence. "Hey, I don't know who you think I am, lady. I'm just a soldier."

"That's not what I've heard." She couldn't see what he was looking at, but suspected that his eyes were doing a circuit over her shoulder. No one was near enough to hear anything. She'd already checked. The pumping music from the bar and buzz of the crowds would have made eavesdropping incredibly difficult. "Fairchild has worked for you before, hasn't he? I'm thinking that he approached the Wong Kai as part of some operation. You didn't want him arrested because you don't want the Hong Kong authorities poking around and finding American fingerprints all over their domestic business. So you swept in and got him out of the way when things went wrong."

Zack sucked on his straw with an air of concentration.

"The thing is," continued Rose, "you can't protect him for ever. You know what happened in the restaurant, don't you? Fairchild accidentally shot Darcy Tang's nephew. Oops. I mean, the guy's not dead or anything. But that's not the point, is it? Saving face, that's what it's all about in those circles. You can't just shoot an important guy like that and get clean away with it. Bad for the reputation. Bad for business. So where does that leave our friend? Getting a ticket out of here, if I'm not much mistaken."

Zack had given up on the straw and was looking at her with some intensity. "Who did you say you were again?"

"I didn't. My name's Linda Duffy. I'm a visiting entrepreneur."

He nodded sagely. "Oh, right. Entrepreneur. I see."

"From our brief conversation earlier, I think I might be able to do business with John Fairchild. I think I might have some information that he'd be interested in."

"Information, huh?"

"Yes. So it might be in his interests for he and I to meet up, and have a little chat. About how we can help each other. John Fairchild travels extensively, does he not? He has bases in dozens of countries, moves from place to place."

"If you say so."

"So, assuming he has the sense to leave Hong Kong, where might he be headed next, do you think?"

"How should I know?"

"Right. You're just a soldier."

"Right." He grinned and gave a mini-salute.

"I imagine," she said it as if it had only just occurred to her, "that it wouldn't be great news if the Hong Kong police knew that it was you in that boat. They were too far away to see, but you never know, it might be that someone who was there could positively identify you and pass the name on. I can't imagine you'd welcome that, if you're keen to avoid the USA being associated with this matter."

Zack's forehead was now registering mild distress and he bit the end of his straw.

"I mean I wouldn't normally be keen to approach the police. But I was just an innocent bystander at the end of the day. It wasn't me that shot a gangster. I just wandered in off the street for a bowl of noodles, and all hell broke loose."

"Yeah, right." Zack's forehead lines were still severe.

"It was definitely you I saw in that boat. Just as you're standing in front of me now. So maybe I should do my duty as an honest citizen and report you to someone."

"That's what you'd do, is it?" Zack sounded far from convinced. But he was watching her closely, as far as she could tell, anyway.

"Sure. I mean, to be honest, I don't have a great memory for faces and could easily forget the details of what I saw. Particularly if I got busy on something else. Found a reason not to be around anymore."

"Such as?" He managed to sound casual.

"Such as running into John Fairchild again. I mean, if I knew if he were still in Hong Kong or had already left. Where he was likely to go. Is he still working for you?"

"Hey." Zack held his hand up in a gesture of defeat. "Fairchild is his own guy. He does what he wants. Our encounters are – episodic. And short."

"So he's gone."

"Gone. Or going. That's the usual state of things."

"Well, you must have some idea where he might go next. Or who else he's talking to? Come on, Zack. Give me some kind of a clue and I'll be out of your hair."

Zack was shaking his head slightly. "You'll never catch up with him."

"Won't I?"

"Not if he doesn't want you to."

"Well, it won't do any harm, then, will it, if you point me in the right direction? Your conscience will be clear, and you'll have got yourself and your country out of trouble. Look, just give me some idea of some place he might go. That's all. He doesn't have to know you tipped me off. I just got lucky, right? And, as you say, he's so brilliant I'll probably fail anyway."

Zack sighed. "Okay, okay. Dragon Fire Tours. Check them out."

"What?"

"Dragon Fire. It's a tour company. They run tours. For – tourists." Zack had momentarily lost his easy way with words.

"And?"

"They got an office in Western district. He'll go in there tomorrow to pick up messages, make travel plans. It's his company. He owns it. They sort out his paperwork in this part of the world."

Paperwork. There was a word that could cover a multitude of sins; false passports and IDs, money laundering, all kinds of things. It was a reasonable lead. "Dragon Fire?" repeated Rose.

"That's what I said, isn't it?" Like a lot of reluctant informants, Zack was getting hostile. "You know, he's not going to like you chasing after him. He can get dangerous when—"

"When what?"

"When he thinks he's being pursued."

"Well, perhaps he shouldn't do the kinds of things that get him pursued, then."

"Don't say I didn't warn you. I don't know who or what you are, but he'll figure you out and if he doesn't like it, you'll know about it. I promise."

"Thanks for the advice. Oh, and I'll come looking for you again if there's no sign of him at this place. In case you felt like tipping him off. I may have another attack of conscience."

"Christ, you people, can't you just leave him alone?" He was suddenly harsh.

"You people? What do you mean by that?"

"You Brits. You did enough harm already. No wonder he hates you all."

"What harm?"

"Oh, never mind. I need another drink." Zack looked weary all of a sudden. "Look, I gave you what you wanted, didn't I? So how about you get lost?"

"If it doesn't work out," said Rose, "I'll be back."

"Well hey! I'll look forward to that." Zack's brash tone had resurfaced, laced with irony this time as he turned away from her to elbow his way through to the bar.

Lan Kwai Fong was even busier as she squeezed her way through again, deep in thought. Zack had given her a glimpse of a John Fairchild which was different from the version in the files. Fairchild's file painted him as an information peddler, a blackmailer, a mercenary. Fairchild the victim didn't really compute. Not that it was her problem. As long as she found him and got what she needed to out of it, why would anything else really matter?

Chapter 5

Maybe for other people today is just another day in the monastery. Mornings are for chores: cleaning, washing, polishing, carrying the breakfast and morning tea, and tidying up afterwards. I find them tedious and gruelling, but I do my share. Today I have worked fast to finish early so that I can walk before prayers. But I have an insight from deep inside me that things have changed forever. Tashilunpo is different today. The world is different. This feeling weighs me down inside. I have not yet fathomed the reason. But I know that this change is because of me.

The main courtyard by the front gate is busy as it often is, as it should be in a monastery of this size and importance. Tashilunpo used to be much more important, when the Panchen Lama was properly in place here and we played our full role as one of the leaders of Tibet, just as the Dalai Lama did in Lhasa. But now much of what happens here is just for show, for the tourists, so that the Chinese government can say that it is tolerant of our religion while posting soldiers on every street corner. I walk slowly towards the main gate, my prayer beads in my hand, and I see the tourist coaches parked outside. I can see that many of the tourists are from other parts of China, and they wander around and take photos with their big cameras of the gateway and our golden roofs, and sometimes of us. I wonder what they do with all these hundreds of photographs that they take. I have six photographs that are mine. They demonstrate who I am and are vital to enable me to fulfil my role in the world. They are all I need.

I will not go out of the main gate. To do so might raise questions. I will walk past the gate on my way to the main hall. But as I approach, I see that the Chinese soldiers who stand on guard just inside the gate are already watching me. Of course they always watch, as that is what they are here to do. But their manner is different. Some of my fellow monks are in the courtyard also, sweeping, carrying things or just walking through. But the soldiers now are watching me in particular. They recognise me.

This is exactly what the Rinpoche was so determined would never happen. He always told me I needed to be one of a crowd, never to be noticed. But because somebody saw me speaking with the Russian, now they are suspicious of me. Dread is curled up like a snake in the pit of my stomach. But I must not show any alarm. I repeat a mantra to myself and look up at the sky as I keep walking at the same steady pace.

Just outside the gate, leaning against the wall and looking in, is a Chinese man with a tour guide's identification badge. He is wearing a red baseball cap and smoking a cigarette. He comes to Tashilunpo from Beijing once every two weeks for most of the year. His tour group is inside. I know that really he should be with his group, but he is friendly with the soldiers at the gate and brings them gifts. So they let him stay here and smoke a cigarette while his group looks around inside. I know that he is not really interested in our religion. He has shown his group the Kelsang Lhakhang main temple complex; he will have explained the meaning of the Wheel of Life and the six states of being. During this tour of Tibet he will expound on the many manifestations of the Buddha and the bodhisattvas; he will show his Chinese customers many of our shrines and statues and murals and thangkas. But he does these things because he is told to do them. He does not feel the truth of it in his soul. I know because he has told me as much. I also know his name. His name is Wei Li.

I walk slowly past the gate, twisting my prayer beads between the fingers on my right hand. He sucks on his cigarette as he gazes blandly around. Our eyes meet for a second then I look away and twist the prayer beads tighter around the three middle fingers. I keep walking slowly and muttering my mantra, but I know he will have seen. The soldiers will not notice the signal, but even so I can feel my heart fluttering as I think of their eyes on me, their hands on their guns. When I am past and they are no longer in sight I stop and crouch on the ground, my back against the cold wall, and close my eyes to calm myself. Then I stand again, because we do not have much time.

Wei Li will take a different route from me. I will get to the entrance of the third chapel of the courtyard by the chanting hall before he does. When I get there I need to see that he is holding his mobile phone in his left hand and a water bottle in his right hand. If he is not, I will turn away and leave. If he is, then I will lift my prayer beads and put them round my neck, if I am sure that no one is watching us. When John Fairchild first told me how we needed to take these steps before we met, I thought that it was all a silly game. But he insisted. Today, now I have seen the soldiers' eyes on me, I am grateful for his prudence.

I take more time than usual getting to the chapel, stopping twice and waiting to see if anyone is walking behind me. I wish I had done the same when I followed the Russian, but I was so keen to speak with him that I was not sufficiently cautious. I stand by the chapel entrance and Wei Li walks towards me. His phone and water bottle are in the correct hands so he is also sure he has not been followed. I lift the prayer beads over my neck and go inside. Behind the shrine is a door to a tiny robing room. I open it using the key which is hidden in the velvet folds of the shrine. Only the Rinpoche and I know about this room and the location of the key. So I know that no one will be inside. Wei Li follows me into the room and I shut the door.

"I've got to be back at the coach in seven minutes," says Wei Li. He speaks Mandarin, like he always does. I am not sure he can speak a word of Tibetan. He looks bored.

"It's important," I say. "I need Fairchild to come immediately. I have some information for him. How soon can you contact him?"

"I don't know where he is. Can't you give me the information to pass onto him?"

Wei Li knows that I will not trust him with the contents of a message. He finds our arrangement tiresome. "No. I can't pass it to anyone else. You must tell him to come straight away. I have some news for him."

Wei Li shrugs. "I can phone today to find out if he's in China. If he's not, he could be anywhere. The office can't always reach him."

"You will try," I say. "It's more important to him than it is to me. I have news from Russia. Tell him that. From Russia."

Wei Li shrugs again. "I'll do what I can."

"You think these messages are foolish." I do not intend to say it. Wei Li is always like this, but today his dismissive attitude upsets me more than usual. He does not understand the situation we are in. I carry on, although I shouldn't. "I would like to send a letter without your help. But if I put it in the mail, your government would read it. I would like to make a phone call, but your government would listen. I would like to send a message on a computer, but your government would trace it. You don't want to take these messages, and I don't want you to take them. But I have no choice."

Wei Li seems amused at my agitation. "Oh come on. Everyone has a choice," he says. "If you didn't resist, you could write all the letters and make all the phone calls you like. You monks, what do you want? Being part of China has brought so many benefits to Tibet. Look at the roads, the train lines, the shopping centres. You have better healthcare, better food through Chinese farming technology. You're free to practise your religion if you want. But you still resist. Why? You have the best of everything."

I do not try to answer this. A man like this is not capable of understanding the value of thousands of years of cumulative wisdom and spiritual awareness, bringing us closer to true enlightenment. Shopping centres! This room we are standing in suddenly feels very small, and it is full of the smell of cigarettes on his breath.

"You must pass on the message," I say. "You have to do what John Fairchild says. Whether you like it or not."

He looks at me curiously. I have never spoken like that before. He thinks I am nothing but a prayer-monger, irrelevant in his world, part of a tradition he can only see as history. But I will do far more than utter prayers. I will be the manifestation of these prayers, my own and those of thousands of people. At times like this I feel the power rise up within me, the knowledge that I can change things, that I am destined to lead, as I have done for hundreds of years. "You don't care for my religion and my philosophy," I say. "And I don't much care for yours. But you are the people who are walking our streets with guns."

"Medieval superstition," says Wei Li. "I look at your pilgrims in Lhasa, in Jokhang Square, and I see elderly peasants, saving up their meagre pennies to journey hundreds of miles so that they can lie in front of a temple. Toothless grandmothers with weathered skin rattling prayer wheels like children's toys, muttering those incomprehensible chants, thinking that it will bring merit and better luck in the next life. How convenient it was for your wealthy landowners to persuade people to put up with misery now so that they would have a better life next time around. What a scam! I sometimes wonder that a world superpower like China has any time for such backward ideas."

He is baiting me. I do not know why he has to do this job. I do not want to trust him but Fairchild tells me I can. A Chinese guide can go back and forth and convey messages without arousing suspicion. And this he does, and has done for years. But he does not like doing it. So he is expressing all his anger at me. This will happen later too, when people know who I truly am. I can expect to be the subject of people's anger and frustration even when I have not caused it. I have learned this from the Rinpoche as he has tried to prepare me for my role. So while his words make me dig my fingers into my palms, I find some strength to put my anger aside, just as the Rinpoche would want.

"My friend, we come from very different places. In my tradition there have been abuses. Life is very hard for some Tibetans. But Communist China has also taken some wrong turns. Many deaths resulted, didn't they, in the agricultural reforms and the Great Leap Forward introduced by the revered Chairman Mao? And even in more recent years, in Tiananmen

Square? Protesters mown down by tanks by your government that says it exists for the people. So I say that we are better, are we not, when we can accept different views and express our religions freely without it resulting in oppression and death. Do you not think?"

Wei Li falls silent. We have spent too long talking. "My friend, we do not have time for this. We are on opposite sides, it seems, but I mean no harm to you. My message, please, you will send to Fairchild at the earliest opportunity. Go, before you are missed."

I open the door and check the chapel. No one is there. As Wei Li steps out, he turns. "I don't know or care what these messages are for," he says. "But you're mad if you think you can win this fight. You can't defeat China. You know that." He turns and walks off.

I put everything straight and join the others in prayer. I will not be able to approach Wei Li again. It is too dangerous now. I have no means of contacting Fairchild any more and can only hope he gets this message and comes to me. I think a lot about what Wei Li has said. China is a formidable power to defy. But our struggle is not about guns and money and soldiers. Wei Li cannot possibly understand that. I know that I will succeed. I will succeed because I must.

Chapter 6

Early the next morning, Rose left her hotel, an unremarkable glass pillar slotted between offices in a side street near the subway. She stopped at a fast food cafe for a doughnut and an iced coffee. Still feeling the effects of jet lag, she had hoped the coffee would invigorate her, but it was unpleasantly sweet with too much ice, and made her head throb.

She turned away from the harbour and the skyscraper zone along the front, and headed into the older Hong Kong, where the streets were narrower and the buildings squat in contrast to the forest of towering glass on the waterside. The roads were less busy, but even this early, people moved at speed along the pavements and the sun's heat was intense enough for her to want to walk in the shade. Shops of all sorts jumbled together here, upmarket fashion boutiques crammed between noodle bars and flower shops. The ground started to slope upwards towards the Mid-Levels, whose plush apartment buildings, including Alastair's, rose above the lower-level Central district. At times, the green tips of the Peak emerged behind them.

Rose turned right in the direction of the Western district, with the Peak on her left. Above her head a steady stream of pedestrians crossed on the Mid-Levels escalator walkway. Suspended in the air along its length hung a solid mass of colourful and chaotic street signs in a mix of Chinese and English, shouting their special offers with arrows pointing in every direction. Stepping off the pavement to avoid a dusty pile of wooden planks, she jumped aside at the blaring horn of a squat delivery van forcing its way along the narrow street. A few yards later she turned off.

This side street was quieter. Even using the map on her phone, the office was hard to find, half-hidden behind a large sagging awning from which was draped a length of blue plastic tarpaulin, fastened to the balcony above with lengths of duct tape. Its only outside presence was a cracked black and white sign with Chinese lettering, and underneath in English: Dragon Fire Tours Limited. A few half-hearted posters of beaches and temples and the inevitable Great Wall graced the window. The shopfront immediately to its right displayed a dense medley of mobile phone cases, laptop power packs, headphones and miscellaneous peripherals. Both shops were still closed this early in the morning.

Rose walked slowly by, taking in as much as she could. Well beyond the shops she stopped and fumbled in her bag for something, then played with her phone for a while, keeping an eye on who passed her in the street. This was all very well for a few minutes, but she would have to find somewhere out of sight to watch the place all day. She crossed the street, looking as if she were trying to get a better signal. There she looked back at the buildings directly across the street from Dragon Fire Tours. What she needed was an empty room, or access to the roof. These windows were too high up to see inside. She checked her watch. It was 7.30am and she had been hoping to be in position by now.

A man in a shirt and tie emerged from a door almost opposite Dragon Fire, and set off away from her, throwing a backpack energetically over his shoulder. A commuter on his way to work. He'd definitely be gone for the day. Handy, if he happened to live alone. Rose waited until he was completely out of sight and no one else was in the street. Then she sauntered back, casually crossing the road, and as she walked past it, gently pushed on the door. It gave under her pressure. She quickly checked that she was still alone in the street, then pushed the door and went inside. She was standing in a tiny lobby facing another two doors. The doors to two different flats. Which one had the man come out of? She stood still and listened. Sounds of talking and a TV or radio reached her, but she couldn't tell which of the two doors they were coming from. The lobby smelled of cooked egg. She listened at each of the keyholes but could hear nothing through them.

From her bag she retrieved her lock picks, stashed away in the inner pockets of a make-up bag. The first door sprung open easily, just a simple single-turn lock. She held the door and waited for any reaction from inside. None. She pushed it open very gently and stepped inside, leaving it open for a fast getaway if needed. Behind the door was an archway into a living area. She could see a laminate floor, a sofa, TV screen on the wall, soft toys on the floor. She took a step nearer and now sounds started to reach her from beyond the archway. A woman was talking in Cantonese with sharp barks as though issuing instructions. As she stood silently by the door, a young girl wearing pyjamas padded into the living area. She picked up a remote control and switched the TV on, with her back to Rose. She sat on the sofa and nudged herself back onto it until her feet were sticking out in front of her. Her eyes were on the screen and she wiggled her toes as she sat and watched, unaware she was being observed by someone standing in her apartment. How vulnerable people are, thought Rose, how oblivious.

Without making a sound she backed out and pulled the door closed behind her. The other door was more tricky to open, with a deadbolt as well as a simple latch. It gave with a loud click and the door creaked a little as it swung inwards. Rose steadied the door and stood without breathing, straining her ears. Behind this door was an upward staircase, steep and narrow. No carpet. Rose crept up the stairs, each time lowering her foot gradually onto the next step. Half way up she paused. The staircase was short and already she would be visible to someone upstairs. She could hear nothing. She carried on. The stairs led up straight into the back of an open-plan room almost filled with a double bed. Blinds filtered out much of the light and the room was murky. It smelled of deodorant, or aftershave. Her heart thumping, Rose stepped forward to take a closer look at the rucked-up duvet on the bed. She recoiled backwards when she saw a dark mass on the pillow, but it wasn't someone's head. It was the edge of a crumpled black T-shirt. No one was in the bed. A tiny stretch of space between the bed and the row of windows at the front gave enough space for a single chair and table. An open door in the back wall led to a tiny toilet and shower room, another into a tiny kitchenette. She relaxed. The flat was empty. She peered into the shower room and looked more closely. One bottle of shower gel. One toothbrush. One razor. This guy lived alone.

After returning downstairs to lock the front door, she pulled one of the blinds back just enough to peer out without being seen. It was a good location. She could observe all approaches to the travel agency with minimal visibility. She pulled up the chair and settled in for a wait. After an hour, a woman in a navy suit arrived and unlocked the door to the office. When she opened it, a faint beeping betrayed that the shop was protected by a burglar alarm, something Rose had suspected might be the case. She could see the woman moving around inside, sitting in front of a computer, answering the phone and speaking with animated hand movements.

Half an hour later, a gangly young man in a T-shirt and jeans arrived and opened up the electronics shop next door. After another half hour, an older man in shorts and flip-flops went into the electronics shop. Its first customer of the day. This was Rose's chance. She slipped out of the flat, leaving the door on the latch, and went across into the electronics shop. The gangly man was at the counter with the older man, both studying a smartphone and looking perplexed. The employee looked up when Rose came in: the other man didn't turn round. The walls of the shop were crammed floor to ceiling with tech peripherals and accessories. On a pretence of searching for what she wanted, Rose turned her back to the counter, bent down low and attached a small microphone to the wall behind a stack of laptop cases.

Taking her time, she finished browsing then slipped out of the shop without looking behind her. The conversation between the two men continued uninterrupted as she left.

Back in the flat, she switched on her listening device and put on the earpiece. It was silent but she'd have to wait until the woman was on the phone again. If she could see her talking but not hear her, she'd have to go over there again and reposition the mic. And of course Fairchild could show up at any time. How difficult all of this was with no support. Rose was used to working in a team, coordinating people with specialist expertise to achieve a common outcome. An exercise like this would be properly planned and prepared. She was having to rely far too much on luck.

Her head filled with a loud, distorted blaring, and she reached for the volume button. It was a desk phone ringing. Rose watched the woman pick up the phone and heard her greeting, then a pause, then a cascade of Cantonese. She made some adjustments to the monitor and the speech became a lot clearer. It would have to do. She set the device to record. If Fairchild spoke to this woman in Cantonese, Alastair was already on stand-by with some discreet translation help. She disliked having to go back to him: he'd already called in a favour to borrow this device for her. When the phone call finished, she switched off. These things only had a limited battery life and she might have to be here all day.

She waited for another three hours, shifting her position every now and then, and recording two more phone conversations. It was coming up to midday when she saw him. Fairchild was strolling along in a light blue short-sleeved Oxford shirt and chinos. He didn't look like someone who was trying to hide, despite the chase of the previous evening. He must be confident that he could distance himself from the police, or that someone else would do it for him. He pushed the door and went into the travel agency. Through the window she could see the woman rise to greet him, a lot of nodding and smiling. In her earpiece their voices joined in a chorus of greeting. They both sat on either side of the desk. The sound was muddy and she had to fiddle with the buttons again to account for the change of tone and position of the people talking. They were speaking in a mix of Cantonese and English, the English phrases broken up and meaning very little on their own. This went on for some time. Rose could only listen and hope that when the sing-song Cantonese was translated it would all make sense. Then the woman said something that did make sense.

"China not safe for you. I see news. I hear what happened."

Fairchild then spoke. "If way lee has something to say, I need to hear it."

Rose put her ear closer to the device. The words didn't make sense. Unless it was a name. Wei Lee?

The woman tutted. "Could just be a story. Nothing. You never find out what happened. You follow these stories all over."

"That's what I do, Molly. You know that. When can you sort it out?"

"When you want to go?"

"Straight away," said Fairchild, as if it were obvious.

Rose could see Molly tap at her computer terminal. She made a comment, back in Cantonese now. Fairchild asked her something. Molly's response: "Beijing?"

"Beijing," Fairchild repeated. It was just one word on its own, clear.

More tapping at the keyboard. Molly was reading something out to him. More Cantonese. Several more exchanges, mainly in Cantonese. Then Fairchild stood, they exchanged final words and he came out of the shop. Before the door had even closed behind him Molly was back tapping at the computer screen. Fairchild walked on, directly below the window where Rose was sitting. She looked down at the top of his head as he strode past. Gotcha, she said quietly to herself.

Chapter 7

Rose got her CSM out of the hotel safe and fired it up. She was absurdly pleased that Walter had managed to get her one of these. The CSM was on the face of it an ordinary and slightly out-of-date laptop, but was loaded up with all manner of hidden encryptions that enabled MI6 officers the world over to communicate securely with each other. It also included a news feed, corporate messages and so on. It was like being connected to the hive mind.

She connected to the bespoke Service software for video calling and waited for Walter to respond. She recalled her first impression of Walter when he'd shown up at her flat that evening and had persuaded her he was a bona fide SIS officer. He'd spoken quietly and fussily but got to the point well enough when he wanted to. His tweedy brown jacket was thin at the elbows and slightly too big, but looked like it had fitted him once. He was sharp-eyed but worn around the edges, like an old pair of garden shears that had been in the garden shed forever and had all its paint chipped away, but still cut like a dream.

When Walter eventually came online, his face on the screen looked washed-out and tired. He was jacketless and in a white shirt, sitting in front of a pale, bare wall. He was, apparently, in Tel Aviv, but she only had his word for that because the CSM masked location by default. He nodded from time to time as Rose gave him a selective update. Walter had no need, she had decided, to know the detail of her little skirmish at the Famous Central Golden Palace and what it gave away about her. So she kept things succinct.

"He's going to Beijing? I see, I see." Walter spoke in the manner of a benign schoolteacher from days gone by. "Any idea when?"

"Straight away. To meet up, possibly, with someone called Wei Lee. To find out what happened. It sounds like this is something he does a lot, trying to find out what happened. That's all I've got." The Cantonese translation hadn't revealed anything further. Rose told Walter about Dragon Fire and Molly's role.

"And how did you get onto that, out of curiosity?"

"The guy who was driving the motor boat showed up in Lan Kwai Fong. That's a popular nightspot."

"Indeed it is." The more Rose talked to Walter, the more she came to believe that this fussy little man had been around a bit. "And this chap, he just happened to be there, did he?" Walter's tone remained mild despite the challenge in the question.

"Most foreigners end up in Lan Kwai Fong at some point. It was a fair bet he'd show up on a Friday or Saturday night." Rose shuddered inwardly at how weak this was. Above his gold-rimmed glasses Walter's eyebrows raised, but he left it there. "He's American," Rose continued. "Name of Zack. They're friends, I think. He seems to believe that Fairchild has been mistreated by the British in some way." She paused, hoping for some enlightenment. "Has he?"

Walter smiled faintly. "He may think he has. It's really a matter of opinion."

Rose shifted on her chair. Her tiny hotel room was airless and smelled of mould. She'd put the aircon on full throttle as soon as she'd come in but it couldn't compete with the sun blazing in through the glass. "Well, it sounds like I need to get myself to Beijing. I've never worked in mainland China before, as you know. Can you source any intel that might help me locate him? Like when and where he enters the country?"

"Not this time, I'm afraid, Rose. We don't want to do anything that might alert the Chinese to what we're up to. This is going to have to stay very much a stand-alone venture."

"Walter," said Rose. "I've spent months on this already and only got as far as a five-minute conversation. This would be so much easier with the proper resources. Is there really no way you can help?"

Her impatience fell flat in the tiny room. Walter, thousands of miles away, sat back in his chair abruptly. "Well, as I said at the start, Rose my dear, if this is a challenge you don't feel you want to pursue, that's always an option. I'd quite understand."

My dear. Had no one told him that people don't talk like that any more? "I don't think you want to see that, Walter. I've got closer than at any time before. But do you really appreciate how difficult this is?"

"Of course. The situation is far from ideal. You know why this little venture of ours needs to be entirely separate from all other operations. And because of the international nature of John's lifestyle, it has to be somewhat wide-ranging. If we could narrow down his activities to a particular city or country or even continent, things would be a lot more straightforward. But I did explain all of this at the start. It hasn't changed since you took it on, Rose. And, as you say, you've got closer than ever before."

Rose sat back. The sun was shining uncomfortably onto her neck but her room was too small to avoid it. "What is this thing that happened? Fairchild says that it's what he does, that he tries to find out what happened. Do you know what that's all about?"

Walter's face stiffened. "Things from a long time ago that are no longer relevant, Rose. It's the here and now that we're interested in. If Fairchild has access to our confidential intelligence and is prepared to pass it on to anyone who wants it, he can do a lot of damage."

"But what's his motivation? You think he's doing this purely for money? He's already got money. He's wealthy, according to his file. Shouldn't we be trying to dig a bit deeper to find out what he's looking for? Then we have some chance of predicting what he's likely to do next."

His eyes glimmered. "What you need to do, Rose, is focus on Beijing. And that will be a challenge, I'm afraid. I was posted there myself many years ago. And it's for that reason that I can't visit mainland China myself. Not for anything operational."

"Why?"

"I was posted in Beijing some years back under diplomatic cover. Unfortunately I became victim of the extreme vigilance of the Ministry of State Security who labelled me an SIS officer and I've been unable to operate in the country ever since. I was watched assiduously wherever I went, and if I were to arrive there now, the same thing would happen again. They will still have me on file, that's for sure."

"You could come in under cover. With a different identity."

"But that would need arranging, would it not? Another opportunity for the word to spread internally that something is going on."

"Well, it's going to be difficult to arrange a face-to-face meeting, then."

"It'll have to happen elsewhere, that's all. But one thing at a time. First you have to find him again."

"Any ideas? I've heard it's a big-ish place, Beijing."

He didn't respond to her sarcasm, which was probably just as well. "As I've said before, my dear. Start with the most expensive hotel. That's where he'll be if he wants to be found."

"And if he doesn't want to be found?"

"I really have no idea. But there's a thought!" He sat back, eyes glinting, looking pleased with himself. "Given it's Beijing, it may be worth trying this place. Make a note of this." He reeled off the details of an address. She grabbed the hotel notebook and wrote it down.

"What will I find there?"

"It's an apartment in central Beijing. He's stayed there in the past."

This was very specific information to have to mind about somebody. Rose was about to ask about it, but Walter's attention was distracted by something happening in front of him off-screen. "Ah. I have to go now, I'm afraid. Things are a little busy here. Get in touch if you need to. You know how." He reached forward with his hand and the screen went blank.

The air conditioning gurgled. She grabbed the remote control impatiently and switched it off. A long judder, followed by silence and the occasional drip. How well did Walter know Fairchild? There were no references in the file to a prior relationship between them. She thought back to Zack, and his frustrated outburst in Lan Kwai Fong, and Molly's references to Fairchild pursuing "stories" about "what happened". There was a lot she wasn't being told. Fairchild's motivations were still a mystery, which didn't help if she were supposed to be reaching out to him.

Anyway, one thing at a time, as Walter had said. This address might pay off, but on the other hand it might not, and she could waste days staking it out for nothing. She needed more options than that, and Walter wasn't the only person who had previously worked in Beijing. She hesitated only for a moment before picking up the phone and dialling Alastair's number.

Chapter 8

Current architectural tastes seemed to dictate that every modern international airport looked like every other modern international airport. John Fairchild traversed the glass-roofed glossy-floored expanse of Beijing International Arrivals hall, looking ahead to the distant taxi rank and dodging waves of well-heeled erstwhile-communist masses. The flight had been delayed, resulting in a long morning confined in Chep Lap Kok's business lounge followed by a suit-crumpling three hours in the air, discomfort that even the complimentary gin and tonics couldn't assuage. It felt good to be using muscles again and he strode at pace, overtaking many of the shorter-legged passengers around him.

His mind, acting annoyingly independently, drifted back to the woman who had unexpectedly pursued him through a building site in Hong Kong, having introduced herself to him earlier as Linda Duffy. He remembered his shock at the sight of her when he turned round and she was there, some distant city light catching her face and the wisps of fair hair curling on her cheekbones. She'd been breathing hard, with beads of sweat on her forehead and her eyes bright. There was something very energetic, very alive about her, yet self-contained as well. And all the while the bloody local police were closing in on them. Once again Zack had been his lifeline, which was as it should be since he'd been doing the job for Zack in the first place, or trying to. Duffy, or whatever her name was, had scuppered it nicely. She was an intelligence officer, that much he was certain of. Assuming she was working for the British, what did they want with him now? The whole encounter was irritating and somewhat embarrassing, which was surely why her image was sticking in his head so much.

Alongside the information desk, foreign currency exchange and newspaper kiosk, he had a familiar creeping sense of being watched. He hadn't used his real passport and all the visa work checked out, thanks to Molly, but nevertheless something wasn't right. A thin man in a tan suit turned away from him as he passed, intent on his phone. Further along, a guy in a blue striped shirt examined the contents of his wallet, glanced up, stashed the wallet and walked away. Just in front of the sliding door exit a woman stood facing away from him wearing black leggings and a pink T-shirt with a picture of a panda on the back. As he reached the exit, she turned towards him, revealing an impeccably made-up face, which held his gaze. Reluctantly, he slowed.

"Comrade Chu!" he said. "What a surprise to see you here. Of all the people to bump into at the airport."

Comrade Chu didn't smile. "Mr Fairchild. So good to see you in my country. I trust you had a good journey." They were speaking Mandarin.

"Very good, thanks. This welcome is overwhelming. It's almost as if you were aware of my impending visit."

"Well, as you know, we like to keep an eye on who is coming and who is going." Fairchild made a note to get all of his identities replaced. He had no idea how the Chinese could have latched onto this one but it had happened before. Chu fell into step beside Fairchild, keeping up with him despite her glittery silver high-heeled sandals. The tan suit and the blue striped shirt lined up behind them. "So what brings you to Beijing, Mr Fairchild?"

"Oh, I don't know, I just felt like dropping in. There's so much to see here. Maybe I'll go up to the Summer Palace, the Great Wall. Since I've only been in the country around seven minutes, I don't yet have a detailed itinerary."

"Tourism? Really?" The serious expression on Chu's face did not break despite the scepticism in her voice. Her skin was a flawless ivory, her wide eyes emphasised in moist black with perfectly separated lashes. She could be any age between twenty-five and forty-five. Fairchild had to admire how she embraced the need to dress appropriately for street work. No one could mistake her for a government servant in that get-up. It did make him wonder why she felt the need to be so rigorous even in her own country. He had heard rumours that Chu liked to steer her own path by means that the party bureaucracy and various of her colleagues might not always endorse. That she had retained her position for many years, nevertheless, was testament to her talents.

By this time they had stepped outside and were standing by the taxi rank. Beijing was as hot as Hong Kong: Fairchild's shirt was already clinging to his back. A black saloon drew up beside them, in a way which suggested the driver of this particular car didn't have to worry about the Taxis Only notices. "Might I offer you a lift?" said Chu, opening the back door.

"That would be very kind." Fairchild got in. He didn't revel in her company, but if he got in a taxi they would surely follow it anyway, so he may as well get a free ride and find out what the woman wanted. He kept his half-empty backpack beside him. He generally travelled light. Chu climbed in the other side and they slid off towards the expressway. The pulsating infrastructure of one of the world's fastest-growing economies accelerated past them through tinted glass. The cool of the car's leather seats was a relief.

"So! I trust you had an interesting time in Hong Kong. Such a vibrant little place." Chu had the standard Chinese disdain for the tiny territory, theirs in name but remaining stubbornly separate politically. Fairchild gazed innocently at the passing billboards. Quicker just to let Chu get to the point. Normally on arrival he'd be checking his phones, but he hadn't even switched them on: they didn't work here anyway. He had a stash of Chinese SIM cards which he'd pick up later. After a pause, she came a little closer to the point. "I understand there was some excitement there recently. A shooting. Very dramatic. Involving the Wong Kai."

Fairchild sniffed. "I think I might have seen something about it."

"Oh, I believe it came a little closer to you than that. You know how you get to hear things." Fairchild did. Chu and her unit were formidably well connected, with inside sources in all kinds of organisations. The Hong Kong police would be no exception. "A Westerner, I am told, pulled the trigger then managed to evade arrest."

Fairchild tutted. "A tragedy."

Chu's elegantly painted lips pursed. "With some help. From an American, we think." Fairchild glanced sideways at her. Zack wouldn't be pleased with that. He'd been fuming about having to come in at all.

"Christ, what's wrong with you?" he'd roared that evening as he knocked the boat into gear and they took off across the harbour. "All you have to do is introduce yourself nicely to the boss, now the whole island's on your tail! I mean, what the hell?" Fairchild could only try and explain that the tense but perfectly manageable atmosphere in the restaurant while he had been waiting had been completely destabilised by the unexpected presence of a kick-boxing British secret agent posing as some kind of upmarket prostitute, or at least that's how he'd described her to Tang's nephew. Zack had respectfully inferred that it might be a while before he offered Fairchild any more work. But of course things had developed since then.

"You know," said Chu, "the Wong Kai is very well established in many parts of China. Including Beijing, of course. So it is of particular interest to our law enforcement ministries. It's a pity none of us knew about this."

"Didn't know about what?" asked Fairchild.

Chu's face registered no expression. "Seems the USA and others were planning to cooperate with a criminal gang in some way on Chinese soil."

"That's a very big jump to make, Chu. I'm sure it was all just an unfortunate misunderstanding. Besides, I didn't realise the Special Administrative Region of Hong Kong was classed as part of China now."

Chu's face puckered with irritation. "You are wanted by the police, Mr Fairchild. SAR may be separate but we operate together to track down criminals trying to hide from justice."

"Well, that's admirable. The Wong Kai will be grateful to you for your efforts. Of course it has been suggested that the Wong Kai has, from time to time, actually worked for the Chinese government, for the more unofficial of your law enforcement operations. There's never been any evidence of course."

Chu looked at him blankly. There had, of course, never been any evidence. "So," she continued as if Fairchild had not spoken. "I should take you in to police headquarters now and lock you up. Then send you straight back to Hong Kong to await trial."

Fairchild looked as if he were giving this idea some consideration. "You're not going to, though, are you?" he said.

"And why is that, Mr Fairchild?"

"Well, because I'm worth more to you out there." He waved his hand as if to take in the whole of Beijing. "Besides, I know a thing or two which it wouldn't do to have revealed. Us having worked together in the past. I'm no loyalist, as you know."

"Mr Fairchild, I know how much you value your freedom. If you want to continue to enjoy it, you will have to pay a price. Of course when I say freedom, I mean relative freedom."

"Relative?" enquired Fairchild.

"Well, you know what this country is like," said Chu. They were nearing the city centre now, and had slowed to crawl through thick traffic alongside pavements packed with bodies moving in every direction. "With one point two billion of us, you are never really alone in China."

Fairchild considered this. Chinese secret service surveillance was indeed thorough and wide-reaching. The sight of Chu at the airport was a real blow. He ran the risk of being watched and followed the whole time he was here. Which was a pity, because it was absolutely critical for what he was doing here that the MSS had no knowledge of it at all. "Well, that's certainly a comfort. And I get this relative freedom in exchange for what?"

They were passing a row of tall, gleaming new apartment blocks. Chu pointed through the tinted glass. "Look at this, Mr Fairchild. New housing, to replace the slums we had before. Do you know how many people China has lifted out of poverty in the past twenty years? Four hundred million. That's four-fifths of the population of the entire EU. Look at life expectancy, literacy, infrastructure, technology. Buying power. Growing middle-class Chinese, travelling the world. The government of the People's Republic is straining every muscle to serve the people." Chu's Communist-era term seemed out of place. Fairchild had heard all this before, and he knew what was coming. "And yet, some people still resist, driven by reactionary ideas and wanting to return to the vested interests of the past. Dissidents, Mr Fairchild. In every town and city. They want our country to fail. They are plotting against us. And you know these people."

Fairchild put on a self-deprecating laugh. "Please, Chu. I don't know all your so-called dissidents. Particularly if there are as many as you think they are. Which I doubt. Most people just want to get on with life. You've managed to buy their cooperation with higher living standards and the internet. You don't seem to be losing the battle as far as I can see."

"Well, you don't know everything about the fight," said Chu fiercely. Fairchild was glad he didn't know everything about the fight. He could imagine how unpleasant it was. "Mr Fairchild, you have friends, contacts, colleagues. You smell out people's secrets. You know people who are disaffected, who want to see us damaged. I know you are a person of pragmatism. You know how to weigh these things up. In exchange for your freedom, some names, please. And we will know if you are dealing with us plainly or not. You know how thorough we are."

Fairchild looked out of the window. He had a pretty good idea how thorough they were. "You're asking the impossible," he said. "These dissidents everywhere, they're in your mind. They don't exist. You're paranoid, all of you. That's your excuse for repressing your own citizens. That you're doing it in their best interests. It doesn't wash."

But Chu was shaking her head. "You know people. What are you doing here in Beijing anyway? Makes no sense for you to come here now. Anywhere else in the world would be better to flee to. But no, you come here, where the Wong Kai is so well established. Why? What are you planning here?"

Fairchild considered touching Chu's knee reassuringly but decided it was not worth the risk. Chu could move very fast when she wanted to. "Rest assured, comrade. I have no ambitions to bring down the Chinese government. I'm merely looking after myself. You know that's my only priority. Tiananmen Square, please." Chu frowned. "Could you drop me at Tiananmen Square? I'll make my own way from there."

Chu sighed, leaned forward and nodded at the driver. She sat back again. "So, it's up to you, then. You can pass me some names, anonymously of course, no one will know where the information comes from. You will then be free to continue your business. Or we will find you and have you arrested. Don't think you can evade us. We will track you down, Fairchild, whatever you are trying to do here."

They were approaching the traffic lights at Qianmen Gate at the south side of the square. The driver swerved over to the pavement. Chu dug a business card out of a small silk handbag that matched her shoes. "I know how you value your privacy, Mr Fairchild. We all have things that are important to us, and your secrecy is that to you. I don't wish to invade it. I really don't. Please, call me, whenever you want." The card remained in her hand as Fairchild opened the door and let himself out. Chu's elegant face looked up at him. "You know, I'm not so bad, Fairchild. Given the view that the Wong Kai have of you, a little help might be exactly what you need right now."

Fairchild found himself hesitating. Slowly, he reached in and took the card. "Thanks for the lift," he said before slamming the door and turning away. As he navigated his way across the road to Qianmen Gate on the south side of the square, he pocketed Chu's card. Not that he needed it. Chu's team would never be more than shouting distance away by the sound of it, unless he made some effort to distance himself. He stood in the shade of the gate and contemplated the mass of people in the square in front of him.

Chu he had known for some years. If he had to engage with the formidable MSS, it may as well be her. Fluent in English and comfortable with the ways of the West, Chu was more talented than most of her colleagues at enlisting the help, reluctant or otherwise, of himself and other non-Chinese, in their obsession with domestic security. He had done business with Chu previously, albeit warily. He had perhaps underestimated the influence of the Wong Kai clan. If Chu was right, this continuing vendetta could make things difficult for him. Hers had been a carefully thought-out offer.

A few moments after Fairchild had melted into the shadow of Qianmen Gate's heavy stone archway, a Western tourist in a white bush hat wandered up to admire the socialist-style statuary outside Mao's mausoleum, and made his way northwards through the vast square, becoming entwined with a large escorted group of German tourists.

Slowing his pace to blend in, the Western tourist found his thoughts returning to Linda Duffy. What did she want? She knew what she was getting into in the restaurant, and it was for him, she said, not the Wong Kai. She seemed prepared to go to great lengths, it would seem, to get his attention. That intrigued him, he had to admit. She'd tracked down Zack in Lan Kwai Fong and leaned on him. Zack had called him, somewhat sheepishly, to own up to that. He hadn't given her a lot, though. Dragon Fire was traceable back to him anyway, and Linda Duffy wouldn't get anything out of Molly, that was for sure. It was unlikely Duffy would know where he was now. He should really be putting her out of his mind but he was finding that difficult, for some reason. The business here needed his attention, and this was a matter that always had, always would have, his highest priority. At the north edge of the square the tourist considered the entrance to the Forbidden City, then, as if on a whim, ran for a bus heading to Wangfujiang and jumped aboard at the last minute.

Wangfujiang's wide pedestrian street was as thick with crowds as ever. A group of Americans came out of a department store and joined the throng, one of their number at the back in a fishing waistcoat and wide-brimmed Tilley safari hat, clutching his purchases in a plastic bag, which happened to contain a half-empty rucksack, and looking a little lost. The shopper gazed around at the neon-clad storefronts and thought about the informally clad Comrade Chu and her offer. Given Wei Li's itinerary, it was likely that the message he had concerned Jinpa. What he'd said to Chu wasn't entirely accurate. Jinpa was a dissident who could be immensely damaging to China, more than Chu could possibly realise. Passing that kind of intelligence to Chu would easily buy Fairchild's escape from the Wong Kai and the police charges. But was that ever, seriously, something he could possibly consider? If Chu thought that he could, it was no bad thing. He liked to tell people he had no loyalty. But first things first. He needed to find out what the young Tibetan wanted. And he needed to do that unaccompanied.

Still clutching his plastic bag and gazing about himself, the American shopper casually wandered into a side street and disappeared.

Chapter 9

Darkness was already gathering as Rose slipped quietly across the bridge onto the island in the middle of Beihai Park. Some boats were still out on the lake, water rippling in the glow of ornamental lamps lining the carved stone walkway. Over by the tea house, ballroom music played from a portable machine while dancers practised their skills, moving gracefully by the water's edge. Couples idled on the bridge, looking out at the water below elegant fronds of willow. Rose made an effort to slow her steps to blend in with the relaxed pace of park life in the heart of heavily populated Beijing.

Never having served in China, she was aware of no reason why her presence would arouse suspicion, but China had such a reputation for the thoroughness of their home security that she was being cautious. This evening she was faithfully playing out the role of the visiting tourist. She had changed into a loose-fitting top and long light skirt as soon as she arrived at her hotel, and come straight here to this expansive formal garden next to the Forbidden City. Plenty of people were around despite the growing gloom, showing no signs of leaving. Why would they? It was still early. The park was open for another three hours and it was a balmy night. Which suited Rose's purposes entirely.

On the island, she walked through an ornate stone gate. Steps rose in front of her up to the peak of the giant Buddhist stupa that crowned the island. Checking that no one nearby was paying any attention, she backtracked around the side of the gate. The densely wooded little island was shaped like a dark green fairy cake with the stupa a white cherry on the top of it. Since most of Beihai park consisted of the lake and its walkway, this island was its biggest area of land. A rough pathway into the woods was just about visible, not an official route but a shortcut formed over time. She took the path which twisted up and away from the steps, round the side of the island. She was in the most densely wooded part of the park, hidden from view. She could smell pine and could hear nothing except her own footsteps. There was hardly enough light to see the ground. After a couple of minutes the path opened out slightly. A small pile of boulders was almost hidden between trees. After checking again that she was alone, Rose fumbled until she found the loose one which revealed a sizeable weatherproof space inside. The contents were bagged in black plastic. Quickly she piled all of it into her backpack and replaced the rock exactly where it was. She brushed the dirt off her knees and emerged from the pathway, like a tourist who had gone off-piste by accident. She climbed the steps to the stupa and spent a few cursory minutes admiring the view of Beijing as lights blinked on all over the city. Admittedly it did look nice, if a little hazy in the smog. She took a few photos and made an effort to saunter at a leisurely pace back to the hotel. How dull it was, it all reminded her, being an ordinary tourist.

Back at the hotel she explored the contents of the dead drop. Alastair had done well. The packages contained quality recording equipment, for bugging a room or several rooms for a period of time, more sophisticated than the single wall mic and monitor she had borrowed in Hong Kong. Again she missed working with a technical team on an operation like this, but needs must. She had to hope that her buddy on the inside hadn't got himself into trouble, or caused any of his old Beijing colleagues grief either. But it was for a good cause, if it protected British interests. All this sneaking around was very galling given they were all supposed to be on the same side.

The next morning she got up early and struggled into her running gear, pinning her hair under a baseball cap. Outside the hotel, she kicked into a run along the wide pavement, the rhythm of her padded running soles a familiar comfort. The air was already warm but with a fresh edge. She loved running. It made her feel light and powerful at the same time. Some traffic passed on the two-lane road but she saw few pedestrians. As the sun rose in the sky, so did the temperature. She covered four blocks fast, letting her mind go its own way, before slowing to a more manageable pace and settling into a rhythm.

Her phone in a pocket on her arm showed that she was nearing her destination. The address Walter had given her was in the commercial Jianguomen district. It turned out to be a respectable residential block on a spacious but busy street. A very suitable pad for a visiting businessman. She ran straight past, glancing in as she did so through the glass doors. Inside she registered a plush, spacious lobby with a thick carpet floor and a concierge desk with two uniformed staff. Two lifts were positioned beyond the desk. She powered on, turning the next corner abruptly then the next. Ducking into a side street, she got out of her bag the skirt and long-sleeved shirt which she had brought with her, and put them on over her running gear. She removed her cap and loosened her hair. Walking back round the corner, she continued away from the flats, stopped in a convenience store and bought a pack of cigarettes. She had noticed from running past before that a McDonald's further up opposite the flats had just opened for the day.

She went in, bought a coffee and the nearest McDonald's equivalent of a bacon and egg sandwich, and went upstairs.

The street was lined with trees on both sides, but she had a view of the door and part way into the apartment building lobby. She ate slowly and most of her attention would have seemed to be on her phone. But she was keeping a careful eye on the street outside, not only for anyone coming out of or going into the building, but anyone who didn't seem to be going anywhere much. The only stationary presence in the street she saw was a man lying in a doorway apparently asleep, his exposed feet showing bare brown toes.

A young woman in casual clothes came up to the lobby. With long dark hair, she looked south east Asian, Filipino or Indonesian maybe. Perhaps a resident, perhaps a cleaner or au pair. Here was the interesting part: she keyed in a code on a number pad next to the door, which then slid open. Inside, she walked straight past the uniforms on the desk to the lifts at the back. The concierge team barely even looked at her as she walked past. Either they knew her, or they weren't particularly vigilant. There was only one way to find out which.

She finished her breakfast, took the coffee outside and lit a cigarette. She moved forward as if restless, idly knocking the tree trunk next to her with her foot while looking up in a bored way. From here she had a clear view inside the apartment building lobby and of anyone approaching. She drew on the cigarette. She was not a smoker but appreciated the nicotine rush, the tingling in her fingers. Smoking was also an excellent excuse for hanging around out of doors.

Things went like a dream. A delivery van pulled up and a driver in a bright yellow uniform jumped out, retrieved two items from the back and waved at the guards inside to let him in. Rose stubbed her cigarette and crossed the road. She arrived at the door as the delivery guy was at the concierge desk, three heads bent over the driver's device as they were asked to sign for the parcels. Rose already had her hand on the decoder, a smart little item that looked like a piece of silicon, another gadget from the Beihai Park dead drop. The last time she had seen one of these was in training. She placed it up against the keypad and gently pressed it into place. It worked on the minute traces of grease that fingertips left behind. Leave it on there for ten seconds and it shows up pink. The areas the pinkest are the buttons used the most. It works on almost all materials. So she had been told. Three seconds. No pink, and it looked like the signing was all finished. But some chit-chat was going on. The weather! The traffic! The ball game! Who knew. Six seconds. Still no pink. The delivery guy was turning to the door, waving at his chums. Rose stepped out of sight of the door and turned her back on him, playing with her phone again. If she were unlucky he would glance up at the keypad and see that something was odd about it, but he'd have to be pretty observant. She heard his steps pass behind her and the door of his vehicle slam.

Ten seconds was long gone, but she had to wait for the van to drive off. Now she could retrieve the silicon but needed to do so carefully so that it didn't smudge. She had no choice but to be blatant and fast. She stepped up to the door without even looking into the lobby, and peeled back the corners of the silicon. Now there was pink. She registered the four areas of smudge, but she needed the silicon itself to know which order they were last used. God knows how it did this. She'd only been told it needed to have been used in the last hour and that it was 85% accurate. But that was a while back. Maybe they were better now.

She had the silicon in her hand. On her other hand was its flexible casing. She laid the silicon flat on top and folded the casing over so it was covered. Only then did she glance up. One of the uniforms was looking straight at her. What had he seen? She turned and walked away without looking behind her, heart thumping. After ten steps she heard the door open behind her and made an effort not to speed up. Her ears were straining for the sound of footsteps running after her. She was making mental notes of who was around her, what her options were. But there were no steps. Maybe he hadn't seen anything. Maybe he had, but had no idea what to do about it particularly given she was a foreigner and probably didn't speak Mandarin. Maybe he just didn't care. But in any case she just kept walking up to the next junction, turned out of sight and slowed her pace, waiting for her breath to return to normal.

In a public toilet she reverted back to her running gear and ran back to the hotel. There she changed into a business skirt and blouse, dark and formal. Hello again, Linda Duffy. She greased her hair a little to darken it, tied it back severely, and dug out a pair of glasses. Like this with heels on, the guards would let her walk straight past them, if they were still on shift when she went back. She didn't want to go too early as she wanted Fairchild, if indeed he was staying there, to be out.

The silicon had done its magic by now. The four smudges ranged in colour from pale pink to a dark red. From morning till night, light to dark, that was how to remember the sequence, she'd been told in training. She memorised it and cleared the silicon by washing it in soapy water. After another coffee she loaded a large handbag with more gear, put on a jacket to match her skirt and set off again, going by taxi this time.

The taxi dropped her a little further along the street out of sight of the doors. Rose walked back to the apartment building, confidently tapped in the key code, and walked in when the doors slid open, nodding briefly to the uniforms as she strode past to the elevators. They met her gaze then looked away again. She loved this. A bit of misdirection, a change of clothes and hair and you can do anything, be anyone you want.

The elevator took her up to the tenth floor and a corridor just as thickly carpeted as the lobby. A camera was positioned at the far end, pointing at the elevator door. On her way past Rose had looked for any evidence of live feeds at the concierge desk. There were none, so either it was recording for future reference or it was a dummy. At the door to the apartment she rang the bell of the door opposite and waited. No answer. She tried again before getting her manicure set out and working the door. She timed herself: twenty seconds before the lock gave and she was inside. If anyone were watching this on a screen she would know about it within the next minute or so. She closed the door gently behind her and waited. Nothing. Anyone paying for these flats thinking they were living in a fortress was much mistaken. After a quick tour of the flat to check that she was alone, Rose opened the front door, rang the bell of what she was hoping was Fairchild's flat opposite, then retreated behind the front door again. Through the spy hole she could see Fairchild's door. She did not want to come face to face with John Fairchild right now, and have to explain how she knew where he would be. She had talked herself out of a lot of situations, but that one would have been tricky. No one came to the door. She waited, then did it again. Nothing. Her manicure set on Fairchild's door took longer. She sweated and her hands slipped twice before it finally clicked and gave way. She closed the door behind her and moved inside.

The first thing she noticed entering the living room was the number of books. An entire wall of the generously sized room was lined with bookshelves. History, politics, economics, art, philosophy, geology, mathematics, fiction – the range of topics was huge. The subjects spanned the globe and a good few were in different languages. Oriental themes were prominent: she could see Chinese astrology, *Thoughts of Chairman Mao*, *The Tibetan Book of Living and Dying*, *Art of the Ming Dynasty*, and a few in Chinese.

Aside from the books, the room was free of clutter. The furniture was a classic contemporary style, no signs of wear or anything personalised. If it weren't for the books it could have been a room in a hotel suite anywhere. Outside the window stretched a passable view of Beijing sprawl and smog. Pulling on gloves, she started checking desk drawers and cupboards. No sign of a laptop or similar device. One drawer contained six mobile phones, all switched off. Had he even been here? Was it even his place? She could be rifling through the belongings of a complete random. She walked through to the bedroom. It wasn't a big place, just one bedroom and a bathroom off it. Bag in the corner, glass of water and a book by the bed. The bed was unmade and a shirt was draped over the end. Someone, a man, was definitely staying in this flat. The book was a recently published journalistic analysis of modern China.

She was about to stick her head into the bathroom when she froze. The sound was of metal on metal, a key turning in a lock. Someone was entering the flat. She already knew that there was no balcony, no fire escape, no other way out. She held her breath as her pulse raced and footsteps came towards her. She had nowhere to go.

Chapter 10

I trudge up the dry path feeling the stones through the thin soles of my sandals. I look down on the gold tips of Tashilunpo's giant white stupas lined up inside the monastery complex. When I was small, the abbot lifted me up so that I could touch the cold rough surface of one of these massive plinths. I remember the sour smell of his body through his sleeveless yellow tunic, and the loose flesh of his bare arms as they supported me.

"Do you know who is buried in there?" the Rinpoche said, smiling as though it were a game. I shook my head. "You are," he whispered. But it was a secret, one of many. Mine was a childhood of secrets.

My brothers are studying philosophy this afternoon. I should be with them, but often the Rinpoche has wanted to use this time to take me aside for additional learning and study. No one has commented on this – no one questions the Rinpoche – although over the years they must have wondered or talked between themselves about it. I sometimes worry that their presumptions are uncharitable and perhaps even lewd. There is a price to pay for having secrets.

I walk slowly, the monastery wall staying on my right side, the sun casting bold shadows of the large bronze prayer wheels lining the kora like a row of drums. The sun is hot but the air is cool once away from its glare. And cold, very cold, at night. We live in mountain air after all. We have planned for this when the time comes.

As I do every time I pass, I set each prayer wheel in motion, feeling its weight resist my hand before it trundles clockwise, releasing a mantra each time it circulates. I imagine all the mantras spoken and spun rising into the air like thousands of tiny birds on the wing. A taxi driver's mutter at the wheel, a cleaner's moment of rest leaning on his broom, a market trader filling time clicking her prayer beads, each adding another little bird which flutters up to join a constant flow of mindfulness and compassion, a quiet collective affirmation of faith in the possibility of escaping the cycle of suffering and finding true peace.

Higher up, the path continues upwards away from the monastery's boundary wall. I hoist the hem of my robe and climb steadily, back bent against the sun. Somewhere on this hillside, I first met John Fairchild. I was just a boy then, angry and resentful. He seemed to realise a lot without my saying it. The Rinpoche thinks that I betrayed my secret to the Englishman, but I did not. We never directly spoke of it. And yet, everything he has said and done suggests that he knows who I am.

Where the path levels off I stop and look down over the monastery below. From here, Tashilunpo looks like a walled village, mud roofs clustered together as if taking shelter. Beyond lies Shigatse town, spreading east and south over the plain as it expands, so fast these days. Across the recently built zones, flashes of corrugated blue and grey blocks of tiled concrete form orderly grids of streets lined with slow-moving vehicles. It is a Chinese version of what a town should be, wide streets laid out in boxes, practical and modern. Are China and Tibet now merging together? Or is Tibet being pushed out, retreating behind the monastery wall to cower in fear? To my left, the kora continues round skirting a hill above the monastery, to the old fort which stands deserted like a mini version of Lhasa's Potala Palace. Shigatse used to be a political force in its own right, the biggest seat of power in Tibet after Lhasa. And the power centred on Tashilunpo, one of the biggest and most spiritually revered monasteries in Tibet. The Chinese would say that the big monasteries were corrupt, that the handful of senior monks were no better than feudal landowners robbing the people. Of course corruption occurred. But an atheistic Communist Chinese state would never understand their spiritual role, the power of prayer itself, the years of study so that only the most devout and determined would achieve what is really important, a true understanding of the meaning of existence. And the merit gained from that understanding would spread by means of the essential connectedness of all things, beyond the walled village, through all of Shigatse, all of Tibet, to all sentient beings. They may pretend otherwise these days, and talk about freedom of religion, but their one real aim was always to stamp out tradition and break thousands of years of continuous learning and growth. And here in Tashilunpo, they almost succeeded. Almost.

I am walking faster now, these reflections giving me anger and determination. These insights I owe to the Rinpoche. As well as a monk's Buddhist philosophy and the state-sponsored history which we all must learn, he has given me another view of the world, a whispered history, a preparation for what is to come. The abbot has always said that we cannot stay for ever under the oppressor's thumb. My education here at Tashilunpo is now complete. We will know when is the right time. Maybe it will be a beautiful rainbow, or the expression in an animal's face, or a reflection in a lake, but some day, when the date is auspicious, indications will tell us that now we should flee. And I will need to understand the world that we are fleeing into.

My mouth is dry from the dust. I sit on a stone ledge and wait. A scuffle of rock heralds the appearance of the abbot, with deep red cheeks and beads of sweat across his forehead. However slowly I try to walk, the Rinpoche is always slower. This concerns me deeply. The old man sits heavily on the ledge next to me. Looking at his tired face, I wonder how many of those lines have been caused by me. How often has the abbot, making that critical decision more than fifteen years ago, wondered if he did the right thing?

We both look out over Tashilunpo and the town beyond. I hesitate, but I need to tell him although I know the pain it will cause.

"Master," I say. I call him Master just as everyone else does. Some day I suppose this will change, and he will be addressing me with the full dignity associated with my status. This is not something we have spoken of. "I fear I may have brought suspicion onto us."

I tell him about the Russian, the conversation we had, the things the Russian told me and why this is so important to my friend John Fairchild. I feel his eyes on me as I tell him about Wei Li and the Chinese soldiers watching me as I passed through the courtyard to give him the message.

"I know you will say that I was foolish," I say. "I know you think I give too much importance to the Englishman. But it was a single chance that would never have happened again. If it was the same Russian, the same Dimitri, I can't say if it was, but such a fortuitous meeting could not have been ignored."

The Rinpoche says nothing, his weary eyes scanning the view. It is often his way. So I continue. "You named me Jinpa when I entered the monastery. Generous, that is what the name means. You wanted me to give whatever I could to help others. Did you not?"

The Rinpoche speaks, the rhythm of his voice less measured than usual. "I gave you that name because you needed generosity of spirit. It would be easy to descend into anger against those who have forced us to live like this. And you have avoided that." He turns to face me, his voice uncharacteristically high. "My child, I know you value your friendship with the English traveller. But you have risked everything! We cannot stay here now. We must leave."

His words hit me like physical blows. "No!" I say. "Not yet. We must wait for the right time, for an auspicious sign. You have said so."

But the Rinpoche is shaking his head. "As long as we were safe. But you are being watched. Someone saw you speaking to this foreigner. They will discover everything in time. You know they will. We must go now, before their suspicions grow any further."

I feel tears in my eyes. I have always known we must flee, but Tashilunpo is my whole life. And I know what hardships lie ahead. "We must wait for Fairchild," I say. "I sent a message for him to come here. I have to give him the message. If I don't do that, it was all for nothing."

"And how long will he be?"

I remember the indifference in Wei Li's face. "I cannot say."

"It could take some days for him to arrive. Weeks, even. We must start to make arrangements straight away. If he comes, he comes, but we cannot wait for him."

My heart thuds. What those simple words refer to, though always unavoidable, terrifies me. I steady myself with a whispered mantra and clasp my hands on my lap. "How long will it take before we are ready?" I ask.

"Four or five days. You must tell the others. You know how."

He takes a breath and pulls himself to his feet. He gives me no more than a look before turning and heading back around the kora. I watch him walk away. His body is stiff and tired. He has given his life to his cause, to my cause, to me. I want to say I am sorry, to gain his forgiveness, to put things back how they were, but I cannot. I hum another mantra, the sound falling dead in the air, and another one, and imagine two birds fluttering up to join all the others in their vast upwards spiral.

I cannot explain it. But despite the consequences, through all of my shock and fear, something in me or through me is telling me that what I did was right.

Chapter 11

Rose looked round wildly. She had a few seconds, no more. Footsteps were crossing the living room. She squatted and slid under the bed, her mind flashing through the last few seconds. Had she left anything visible? The bedroom doorway darkened. She didn't move, every muscle tensed. The footsteps passed the bed and went into the bathroom. A tap was running, water was being splashed. That stopped. Then the unmistakeable sound of a man urinating into a toilet bowl. Lovely. A toilet flushing, more running water and splashing. The hiss of a deodorant can. It was good to know Fairchild sweated in this muggy climate just like everyone else, assuming this was Fairchild of course. Then, from further away, the sudden sound of piano music. Chopin, maybe. Or possibly Brahms. The footsteps passed by the bed again. In the living room the music stopped and was replaced by a man's voice. John Fairchild's voice, answering the phone. She couldn't understand what he was saying: it sounded like Mandarin. The voice went on and became quieter, then louder again. He was circulating the living room while talking. Just as she was starting to wonder how long this would last and what her options were if he stayed in for the rest of the day, the conversation stopped. Drawers opened and shut. A pause, then a definitive slam. That was the front door closing.

Rose stayed unmoving for several minutes before silently emerging and checking the living room. No sign. He had gone out. She may just have been lucky, very lucky. What now? He would have left the building already so she had no chance of picking up his tail. She may as well stay and do what she came here to do. As her mind turned to her stash of listening equipment, her stomach did a backward flip. She took three steps and saw it, her bag, sitting on the floor behind an armchair where she had put it down. If Fairchild had been focusing entirely on the phone call, he could have missed it. On the other hand, he might not have done. He could be fully aware she was there now. He could be right outside the door. Christ, he could be *inside* the door. Well, if he were in the flat, he could only be in the kitchen. Rose crept forward, ready to move quickly and defensively if need be. She paused, then stepped into the kitchen doorway.

The kitchen was barely more than a cupboard. And it was empty. Rose breathed out slowly, waiting for her pulse to return marginally closer to normal before resuming her task. Very, very lucky. But this kind of luck didn't hold out for long.

Chapter 12

The words of the Rinpoche are still in my ears. We have only four or five days. I need to tell the others in our small group as soon as possible, secretly and quietly, without attracting attention. They will be uprooted from everything they know, and it is down to me to uproot them. I wish it were otherwise.

To find the strength, I walk round to the huge white chortens by the monastery wall. I reach up and rest my hands on the plinth of the tenth Panchen Lama's resting place, feeling its cold touch and looking up at its ornate golden decorations shining in the sunlight against the blue sky. I hear a whispered voice in my head. *Do you know who is buried here?* I close my eyes and empty my mind to listen, and feel, and sense the bond between us. Now I am ready. But I never get the chance to carry out my task.

I hear noise, the muttering of a crowd of people. It is coming from the debating courtyard. But this is not the relaxed chatter of students engaging in debate. The sound causes the skin on the back of my neck to prickle, and my pulse to race. It is the sound of voices raised in anger.

I run round to the back entrance and slip in, hovering by the wall. A multitude of my brothers have gathered here. Many of them are sitting down. Surrounding them is a ring of Chinese soldiers, clutching their weapons. Some of the monks are on their feet, shouting at these soldiers, raising their arms aloft in defiance.

I understand this anger and feel it too. These soldiers should not be here, in this place of peace, with their weapons and their spies. A feeling of dread spreads through me. This is happening because of me. Since the day I spoke to the Russian, right here in this garden, the surveillance has increased. The soldiers have been heavy-handed and ever-present. I have heard my brothers complain about it, their resentment growing. And now, I do not know how, a big confrontation has built up. And now these black-clad soldiers, armed and protected, encircle my countrymen, staring with hatred or indifference as they gesticulate and shout in their bright flowing robes, not caring about their own safety as they express their frustration and their determination and give true voice to their faith, as all of us long to do.

The Rinpoche has always said we must protest with the heart, not with the body. It is futile, he says, to try to rise up when our nation is so heavily oppressed with such force. Watching this scene, I want to run forward and join my fellow monks, adding my voice to theirs. But I know I cannot. I must not put myself in danger, for the sake of the future of Tashilunpo itself. So I shrink back like a coward, concealing myself behind a tree trunk, instead of running forward with reckless joy as I long to do.

A small group of monks are goading one of the soldiers. They have surrounded him, shouting. He is young, red in the face, shouting back at them. With a shock I realise that one of the monks is Sonam. This is very dangerous. I see him mouth wide, eyes blazing, his finger jabbing the air as he closes in on the young soldier. He should know better. I tense, ready to go over there and pull him to safety, but he is too far away, right at the other side of the courtyard. I cannot risk myself.

Now more soldiers are joining in. A scuffle starts, people pushing each other. A monk falls to the ground and a crowd gathers round him. The shouting in the courtyard becomes a defiant chant. People get up on their feet. The soldiers look at each other and take a step back. They are outnumbered, and the monks are angry.

A deafening crack splits the air. A soldier has fired his gun up into the sky. Silence falls. Two or three others do the same thing. Then the silence is replaced with jeers. The first soldier lowers the barrel of his gun and aims at the crowd. Someone screams. People run, this way and that. He fires again. So loud! A bullet hits the wall not far from where I am standing. I cower behind the tree. In panic, monks are gathering round the gates to try and get away. More shots are fired but all I can see are my brothers, running and pushing to get away from the gunfire. I am caught up in the crowd squeezing towards the gate. People are pushing from all sides as others join from the back and shove forward in their fear. I hear more shots but cannot even turn my head. In a blind mass of panic we squeeze through the gate and fan out on the other side. Bodies are running in different directions, some wanting to hide, some to escape. For myself, I want to find Sonam.

I try making my way to the other entrance to the garden but I am swimming against a tide as people run along the narrow passageway. I press myself against the wall, watching. I do not see him. The gunshots have stopped. I say a mantra and pray that nobody is hurt. Not because of me, not because of me, I plead. Then the soldiers start to emerge.

They have handcuffed some of the monks, those who were involved in the fight. Each monk is pulled along by two soldiers, and others come out around them, guns raised, looking about as they make their way to the main gate. One of the soldiers catches my eye. I shrink back into the shadows. He turns and moves on.

Then I see Sonam, in between two of the soldiers, his arms behind his back. Our eyes meet and he turns his head away as they pull him along. He knows he should not have been a part of this, but he has feelings like all of us. And now he is in their hands.

With my heart, I am with him. With my heart, I sat and shouted with the protesters in the courtyard. But as the arrestees are marched out of the monastery gates, I slip away ashamed. It is the only right course, but now more than ever I know that we cannot stay here and continue like this. Even before speaking to the Rinpoche, Sonam's arrest makes it clear. As our master has said many times, we can trust each other forever, but what is done to people behind closed doors might make any of us say anything.

We must leave, and we must leave tonight.

Chapter 13

Mid-morning, a single figure with a rucksack over one shoulder emerged into the street from a prestigious-looking apartment block in Jianguomen. John Fairchild turned towards Wangfujiang, walked for ten minutes along the boulevard and descended down a long ramp into an underpass. Out of sight from the street with no other pedestrians nearby, a movement from above caught his eye, too late for him to react. The body landed on him like a dead weight, pushing him into the ground and knocking the breath out of him.

A fat hand gripped his neck. He clawed it off. It clamped back again. He twisted and worked free enough to push up into his assailant's chin. The jar provoked an involuntary groan and gave him enough space to get to one knee. His attacker, short but solidly built, recovered and lunged forward with his fist. Fairchild ducked and rolled away. He got to his feet and took several rapid steps back, preventing the stronger man from landing any blows. They came to a halt, staring intensely at each other, both waiting for the other to move.

It was no more than a glance, but enough to give away that he had seen the second attacker over the shoulder of the first, approaching down the ramp. Fairchild surged forward as if to barge straight past. A solid push in the stomach took some wind out of his thickset opponent but was not enough to clear him and they both fell to the ground, the stout man with his arms gripped around Fairchild's waist. Fairchild turned, twisting against the force of the grip, to get the briefest glimpse of a stiletto knife in the hand of the second assailant who, quick on his feet, was almost upon him.

The stocky man pulled his hand back and punched Fairchild twice, fast, in the jaw then in the stomach, the pain making him groan and winding him long enough to see the knife raised above him. But his hands were free and he brought both of them together in a sharp movement which knocked the knife clear. It went clattering down the ramp. The second man watched it disappear with a look of surprise and glanced down at his empty hand.

The next blow to Fairchild's stomach met more resistance and a faster recovery. He kicked up with force, preventing a third punch and giving himself enough time to get to his feet. The knifeman, having lost his weapon, had his arms raised in defence, not attack. A kick to the face of the stocky man as he lumbered forward sent him staggering back. Fairchild turned to the knifeman and shoved him hard against the concrete wall. He grasped and yanked hard on a raised arm, twisting until the smaller man was on the ground screaming, then quieted him with a precise kick to the head. He turned and dodged the first man's power blow aimed from behind, unbalanced him with a kick to his knees and pulled him to the ground. The stocky man's head banged into the concrete as a single punch from above stilled him.

He looked up. A pedestrian at the top of the ramp slowed, registered the two inert bodies, turned and backtracked. John Fairchild brushed off his clothing, straightened his collar, picked up his rucksack and stepped over the bodies to continue on his way.

The noodle bar was as busy and noisy as it always was. The windows were usefully steamed up, although Wei Li was savvy enough to sit somewhere near the back. Fairchild walked in and entered a cloud of steam smelling of ginger, fried garlic and oyster sauce. He ignored the makeshift handwritten menu pinned to the wall, called for tea on his way past the counter and sat down opposite Wei Li. On the table between them sat a steaming bowl of soup and a plate piled high with ribbon noodles fried with beef and green vegetables.

"Try the soup," said Wei Li. "It's very good."

"I've already eaten," said Fairchild, avoiding any direct contact with the food-stained table. They spoke English. There was less chance their words would be overheard and understood by anyone. Fairchild let his gaze rove around the room. No one here looked as if they associated with mobsters, although all kinds of people in this city owed favours to the Wong Kai.

"Is that why you're so late?"

"I bumped into an old friend."

"An old friend!" Wei Li laughed. "Fairchild, you have so many old friends. Everywhere you go, old friends. Some of them are not so friendly, though, hey."

Wei Li was looking at his face. Fairchild touched his lip with his finger where it felt slightly bloated and checked for blood. There was none. Wei Li had learned to be observant. A teapot and small cup were placed in front of him. He poured while Wei Li sucked ribbon noodles into his mouth.

"Your boy has a message for you. You need to go visit. He says he has news from Russia."

The teapot hung mid-air. "Russia?"

"That's it. News from Russia."

"That's all he said?"

"Yes. That's all. And he made a big noise about bad China oppressing the poor. Crazy people. Tibet is richer now than it's ever been. I see plenty of gold left on the roof of that monastery." Wei Li guided another slimy mass of noodle into his mouth and continued talking through it. "He doesn't normally shout all that stuff. Usually he's all peace and smiles. Something not right there. Your boy's in trouble, maybe?"

It was phrased as a question, but he didn't look as if he realistically expected an answer. He picked up the soup bowl and slurped from its rim, a dribble escaping down his chin.

"Did he say that?" asked Fairchild.

"Of course not! He doesn't trust me. I'm the enemy! He uses me because he has to. I'm just the courier. But nervous about something."

He flicked his chopsticks dismissively, resulting in another spatter of beef to decorate the table top.

"When was this?"

"Two days ago. I called into the office straight away." He sounded petulant.

"Yes, I got the message. When are you back in Tibet?"

"Flying back to Lhasa tomorrow. Another tour arriving. Always another tour. You must be making good money, hey."

Fairchild was doing calculations in his head. "Can I get on that plane?"

Wei Li shook his head. "I already checked. All booked for the next week. It's the busiest time of the year. You know that."

His head disappeared behind the soup bowl as he took another draught.

"What about the train?" asked Fairchild.

Wei Li re-emerged. "Train is possible. Beijing to Xining then Lhasa. They can book it in the office." He meant Dragon Fire, their Beijing office. Wei Li counted in his head. "Leave Beijing tomorrow morning, Xining is twenty-four hours, almost. Earliest you could get the Lhasa train is the afternoon day after tomorrow."

"Can't I get a train direct from Beijing?"

"Sold out long ago. Xining is difficult enough. No seat reservations. You will be standing, crammed in with the proletariat. Migrant workers."

"What about the permit? Can they sort that out?"

Wei Li winced. "It's very late. Very expensive."

Foreign visitors to Tibet needed permits. In the high season there was a waiting list. It could take six weeks to go through, assuming they were giving any out at all. Unless, of course, your travel agency had someone on the inside who could get your permits processed as a priority, for the right price.

"And here's the other thing. I'm under surveillance." A clump of noodles fell off Wei Li's chopstick. "Don't worry. I've shaken them for now. But I can't have them knowing where I'm going. I'll need another ID."

Wei Li sucked his teeth, taking in several small pieces of meat at the same time.

"Very expensive, if you want it fast. What's your top price?"

"For a permit and the earliest train to Lhasa, whatever it costs."

Wei Li stared at him. Fairchild sipped his tea unperturbed. "Just get everything sent to my apartment. I don't want to go into the office. They'll be watching it, but they don't know where I'm staying. Yet." He was confident he had avoided leading Chu's surveillance team back to the apartment, but the incident in the underpass concerned him. The Wong Kai could make use of the shops and businesses under their so-called protection to give themselves lookouts everywhere. Hopefully it was a coincidence that they jumped him so near to where he was staying, but at the very least they knew he was in Beijing. He needed to get out of the city as quickly as he could. "Text me to let me know when," he said.

"Okay. Whatever." Wei Li drained his soup and wiped his mouth.

"How's Daisy?"

"Daisy? Fine, fine. Never mind Oxford. Now it's Yale she wants. Yale, Yale all the time. Yale! You any idea what that costs?"

"I can imagine."

It was not an idle question. Thousands of middle-class Chinese parents were looking abroad for university places for their precious only children. To send a child abroad, however, required the family to have a spotless record. Nothing suspect, no strange associations, no inappropriate gatherings or protests, and certainly no protracted love affairs with the wives of senior politburo members. To keep his daughter happy, not to mention his wife, Wei Li needed to keep that delicious episode of his life a well-kept secret, as it had been so far. Which made Fairchild his friend. His old, dear friend. An occasional reminder of that was no bad thing, particular when Fairchild needed his help for something as critical as this.

Wei Li was still looking curiously at his face. "So our security people getting physical now, is it? What did you do to upset them?"

Fairchild touched his lip again. The swelling was bigger. "That was something else."

Wei Li laughed, displaying a mouth of half-chewed noodle. "You lead a very complicated life, Fairchild."

The phone in Fairchild's pocket beeped. Zack was calling. He stood up. "Meet me in Lhasa. Off the train."

Wei Li shrugged while blandly sucking up the last lengths of noodles into his mouth. Fairchild answered his phone while stepping out into the street. "You again?"

The line crackled. "Hey, Fairchild! Good to hear you again too!" Blustering his way, not for the first time, past Fairchild's lukewarm greeting. "You busy?"

"Yes." Zack was still trying to find out what he was doing in Beijing. Fairchild stopped in a doorway a short way from the restaurant and checked out the street.

"Yeah, well, you're gonna want to stop what you're doing to listen to what I've just found out. The Wong Kai are offering a reward. For your life."

"So that's what's driven the rats out of the drain."

"You already noticed something then?"

"You could say that."

"John, you should get out of Beijing." Zack was trying to sound serious. "Not kidding now. That's the worst place for you to be."

"Thanks for your concern. I'm already making plans. I'd be grateful if you didn't share that with anyone, though."

"Yeah, her." Zack sounded as close as he ever got to contrition. "Well, I told you she put me in a difficult situation, Fairchild. Threatened to sell me to the police."

"So you said."

"Anyway, that's the other reason I called. I've kept an eye on arrivals at Beijing in the last couple of days. Like you suggested."

"Thank you, Zack. I appreciate it."

"Least I could do." Zack entirely missed, or pretended to, Fairchild's sarcasm. "Anyway, no sign of a Linda Duffy. But another name triggered an alert. Rose Clarke. I got a photo through. It's her. British. Diplomatic service. You know what that means."

"Right." Many of those involved in espionage abroad were employed officially as foreign diplomatic staff. As he thought, a spook.

"At least she was."

"Was?"

"A former employee, apparently. No longer in the service."

"Really?"

"Really. Interesting, huh? Want to know what else I got?"

"Please."

"I know which hotel she's checked into."

"That's excellent, Zack."

"Yeah, it is. And I could tell you, if I wanted to."

Zack's attempts to trade information and find out what Fairchild was up to in Beijing failed, as they usually did. Eventually Fairchild guilted him into giving him the name of the hotel anyway. It was, after all, Zack's fault that Rose Clarke was in the country in the first place.

After the call, Fairchild, on the move again, made some checks that he wasn't being tailed by any of the various people who wanted to disrupt his business. While dodging Zack's questions, he had formulated a new plan. He made for the hutongs, beyond which, in a very discreet penthouse, he would find his young and rather shy friend Zhang Lao. After that he'd be heading straight for Rose Clarke's hotel. Zack did have his uses. Fairchild checked his watch. The UK was eight hours behind, which meant he could get answers tonight if he put a call in now. Persuading SIS staff to access secret personnel files was treasonous, he supposed, but he didn't much care. They were coming after him, not the other way round. That was what made him angry. Angry enough to pay Zhang Lao a visit.

Navigating the haphazard maze of hutongs, he passed through the sanitised cobbled tourist zone into older, narrower streets full of one-room homes. Here people lived outside in these tiny streets: small children urinated into the gutter, old men sat on plastic chairs staring at strangers, and women squatted by doorways chopping vegetables into metal bowls. His footsteps slowed. He was thinking about Linda Duffy again. Or Rose Clarke, as he now knew her to be. He was thinking about her in the restaurant, her voice, the quizzical expression on her face, her figure as she leaned over the chair to speak to him, compact yet feminine. These details came easily to mind. Truth be told, they had never really left his mind.

His plan for Rose Clarke wasn't nice, he had to admit. But sometimes in this line of work you had to settle for not being very nice. And she wasn't going to suffer anything she didn't deserve. She'd put the Wong Kai onto him, for God's sake. He didn't need a price on his life. He needed to be free to operate in privacy, particularly at a time like this.

His pace quickened again. The Zhang Lao treatment was necessary, albeit drastic. It was quick, you could say that for it. Once it was done and finished, she would be out of the game. He could stop thinking about her. At least he hoped he could. Because right now he had enough to think about.

Chapter 14

After the riot the monastery falls silent. We carry out our duties listlessly, each in our own world. The main courtyard is deserted as I cross, my slow heavy steps echoing in the silence. The Chinese have barred visitors from entering. Some disappointed tourists and pilgrims are gathered outside, but we have heard rumours of a roadblock on the road to Shigatse and travellers being turned away before they even reach the town.

Rumour has done its job. Those who were not present know exactly what happened. No one was hurt, but ten were arrested. I have spoken briefly with the Rinpoche. I know what to do.

I find Palden at his desk, as usual staring at a mass of figures on a ledger through small round glasses. He is our changzho, treasurer of Tashilunpo, diligent and methodical, not satisfied until everything is exactly right. But everything is not exactly right. The Rinpoche took Palden, one of his oldest friends, into his confidence right from the start, and now Palden's position enables him to smooth out certain small irregularities so we can put some of Tashilunpo's money aside without our Chinese overseers noticing. We were once one of the wealthiest monasteries in Tibet, but Tashilunpo's funds are now a fraction of their former size, and the Chinese demand bigger and bigger chunks. With great skill Palden manages to squeeze out some small amounts which can be used to buy supplies and transport when we need it.

It is a role which causes the obedient little man considerable stress. His hesitant manner belies a great aptitude for planning which stems from an obsession with detail and an insistence that everything, however small, be matched and resolved and tidied away. These qualities have enabled the daring substitution so many years ago to pass without hitch. But our biggest challenge is still ahead of us.

As I stand at the doorway of the changzho's tiny office, Palden looks up at me over the rim of his glasses.

I say one word: "Tonight."

I wait for the slightest nod of his head in acknowledgement, and walk off immediately, not wanting to see any further reaction to my news in the tired old man's face.

I make my way to the chanting hall, where I have to wait for my eyes to adjust to the dimness. Yonten is near the back of the hall polishing butter lamps. His huge frame is facing the shrine, and he is rubbing the lamps so vigorously his whole body shakes. I think of Yonten as the youngest of us, but in fact we are the same age and the Rinpoche used to bring him into our lessons when we were smaller. I think he was supposed to be a childhood companion and playmate, but we never became close friends. Built like a bull, Yonten did not share a passion for learning and found the intricacies of philosophical debate difficult to comprehend. Silently and slowly going about his own business, Yonten just wants, I think, to lead a simple life. Nevertheless, he is one of us, fiercely loyal, and his size and strength will be an asset to us on our journey.

Yonten looks up as I approach, coming back from a place of reflection. I feel that they all look at me a little warily, those in our group, as if they are not sure how to behave around me. Of course we know they have to treat me just like any other monk, but normally there would be strict formalities of address to follow even from a young age. The Dalai Lama was brought up on his own in an enormous palace, surrounded by servants and advisers. That would be my destiny if it were not for the necessary secrecy. So perhaps it is difficult for those in our group to act entirely normally with me. It is one of the reasons, aside from pure prudence, why I do not seek out these particular people for company. With the Rinpoche, of course, it is completely different. There has never been anything held back between us.

Not wanting to draw attention, I pass the message on in an undertone and wait for a nod of understanding from the larger man. Then I move on, pressing my hand into the back of his broad shoulder as I pass.

Before leaving the chanting hall I stand for a moment in front of the Sakyamuni statue, feeling calmed by the placidity of its enormous eyes and beatific smile. I will miss looking on this uplifting golden sight. I make an effort to notice every detail. Then I move along to gaze up at the empty throne of the Panchen Lama. Its sight prompts many emotions: pride, sadness, guilt, anger, fortitude. Outside, I pace the length of the courtyard reflecting on the meaning of the intricate murals, the thousands of Buddha likenesses lining the walls. I go into each tiny chapel in turn and light a butter candle, saying a prayer as each wick sputters into life.

The Thongwa Donden temple is where I find Choden, attending to the offerings. It is appropriate to find him here, at the shrine containing the remains of the first Dalai Lama and the early Panchen Lamas. I have spent much time here myself, trying to reach with my mind the collected wisdom of all the years of my being, to help us now in the present.

Choden, always quiet and determined, hears the message and smiles. He lost his entire family in the Cultural Revolution and would happily give up his own life for Tibet to defy China, as the Rinpoche realised many years ago. Our plan means that out of the six of us, Choden is the most likely to lose his freedom and indeed his life. It touches me deeply to see how willingly he faces these prospects. I wonder if I myself would have the strength to do the same.

From the courtyard I make my way to a huddle of outbuildings by the monastery wall. I pause and look back to check that no one else is in sight, then I open a flimsy wooden door and step inside. I am in a small storage room, little used. A number of wooden planks lean lengthways against the wall, and a pile of old awnings gathers dust and cobwebs in a corner.

I close the door behind me and sit on the floor facing the door. I feel along the wall behind me, reaching behind the lengths of wood. My fingers find what they are seeking, a loose stone which I prise away from the wall with difficulty because of the awkward angle. From the cavity behind, I pull out a small rusted tin box which I put on my knee and open up. This box is so important to me that it may as well contain my heart.

The main object inside is a bundle of photographs held together with an elastic band. The oldest one is dated and time stamped: May 12th 1995. I am six years old. The Rinpoche is holding my hand. Standing behind him are two other adults and an older boy. Next to me is another boy, the same age and height as me, the same round ruddy face. It looks like a family snapshot.

The next photograph was taken a few months later. Now I am amongst a group of boys who all entered the monastery at around the same time. We are in the debating courtyard, smiling mischievously. Behind us are the golden roofs of Tashilunpo against the mountainside behind. Every few years sees another photograph. We are always photographed as a group, all unmistakeably at Tashilunpo, all date and time stamped.

These photographs are my passport: my proof of identity when I reach the outside world. I have a sudden vision of myself in the future, in the company of the Dalai Lama, in India, a land I have heard so much about. There are garlands of flowers, so they say, and wide rivers gushing through green valleys, and so much rain. I will go to the mountains, to Dharamsala, Tibet in exile. I will show the Dalai Lama these photographs. His Holiness will recognise me and bless me, and we will work together, both stronger through our connectedness as we have been through time, as we should always have been.

I mouth a mantra with barely a whisper of breath and put the bundle in my satchel. I think about my English friend. I have destroyed all the letters and messages Fairchild sent me. In some ways he is a very wise man. He can see the patterns that hold things together, that to most people are invisible. But sometimes, I fear, his thirst for answers causes him to do things he should not do. I had so much hoped to see him again.

I pause for a moment, bowing my head and closing my eyes in concentration to experience this moment, and then I stow away the empty box. I open the door cautiously and slip out into the sunlight, feeling a new resolve. Tonight is the night. We have much to do to be ready.

Chapter 15

Rose spent several hours sitting in her hotel room monitoring the sound equipment on her CSM. She'd discreetly installed tiny microphones in the living room, kitchen and bedroom of Fairchild's flat before slipping out half an hour after he did. The feeds were recorded on a secure online drive and downloaded to the CSM. Everything seemed to be working, but so far she'd picked up no sound. No one was in the flat. Fairchild was still walkabout. And now she had another problem: the battery on her laptop was gradually draining even though she had it plugged into the mains. The same thing happened with the other power sockets in the room. She'd had no problem like this in Hong Kong. The only thing that had changed was the international adaptor she'd bought at Beijing airport when she'd arrived. It must be faulty.

Everything was being recorded onto the online drive, but without a powered-up laptop she wouldn't be able to retrieve the information. She stowed the laptop in the safe, went down to the lobby and got directions to a nearby convenience store. It was only a block away. While there she stocked up on some "stake-out" junk food as well as the adaptor itself: she could be in her room listening to these feeds for quite some time. As she turned to leave and go straight back to the hotel, the breath was sucked out of her body by the sudden appearance, standing in the doorway, of John Fairchild.

"Well, goodness me! Isn't this the most amazing coincidence? Fancy seeing you here, of all places... Linda, wasn't it?" Fairchild smiled generously. Rose kept her expression as neutral as possible. Her heart was racing and her mind was turning over rapidly. No way was this a coincidence. He had been tailing her. *He* had been tailing *her*. For how long?

"John Fairchild! Well, how nice to bump into you."

"Yes indeed. You know, I think this is far too much of a coincidence to go unmarked. There's a bar I know just round the corner. How about a drink?"

Part of her wanted to flee to the safety of her hotel room. But what was the point in that when the person she was trying to track was standing in front of her? She needed to get on top of the situation and find out what he knew. "Sure. Why not?" she said.

The five minutes they walked together she managed to fill with a few bland travel-related pleasantries before they arrived at some extravagantly themed gothic bar with red velvet seats, fake candles on sticky wooden tables and only a smattering of other customers. Fairchild ordered a gin and tonic. Rose ordered mineral water.

"So!" He sat back and crossed his legs, casual and relaxed in an expensive-looking pink shirt. Questions crowded Rose's mind. Where had he picked up her trail? Did he know she was in his apartment? Had he been waiting for her outside the building and followed her to her hotel? But she was careful, or thought she had been, double-backing several times. The only other option was that he knew where she was staying some other way. But that would mean knowing a lot of other things as well. Her real name, for example. She would have to proceed with her cover and find out what he knew.

"So, you got away, then?" she asked. "With your friend in the boat? Were you heading off to mainland China?"

He was holding her gaze. "No, it was just a short trip in fact. As you know, since you bumped into my friend Zack in Lan Kwai Fong later on that same evening."

"Did I?" Rose had been hoping Zack would be reluctant to reveal to Fairchild that he'd tipped Rose off about the travel agency, but clearly not.

"Indeed. So you also avoided arrest, it seems."

"No thanks to you. A lift would have saved me getting wet. I had to buy a new outfit."

"And now you're in Beijing. It's almost as if you knew I was coming here."

"That happens a lot, does it, women following you around the world?"

"Every now and then." He paused while their drinks arrived then continued after the waiter had gone, keeping his voice low. "I know who you are. I know who you work for. Well – worked for. That was a bit unfortunate, wasn't it? A promising career at MI6 coming to a sudden end like that."

Rose concentrated on showing no response, but her mind was spinning. He'd already realised she was some kind of spook, but this was way more specific, something only someone on the inside could have known. What kind of contacts did he have?

"Still, one door closes and another one opens." He sipped his drink. "This is very important to you, isn't it? I mean, your whole career rests on this little mission being a success. That's the carrot they're dangling, isn't it? They've got you right where they want you."

He was reading a script of her thoughts over the last few months. His softly spoken words crystallised her inner resentment. Walter was right about this guy: he had friends deep inside SIS. But he could read people as well, with startling accuracy. She suddenly felt very vulnerable. Fairchild folded his arms again.

"I'll give you some credit, though," he said. "Tracking me down here. I can't help feeling you're not working as solo as you're supposed to be."

Rose drank some water, realising her mouth was dry. Another thought had spun out of her madly whirring brain: he could have been tracking her since she arrived in Beijing. In which case, he knew not only where she was staying but the location of the dead drop in Beihai Park. She'd have to fess up to Alastair. And he'd have some explaining to do. Damn all this. What a mess. She could feel her face burning. The ice had almost melted in her water. She drank some more.

"So what exactly is your task?" asked Fairchild congenially. "Find me? Well you've done that, ten out of ten. Now what?" He leaned forward conspiratorially. "You're not going to kill me, are you?"

Rose managed a faint smile. She wouldn't have minded. What they called self-defence had been her favourite part of the training they'd received. It gave her great inward satisfaction to know that she could, whenever she chose, inflict great pain on people, or worse. Who would come out best in a fight between her and Fairchild, she wasn't entirely sure.

Fairchild settled back again. "Well, I'm still here, so I assume not. How about an easier question? Who's your handler? I suppose you have a handler now that you're on the outside. Is it your chap in Hong Kong? Alastair, is it? That must be a bit strange, taking orders from him. You two go back a long way, I understand."

This was not good. How could he know all this? She stayed expressionless, but he continued as if reading her thoughts. "Unless Alastair is the person who's been helping you, of course. Unofficially. That might make more sense. An old buddy. How could he say no? I'll bet, though, that he shouldn't really be doing that. Pity if someone found out." Time seemed to have slowed down. Rose drained her water. She couldn't drop Alastair in it, not for anyone. Her pulse was racing. She felt blood rushing to her head and fingertips. Fairchild leaned back and tutted. "Come on, Rose. I can call you that, can't I? Rose Clarke? It's good to know your real name."

Her whirring mind had slowed down. She was struggling to process what he'd just said. She placed her empty glass on the table. "I'm afraid you must be muddling me up with someone else." She almost fell over the words. *Mudduln-me-up.* What was wrong with her?

Come on, Rose," Fairchild was leaning forward now. "You've pursued me here under false pretences, making threats to my friends on the way. Now I'm asking you nicely to tell me, please, who is it within MI6 that you're working for?"

"How about another drink?" She kept her tone casual. Her throat was dry again. She raised her hand to call over the waiter. When he arrived, he and Fairchild exchanged the smallest of glances. It was enough to make her realise what was going on. And to work out that she was in a lot of trouble.

"Never mind," she said to the waiter. As soon as he left, she picked up her bag and made to stand up. "I'm not feeling well," she said. "I'll be leaving now. Goodbye."

He put his hand on her arm. "I don't think so. Not yet."

She assessed the firmness of his hand on her arm, the distance between her knee and the table. She could feel herself swaying. He was watching her.

"Don't think about doing one of your party moves. With the dose you've just drunk there's no way you can get away or outrun me. You may as well make yourself comfortable."

That was the last thing she wanted. This was bad and was going to get worse. She needed to get away from him and to a hospital, fast.

"You're not going to die, by the way." He spoke pleasantly, as if asking her how her flight was. "I just want to ask you a couple of questions, that's all. Nothing to worry about. So who is it that you're working for? Is it the new head honcho? Marcus Salisbury? Is he after me?"

She steadied herself by putting her hands on the table and stared down at her fingers. She focused on breathing evenly, trying to block out everything else including the growing buzzing sound in her head.

"Right. Okay, then," he said. She could feel his eyes on her. "Is it Walter? Something to do with him?"

She could no longer entirely master her expression. It couldn't have been much, just a slight widening of the eyes, a tightening of the mouth. But whatever she'd done, it was enough.

"Walter! Oh, I see! And what does the meddling little Walter want now?"

She had to end this before losing control entirely. It was time to do something desperate to get out of this. His grip was still firmly on her arm. She centred her feet on the floor and lifted her head.

"I need to leave now!" she shouted. "I've been drugged! I need the police!" She slammed her fists onto the top of the table. "Someone call the police! I've been drugged!"

Her arm was jerked upwards abruptly. "We're leaving," said Fairchild. He pulled her to her feet. She tried to free herself, but seemed to have no strength. He was walking her to the door. She staggered.

"I've been drugged!" she cried out again. She could hear her words slurring. A group of customers was looking at them. "Call the police!" she shouted at them. Fairchild said something to them over her head, in Mandarin. They didn't move. As he pushed her outside she turned back to see the waiter watching them with wide eyes.

Fairchild was half carrying her. She tried to look around but the street outside had an unreal quality, like a film set. Traffic went by without slowing. No pedestrians. But someone else was there, someone hanging back behind them. She could feel their presence. When she tried to turn round he pulled her back sharply. She couldn't focus enough to free herself from him.

He bundled her into a side street then an alleyway behind shops. Things were becoming increasingly unreal, out of sequence like a dream. Her back was against a wall and he was standing over her. No one else was there now.

His voice was short and rough. "No more messing about, Rose. What do you want with me?"

Rose had trouble understanding the words. "I didn't—"

"Now, for God's sake!" The stone wall was rough on her back. He was standing very close to her. His hands gripped her shoulders hard, pushing her back into the wall. A finger and thumb grabbed her chin and held it up so her eyes met his, grey and cold. She could smell gin. "Come on, Rose. Why's Walter after me? What does he want? What have I done now?"

She could hear herself speaking, but it was as if someone else were saying the words. "He wants to meet with you."

"Meet with me? Is that all? Come on, Rose. What for?"

"I – I don't…" She couldn't explain.

The back of her head hit the wall as her chin was jerked up. "What is this about, Rose?" He emphasised every word.

"You buy and sell information. You're a mercenary. A blackmailer." It was that voice again, that other voice.

"Yes, yes. So they say. I already know that."

"I've seen your file."

"All of it?"

"No, not all." She shouldn't be saying all this.

"So why are you here?"

She was finding it hard to draw breath. "He says you have friends inside SIS. That you know stuff. Identities, operations." She couldn't phrase things properly. *You know stuff.*

There was a pause. "And?" Rose didn't understand the question. She shook her head again. "That's it? I know stuff? Why now? Why you?" She still wasn't getting it. The hand released her chin, but she still felt the pressure where his fingers had pressed on her jaw. Her legs were shaking and the wall dug into her back.

"Is this to do with my parents? With Vienna?" She couldn't make sense of the words he was saying. It must have shown. "You really don't know anything, do you?" The voice was distant and blurry. "Why did they send *you*? You're nobody. You're not a player. You're just a fuck-up."

She was having to concentrate on trying to breathe. Her eyes were squeezed shut. "I'm not!" The voice that spoke was tremulous and high. She thought she was angry. She tried to push him away. She ought to be able to fight back, defend herself. But she was just flailing her arms about. Now he was gripping both her shoulders, pressing her up against the wall so that she could not move. The buzzing was getting louder and louder. His face was next to hers and the gin on his hot breath stank like medicine. Then the pressure on her shoulders lessened and she felt her knees buckle. The wall scraped her back as she slid down. She fell forwards onto her knees. She was on the ground, curled up.

He was crouching right next to her. His voice, expressionless, spoke directly into her ear. "Remember this, Rose Clarke. I could kill you now. I could have killed you already. But you're not going to die, not this time. When you come round I'll have gone. Don't try and follow me. Give up and go home. Learn from this. Look after yourself. Walter and the rest don't care about you, and neither do I. Leave me alone. That's a warning. You should listen."

He stepped back. "Have a nice flight home," he said, from further away. She heard footsteps. A roaring sound filled her ears. Then there was darkness.

Chapter 16

A large moon illuminates the compound between passing swathes of thick cloud. I have not seen moonlight like this before. It is almost as bright as daylight, cool and clean. Perhaps it is a sign from which we should take heart, although it makes our progress more dangerous.

I hear no sound except a dog barking in the distant town. As the moon disappears behind a bank of cloud and the light fades, we emerge, five grey figures, from the shadows of outbuildings. We are dressed now in everyday rural clothing: worn woollen sweaters, long coats, solid leather boots. Our heads are covered with woollen hats and we carry well-laden backpacks on our shoulders. We do not talk. The biggest of our group carries a wooden ladder.

He plants the ladder firmly against the white monastery wall, but the clouds have drifted. We all retreat into the shadows as the moon suddenly brightens, beautiful but dangerous. As the cold light dims again behind wisps of cloud, we advance on the ladder. With Yonten's foot on its base, Choden ascends first, drops a rope down the other side, struggles awkwardly over the top of the wall and disappears. The others follow. My older brothers climb stiffly, pulling themselves onto the top with difficulty. I am more nimble and can scale rapidly up and over. Yonten ascends last and, straddling the top, reaches down with one hand to retrieve the ladder and stow it at the foot of the wall. Then he too slips down, and we are all out of sight of the monastery.

The white wall, the clustered buildings, the golden roofs and the hillside above us again emerge, bathed in a sea of silver. We huddle at the foot of the wall. When again the outlines fade and become indistinct, we dare to make our way quickly up into the hills, our only sound the occasional crack of a shoe on rock. Then we are out of sight. I have no chance to look back.

So that is how the jewel of Tashilunpo, the culmination of its spiritual knowledge and enlightenment, slips away quietly in the middle of the night while the monastery sleeps, as ignorant of its loss as it was of its presence, leaving the golden throne as empty and the sleeping souls as leaderless as they were before.

Chapter 17

"Zhang Lao!" It was no more than a whisper, but an insistent one. Zhang came running out of the shadows and knelt, rested his fingers on her neck and leaned over her to check her breathing.

"How much did you put in?" Fairchild asked, standing over him watching.

"Not much. Small dose, like you asked. Small dose."

"Not small enough. She's not supposed to pass out this quickly."

Zhang sat back. "She's okay. Pulse is normal, breathing steady. Must be an extreme reaction. Very rare. So fast, wasn't it?" He sounded fascinated, like a scientist conducting an experiment.

"We have to get her back to her hotel. Someone in the bar might have called the police."

"In that place? I don't think so."

Zhang had a point. It hadn't taken much to bribe the waiter to put Zhang's drug in Rose's drink. Fairchild didn't do this very often, but circumstances demanded it from time to time. It was not, he reasoned, that different from getting someone drunk, only more efficient. Zhang was his go-to chemist in this part of the world, a twisted individual, sure enough, but he knew what he was doing. Always before, it had resulted in a hell of a night, with back-slapping and confidences and a few staggers on the way home but no more. Always before, he supposed, it had been a man. He had always made sure his companion got to a bed safely to sleep it off. And he paid extra – a lot extra – to have Zhang lurking nearby in case of emergency. Zhang agreed to this under duress, partly because he insisted that all of his solutions, as he liked to call them, were completely safe, but also because he had an extreme reluctance to leave his apartment, ever.

Even now he was looking around nervously. "She'll sleep it off," he said.

"I can't leave her here. I've got to get her back to the hotel. How am I supposed to do that?"

Zhang seemed surprised. "Okay. I can wake her up a little. Not much. Enough so she can walk. Like a cold shower. She won't remember."

A cold shower. Zhang was full of euphemisms. A wild night, a chill-out, a heart-to-heart. He had a control panel of human mood inside that briefcase. Fairchild was irritated by the suggestive expression on his face. "Do it. Quickly."

He watched Zhang peruse his collection of vials, pill bottles and sachets. Zhang had been a chemistry student when he realised he could make serious amounts of money through his specialised knowledge without having to go to the trouble of studying. Word had spread rapidly, and business was so successful that instead of graduating he moved into a penthouse apartment and let clients come to him from far and wide. Even now he remained young-looking with his skinny frame, unnaturally wide eyes, goatee beard and black T-shirts, but it was impossible to age him. Zhang Lao – Old Zhang – was an ironic nickname, but Old Zhang might not be as young any more as he looked. He took to staying indoors after carrying out a few jobs for some of the less savoury characters in Beijing's criminal underworld. Now he was permanently pale and could only be coaxed out after dark when large sums of money were on offer. Even then he hovered nervously, hyper-vigilant, clutching his briefcase, ready for a quick getaway. Fairchild had never, until now, needed his intervention. Before, a moment had always come at which he would give a signal and Zhang would slope thankfully off.

Zhang flipped open a small bottle of clear liquid, leaned over to Rose's face, pulled her lip back and squeezed a single drop carefully onto her gum. Fairchild's hand stopped him from rising to leave.

"Not yet. Not till she's moving."

They both stayed still, watching until she moaned slightly and her leg twitched. Her head started to move.

"That's all you get," Zhang murmured. "Enough to move. Want me to help?"

"No. Two men with a woman will look suspicious. I'll take her. You go."

Needing no further prompt, Zhang melted into the darkness. Fairchild knelt behind Rose and pulled her up, getting his hand behind her waist to raise her to her feet.

"Let's walk." he said.

She could barely put one foot in front of another, but it was enough. He supported her round the waist and smoothed down her hair, wanting them to pass for a couple who'd overdone it. At the hotel, he got her to her room and pushed her gently inside. She stood, dazed, in the middle of the room, looking at him with uncomprehending eyes. On another occasion, with someone else, this might have been a good opportunity to have a look around, but not this time. He stared at her for a moment, closed the door silently and left.

In the street outside the hotel, he stopped and turned. He looked up at the glass frontage of the hotel, thinking about the dazed expression on her face. He'd been harsh on the woman. Too harsh? She didn't seem to know anything much. But he couldn't be sure about that. And it was because of her unwelcome appearance in Hong Kong that he was now under threat from the Wong Kai. More importantly, he couldn't have anyone following in his wake when he went to Jinpa. He had to be clean for that. He paused, reviewing the whole episode in his mind. It was the right thing to do. It was necessary. And it was finished, now. She should heed his warning and go home. He could forget about her and move on.

He turned and walked away.

Chapter 18

Rose woke with a start. She was lying on her hotel bed fully clothed. It was dark but the curtains were open. She half sat up and retched. Her mouth tasted bitter. She sat up fully, and had to bend her head down between her knees to fight a wave of dizziness. The nausea grew. She crawled to the toilet and sat in front of it looking at its stark whiteness in the fluorescent light. A memory flashed in her mind: her back against a rough wall, hands holding her up, the stench of gin on a man's breath. She leaned over and vomited. She got up, washed her face, cleaned her teeth and washed her mouth out several times. In the full-length mirror she checked herself, feeling up her arms and legs. No redness or bruising anywhere, no rips in her clothing, no stains. She sat down on the bed until another wave of dizziness passed.

She badly wanted to lie down, but needed to work out what was going on. The red letters of the bedside alarm clock said 2.30am. She turned all the lights on and sat on the bed. She went through the evening in her head. She remembered the shock of seeing Fairchild in the doorway of the convenience store. The gothic bar. Ordering mineral water. It had arrived in a bottle: she was careful about that. But she'd poured it into a glass with ice. The waiter must have dosed up the glass before he'd even brought it to the table.

Fairchild was not a nice man, clearly. But what did she expect? This line of work didn't bring you into contact with saints. She was more angry with herself for letting it happen. How had she even got back to her hotel? Parts of the conversation started to return to her. He'd used her real name. He knew she was formerly SIS, but had been thrown out. Alastair. He knew about Alastair but she hadn't commented on that. Walter. She'd given away she was working with Walter. After that things were a little hazy. All the anti-interrogation training she'd done counted for nothing if the right concoction was coursing round the blood stream. The only thing to do in that situation is get away. But it happened incredibly fast. It must have been quite a dose. She went back into the bathroom and retched again, but nothing much came out. She rested her head against the cool of the toilet bowl.

He already knew who Walter was. He seemed to know who everyone was, in fact. But Walter had generated a certain reaction, one of annoyance. It chimed with her realisation that the two of them had some kind of history. Fairchild had expected more of a reason for Rose to be pursuing him. The specifics he'd mentioned meant nothing to her. His parents, and Vienna. She'd read his whole file, and it contained no mention of either. As she'd already realised, what she'd been given was not everything the SIS knew about John Fairchild.

She poured some water, gargled and returned to sit on the bed. The questions that were firing off in her head earlier in the evening were coming back again now. Had he tailed her right from the airport? If so, he'd know about the dead drop, and that she'd been into his apartment. But it might be that he only picked up her trail at the hotel. If he knew about his apartment, would the bugs still be there? He could have taken them. He could have been in this room and taken her laptop as well for that matter. Hands sweating, she wrestled with the hotel safe keypad. The CSM was still inside. She checked inside the battery casing for bugs or trackers. All seemed intact. She booted up with the new adaptor and logged into the sound feeds. They were still receiving, and hours' worth of recordings from when she set them up had been registered. Either he'd left the bugs deliberately to try and use them to deceive her, or he didn't know they were there.

She returned to the file where she'd stopped listening earlier and started scanning through. The monitoring system displayed a graph of noise levels over time. Where she'd stopped listening before, the line was flat. She scanned forward looking for peaks in noise level. For several hours there were none. Fairchild had showed up at the convenience store at about eight in the evening. No sound at all up to that time. So he hadn't been back to his apartment since he'd left earlier, when she'd been there. For at least some of that time he was probably outside her hotel waiting for her to appear. She scanned forward to cover the time they were together. It couldn't have been more than an hour at most although the gaps in her memory were not helping. She started scanning for noise from nine pm onwards, at the same time racking her brain for more snippets of memory. She remembered that they were in an alleyway. What had she said to him? Then these words came back to her. *You're nobody. You're not a player. You're just a fuck-up.* Whatever she'd said to him, he hadn't been very impressed.

At around ten pm, a cluster of peaks came into view on the screen. She put Fairchild's words out of her head to focus on the recording. The slam of a door, footsteps. Very little else, but at least it was working, and it was no more than three or four hours ago. This seemed to suggest that he didn't know he'd been bugged. Despite their disastrous encounter, maybe she still had something on him. She carried on scanning through looking for bumps in the graph. Domestic noises, a tap running in the kitchen, the shower in the bedroom. No dialogue. At around midnight the graph peaked, visualising a sound like the chiming of an antique clock. Then Fairchild's voice: "Yes? Okay, come on up." The intercom. John Fairchild had received a late-night visitor. Rose hoped it wasn't the personal variety. Her stomach couldn't take listening in on something like that right now.

The graph line leaped up again to show a knock at the door of the flat. A door opening then the murmur of voices, both male. She couldn't make out the words. Not all of it was English. It also sounded business-like, not a romantic encounter, thank goodness. The graph shot up again as the door slammed shut, and that was the end of that. Rose rewound to listen again. It was an indistinct muddle of words, some English, most Chinese. Eventually her ear picked out a particular phrase. She ran it back and replayed it. She did the same thing again several times. The words were clear but it didn't make a lot of sense.

She checked the time. Three in the morning. What was the time in Tel Aviv? It didn't matter: a crash call was a crash call, he should expect them twenty-four hours a day. She opened up the secure CSM video link and entered the protocols she'd been given for emergency use only. The screen stayed blank for no more than three minutes before Walter's face appeared, his hair a little ruffled but otherwise as calm as usual. Behind him she could see patterned wallpaper and the edge of a window frame.

"News, my dear?"

"That address you gave me paid off. He's staying there. But he's on the move again. He's going to Tibet. He's getting a train to Lhasa in about four hours."

"I see. And do we know why?"

"No, we don't know why. Why on earth would he go there? What's in Tibet, of all places?"

Walter smoothed down his hair as he thought. "My guess is that he's working for the Chinese government. Tibet's of some strategic interest to them. The region has natural resources, minerals and so on. As well as space for Han Chinese to settle, away from the overcrowded east. It has security issues as well of course, calls for independence, the Dalai Lama in exile being a thorn in their side. I can't see who else would be at all interested in Tibet. Who has he been talking to?"

Rose braced herself for Walter's reaction. "Well he's certainly well connected in some way or other. He knows who I am, Walter. He knows my real name. He tracked down my hotel. And he knows a whole lot of other stuff besides."

She gave him a taster of what Fairchild had said. Walter seemed thoughtful, but took it in his stride well enough. "As I said, this is why we're so keen to talk to him. We need to know who in our organisation is furnishing him with this kind of information. What's your situation right now?"

"I'm back in my hotel room."

"So after you had this conversation, you both just went your separate ways, did you?"

"More or less." Rose wasn't ready to say well, actually, he spiked my drink and interrogated me before dumping me in an alleyway, and I have no idea how I ended up back in my hotel room. Some things were best glossed over. "He mentioned a couple of things, though. Like you, for example. He seems to know all about you" She was taking some liberties with her account of events. Walter didn't seem surprised, though.

"Well, yes, I must confess we do have a little bit of history."

"He also mentioned Vienna."

"Ah. Vienna." Walter suddenly looked tired.

"Yes. Vienna. Is this to do with Vienna, he asked. Or his parents. There's no mention of either in the file you gave me."

Walter was looking down. He seemed lost for a moment. Rose looked at the alarm clock. "Walter, the man seems to know everything about my history with MI6. That's way more disclosure than we were expecting. That could make me pretty vulnerable, depending on what he chooses to do with the information. You haven't told me everything you should have done. Now he's getting on a train to Lhasa in four hours. If you want me to go after him you need to fill me in. And fast, if I'm going to catch up with him in time."

Walter looked up again, scrutinising her. "Are you in any danger? Is there any evidence at all he's passed anything about you to the Chinese? Believe me, if they knew you were connected with us and operating in their country without diplomatic cover, we wouldn't be having this conversation right now. I doubt you'd still be safe and sound in your hotel room."

This was a good point. Reprehensible though it was, Fairchild could have made things a lot worse for her if he'd chosen to. "I do need to know, though, Walter, if this is going to carry on. What is it that you haven't told me? Why does he hate the British so much? He doesn't seem to have a particularly high regard for you, I have to say."

Walter sighed. "How much time do you have, my dear?"

Rose glanced again at the clock. "Not much."

"Well, you'll have to make some time I'm afraid, if you're going to hear this. It isn't short."

Walter knitted his hands together on the desk on front of him. Rose tried to summon some patience. Hopefully it would be worth the wait. After the first thing Walter said, she knew it would be.

Chapter 19

"Fairchild's parents were with us."

Rose blinked. "Fairchild's parents were SIS? What, both of them?"

"They worked as a team. His father was an academic. Like a sponge. Soaked up anything and managed to connect it all together. His mother was the linguist. Phenomenal talent. John ended up with both, as you might have noticed by now."

"You knew them then."

"We worked together. I was also something of a family friend. Used to visit regularly. Brought presents for John. Well, I didn't have any family of my own." His voice became misty with reminiscence.

"So what happened?"

"Well, that's the big question. The Fairchilds were employed by us from the late fifties until August 1980. Under cultural diplomatic cover they held a number of postings worldwide. John spent much of his early childhood in boarding schools in the UK."

"And what happened in August 1980?"

"That's when they were last seen."

"They went missing?"

"The last time anyone saw them was in Vienna. They disappeared from their apartment one evening with no message or explanation. Unfortunately, John happened to be staying there at the time. He was the last person to see them. And it was me that John phoned, when he realised they were missing. I was in Vienna as well, you see."

"You were in Vienna as well?"

"We were all working together on an operation. The Fairchilds reported into me, actually. I was a fast riser in the Service. Young and keen. Too young, probably."

"And?" Rose didn't want to sound unsympathetic about this confessional trip down memory lane, but time was ticking by.

"And, the call came out of the blue. John was ten years old and was staying with mum and dad during the summer holidays. They'd had some kind of row and he'd gone out on his own, leaving his parents at the flat. When he returned an hour or so later they were gone. He'd waited for a while, then called me. I went over there straight away. No sign of them, no sign of a struggle or a break-in, nothing. I escalated it, kicked off the manhunt, and so on. I took John over to my hotel, and the ops team came round to take the flat apart. That's when they found the radio hidden under a floorboard, and some dossiers the Fairchilds shouldn't have had access to. I was called into the office. Then it all went somewhat haywire."

"Whoa. Hang on. A hidden radio?"

"Yes. I'm afraid the accepted theory is that they had been informing on the Service for some time, and they took an opportunity to slip through to the east to avoid being discovered."

"They were double-agents?"

"Suspected of being. After the event, that is. They hadn't been under any suspicion up to that point. As you know, there'd been some negative publicity over the years about infiltration of the secret services. High-profile defections and so on."

"Yes, that's for sure."

"Not very good for our image. So the main concern at the time was to keep the whole matter as quiet as possible. The investigation was highly restricted, and for anyone who wasn't involved it was a complete blackout."

"But what did you tell Fairchild?"

"What could I tell him? I said we were looking for them. Of course I asked him what he'd seen, but it was nothing. Just a man hanging around in the street outside. He gave a good description – had a missing finger, I think he said – but it wasn't enough to go on. We were reaching out to everyone, using all our contacts, but nothing was coming up at all. The decision was made to keep it under wraps, tell as few people as possible. I had to take him back to London. Drag him back, pretty much. He had no other family members, so I ended up acting in loco parentis for him. I can't say I did a very good job."

Walter lapsed into silence. To get things moving again Rose put on her best voice of concern. "What makes you say that?"

Walter shook his head slowly. "He kept asking, asking, asking, and I had nothing to give him. I was given the job of managing him, but he couldn't understand why we hadn't called the police, why we left Vienna so soon. Eventually he stopped asking. I thought it was a positive step, but he'd just retreated into himself. Term started and he went back to school. I saw him sometimes in the holidays, arranged for him to stay with various friends. What I didn't realise is that he'd lost trust in me entirely."

"He wasn't told that his parents worked in intelligence?"

"You wouldn't normally tell a child, so we didn't tell John. I was always going to confide in him, when he was old enough. But I underestimated him. I'm not a family man, Rose, never have been, never will be. I thought of John as a child, but the day his parents disappeared was the day his childhood ended. I had no inkling how it affected him. It was the biggest mistake of my life, as it turned out."

He looked at her mournfully. Rose resisted the temptation to look at her watch. "Go on," she said instead.

"After a few years, he started looking into his parents' past, trying to get in touch with people who knew them. He soon realised that things didn't add up. Some parts of their life story didn't quite fit, as you can appreciate. Eventually he confronted me about it. I had to concede that they were working for me and that some of the details around their disappearance were kept from him. He was furious."

"How old was he then?"

"Fourteen, fifteen. Of course, he kept on hunting. He was totally single-minded about it. Not just uncommunicative but becoming pretty devious as well, lock-picking, housebreaking, that kind of thing. I caught him following me once. I gave him a sound talking-to and hoped that had done the trick."

"He didn't do it again?"

"I never caught him again, my dear."

Rose thought about how careful she'd been in Beijing, or thought she had. Walter was explaining a lot, even though it was costing precious time.

"It got worse," Walter continued. "At one point he stole contact details from me of other officers and started approaching them directly. There was a danger the whole story of their disappearance would get out, after it had been so carefully buried. I had to block him. It was rather embarrassing for me, to put it mildly. But he had managed to find out that his parents were being treated as double-agents." He sighed. "Another big confrontation. Then, when he was sixteen – his sixteenth birthday, in fact – he skipped out of school and visited a specialist tobacco shop in central London. Then he came to see me, or, more accurately, I went home and found him sitting in my house. He said that the man he had seen in the street had come from over the border. He had been smoking a Russian brand of cigarette, he said. He had identified it. It was only for sale behind the Iron Curtain. He was excited, said it was a lead I should follow. Maybe they were abducted. Maybe the evidence was planted. I'm afraid I cut him down."

"Why?"

"It didn't tell us anything new. And it could equally well have supported the idea that they defected. I suppose I was rather dismissive. I rather just wanted it all to go away, I'm afraid. And the Service didn't want to know. Anyway, when I refused to move it forward he just got up and left. I didn't seem him in the flesh for years after that. I sorted things out for him, education and so on, but it was hard to keep tabs on him. I was often abroad myself, you see. Sometimes I honestly didn't know where he was. He'd disappear for weeks at a time. From what I can gather, he didn't confide what he was doing to anyone. He must have read voraciously. He also picked up a number of languages. As I said, he inherited the talent. It was all for this one thing. All to help him find out what happened to his parents. That's what I didn't understand.

"I barely heard from him the years he was at university. Of course the Service funded his education and was generous with his living costs. At eighteen he gained access to a trust fund set up by his parents. When he graduated, he went into business. It was only through other channels that I found out that he was using it as a front for his own network. It was an impressive system, I have to say. Astonishing what he was able to unearth. In fact, there have been times when we've been to him ourselves."

"Seriously? We've asked him to supply intelligence to us?"

"He has been known to help. For the right price, of course. The truth is, opinions of Fairchild within the Service fall rather into two camps. Some people have time for him and feel he's been dealt a pretty poor hand, and others – well – it can't be denied that he has no particular reason to be loyal. I see him as family, I suppose. I'm at least partly responsible for how things turned out. If his name ever comes up, I'm the one people come to. Fairchild is uniquely my problem."

Not, thought Rose, uniquely your problem. Fairchild is my problem too now. "He wanted to know," she said, "why we were going after him now, and why me. I think I get why me. I've been kicked out after all. But why now?"

"Well, the official reason for that is the fallout we're getting. Too many ops going wrong for it to be incompetence. Someone is leaking. We know Fairchild has access. So we shouldn't ignore it."

"That's the official reason? So what's the unofficial reason?"

"You've heard, I take it, that MI6 has a new chief?"

"Marcus Salisbury? Sure. It's been in the press. He's the public face of MI6. It's not a secret."

"Absolutely. Well, there aren't that many people left in the Service who remember the Fairchilds, you see, but those of us who do are quite well established by now. As I said, opinion is somewhat divided about John. Marcus Salisbury is a man who has a fairly strong view."

"He doesn't like Fairchild?"

"I doubt they've ever met, Rose, but he doesn't like what he's heard of him. He doesn't like the idea of him. And he's inclined to believe the worst of John's parents, which is perhaps where this comes from. His elevation has somewhat brought this to the fore, to the extent that we can't ignore any longer the fact that Fairchild clearly does have the kind of access he shouldn't. It's become a priority. I have to say I volunteered myself to be the one to try and catch up with him. Really, who knows what he's been up to, but if I can manage this, I can at least make sure he gets a fair hearing."

He paused and rubbed his eyes. "So there you are, my dear. Not a saga to be proud of, but that's what happened."

"So, what you're saying, is, you've got me caught up right in the middle of some kind of internal SIS personality clash."

Walter's face hardened a little. "Well, as I said, it's a way back in for you. If you're still interested. This is an important matter and a very sensitive one. No one has lied to you, Rose. But if you want to walk away, you can."

His words dropped like lead. The silence that followed said what they both knew already: no way was she going to give up now. A question came into Rose's head.

"How come you knew about the flat in Beijing? That he would be there?"

"Well, I didn't for sure, but it was a possibility. You see, strictly speaking, that apartment belongs to me."

"To you?"

"I said I was posted in Beijing some years ago, and I bought myself a place. Not in my own name, you realise. Through a company, that's how it was done then. But effectively it was mine. I didn't use it for a while, then one time I dropped in and realised that he'd rather taken it on. Must have found the keys and decided to help himself. Or just broken in. Well, I wasn't there much, so it seemed easier to just – leave him to it."

"You just let him take over your apartment?"

Walter suddenly looked very tired. "As I say, Fairchild's family, and family is rather complicated. I do wish – well, I wish I'd done things differently, that's all."

He looked, in that moment, more like a despairing parent who'd run out of ideas than a senior MI6 officer. Rose didn't care much about thirty-year-old regrets. But Walter's story made her realise that what she'd taken on was going to be a lot more difficult than she'd thought.

Chapter 20

We stand and watch the jeep as it drives off, leaving the smell of diesel hanging in the air. We are alone in the silence. Behind us, the narrow road snakes away empty. Before us, rocky land rises up, still dark under a sky touched with a pre-dawn glow. We know how high the land will rise. The ascent in front of us is nothing compared to what we will have to endure to reach the border. At this moment that seems an impossibly long way away.

We have said farewell to our good friend Choden. Quiet, dependable Choden has gone in the jeep, heading back to the main highway and then on to join a convoy to the border town at Dram. That is where many people try to cross the border, smuggled inside a truck or using bribery to get past the Chinese guards. Choden will quietly whisper his business to anyone along the way, interested villagers, fellow travellers. He will tell them that he is one of the disaffected refugees who fled from Tashilunpo after the riot. News of that terrible thing has already spread far and wide. He will tell anyone who wants to know that the rest of the group is in hiding and that his job is to go ahead to the border and secure a safe route through Dram. He will tell people that the rest of us will follow. The Chinese have spies everywhere and this news will get back to them. It will mean, we hope, that they will focus their efforts on the border bridge at Dram to try and catch us. Our valued and loved friend Choden is a decoy. He will almost certainly be arrested while carrying out this task. Our hope is that before the Chinese can do their worst kinds of interrogation that the four of us will be over the border, beyond the reach of the army. Tibetans are mountain people: our Han Chinese oppressors are not. So we will elude them on our territory which we know best. And in the meantime we will pray for Choden and for his inner peace, whatever he may have to endure.

The four of us stay here for a moment in silence, each of us saying a silent goodbye to Choden before we continue. We are well prepared. We have good boots and packs containing supplies. Our guide has been carefully chosen and paid well for his discretion. As well as that, we have each tried to study the route so that we know what lies ahead. All of this has taken years of preparation. Many Tibetans undertake this journey with nothing but the inadequate clothes and shoes they arrived in, completely unaware that the guides they paid to secure their freedom would lead them on such a difficult journey. Many of course do not complete the journey and turn back.

But we will reach freedom. I feel that in every part of my being, and through all of my senses. We must.

Nobody says a word, but I can see each of my comrades' souls written on their faces. Palden is worried and frets about the detail. Yonten stares up towards the highest peaks as if they are a personal challenge. The Rinpoche, whose plan we are following, is gathering his thoughts and checking that everything so far has fallen into place. He hoists his pack onto his back, as we all have done, and I can see that he is trying to hide how heavy he finds it. This is even after Yonten secretly took some weight out of it to add to his own, to lighten our leader's burden. Now we are all ready and no longer have any reason to delay our long walk out of Tibet. The Rinpoche looks at me and nods. We turn and set off across the dry rocky ground, upwards into the mountains.

Chapter 21

Rose checked out of her hotel. She binned what she didn't need and deposited all the sensitive equipment, including her CSM, in the dead drop in Beihai Park. Alastair would be able to account for it somehow: she needed to travel light. She took with her little more than a change of clothes, plenty of cash, a passport and a phone. She got on a train to Xining, the most western city she could buy a ticket to in cash, without needing permits or passports. With no free seats, she stood for the entire night packed in amongst Chinese migrant workers, solemn hard-faced men in worn clothing, hauling bulky packages wrapped with tarpaulin and plastic, with more of them pushing themselves in at station stops in the early hours of the morning. All she could do was gaze out of the window at the passing blackness for hundreds and hundreds of miles. It was only during the following day that the crush lessened and she found space to shift position, if not sit down.

Exhausted though she was, arriving in Xining was a relief. The air was fresher and cooler: padded jackets were the norm, even in the sun. In Xining, local people had darker skin and bonier cheekbones. The food offered at street stalls included yoghurt, mutton, pastries, fried sweet biscuits. When people spoke she heard a softer local dialect competing with Mandarin. Of course it was different here. This was well on the way back to Europe, along the old Silk Road. This area of northwest China had more in common with Muslim Central Asia than the oriental Far East. It seemed insane that this was part of the same country, the same time zone even, as Beijing. And the west had so much space, streaming past the train window, even though efforts were being made to fill it with office blocks and housing and roads as part of a surge of investment and migration, Beijing reaching out to its most far-flung regions to colonise and influence as far as it could. But much of it remained unconquered, rocks and water, empty of everything except the occasional power line trailing off into the distance.

From Xining train station she got a bus to the end of the line. A long way from the impressive new high-rises and expressways of the city centre, this area was practically a slum with metal-sided lean-tos and electric cables slung from roof to roof. She walked down the street, stared out by dark-eyed women in shawls and men wearing white Muslim skull caps. Visitors to Xining didn't come to the outskirts, at least not Western tourists. Being watched always made her uneasy but at least no one was trying to hide their curiosity. To get into what the Chinese had termed the Tibetan Autonomous Province without a permit, she would have to smuggle herself across the border. So, she needed to find smugglers. No easy task in a city she'd never visited before where she didn't speak the language, but Alastair had had a word with a former colleague or two and suggested a couple of places where she might start. While she'd prefer not to continue to involve Alastair, no help seemed forthcoming from Walter despite his having finally told her who it was she was pursuing. She now realised more than ever that she needed all the help she could get dealing with Fairchild, however unofficial the source.

Eventually she came to what she'd been looking for, a vast informal market, vehicles parked with their rear doors open and people wandering through, buying and trading straight from the crate or off the pallet or out of a cardboard box. It was early evening and busy. A lot of people seemed to be shopping for themselves, bargain hunters, keen to cut out the retailer and all that overhead. They weren't wealthy or they wouldn't be here. Others, men on their own, doing deals but not actually taking anything away, were probably buying in larger quantity to sell on elsewhere at a marked-up price. And in here, she'd been reliably informed, were people with off-road vehicles who knew how to evade the border posts. All borders are porous, particularly when they're thousands of miles long in sparsely populated hinterlands. She just needed to find the right person and put on show the right amount of cash.

A man with a cigarette hanging out of his mouth glanced around in all directions before opening the boot of a car and starting to unload crates. Rose approached him. She wasn't expecting him to understand much of what she said, but the word "Lhasa" got a reaction. She repeated it a couple of times. Without showing expression, he shook his head slightly. Rose opened her palms out and looked around. The man nodded in a direction over her shoulder before turning away and continuing to unpack.

Rose followed the direction he'd indicated and the scene replayed several times until another furtive trader, having looked her up and down, gestured her to follow him. They left the market and took a route through back streets, ending up in a small yard where a pickup truck with large dusty wheels was parked, half loaded. The man she was following called out and a solidly built guy in a grease-stained sweatshirt came forward. They had a conversation, then both looked over at her. Rose pulled out a wad of cash.

She had Chinese Renminbi and US dollars. The greasy sweatshirt guy was more interested in the dollars. He held out fingers showing how much he was asking. It was a lot, way more than she'd been expecting. She held up fingers offering half that price. The man smiled. They exchanged gestures but Rose could not get the price down to anything like what she'd hoped. The exchange petered out with the man folding his arms in front of him. Rose sighed and counted the money out. It left her with less than she'd have liked, but what choice did she have? She handed over half and stowed the other half in her bag to be clear he'd only get that on arrival.

The man took the money, pointed at his watch and held out two fingers. Two hours? Two o'clock? Two days? She tried to ask but it was hopeless. The man from the market had sloped off. Greasy Sweatshirt made a "stay here" patting down sort of a gesture, his eyes returning frequently to her bag. He then disappeared round the back of the truck and started moving crates and boxes.

She had little confidence in this guy and didn't like how he was looking at her. Her instinct was telling her to leave. But she had limited options. She had to catch up with Fairchild whatever the risk. Making sure she had a good hold on her backpack, she settled down in a corner of the yard to wait.

Chapter 22

I know I shouldn't cry. I crouch over the body, whispering in silent prayer. Behind me, two figures, one large, one slight, stand with bowed heads. The air is cold and the moon is bright. We were careful on the way here, keeping to the shadows as much as we could. Yonten took the abbot's lifeless form over his broad shoulder, pacing slowly between two of us. We have laid him here on a ledge. The birds will come for him.

Things started well. We set off from the roadside as planned, and had been walking for no more than a day when the Rinpoche collapsed, doubled up in pain. We could call on no doctor and had no way of going back. Our plan, so many years in the forming, had gone wrong.

For two days or more we hid in a mountain hut while the Rinpoche shivered on the floor, and Palden paced up and down with worry, and Yonten sat and stared, and the food supplies dwindled. Our guide, increasingly jittery and resentful as he realised we are no ordinary refugees, mumbled shamefaced instructions for the journey ahead, stuffed his final payment into his pocket and sloped off into the night. While he could still speak, the sick old man urged us all to leave him there. He was ready to pass into another life and was not afraid, he said. He spoke a few private words to each of us, and I could see that we were all affected by them. Even the stoic, inexpressive Yonten was visibly moved. To me the abbot said that I should be prepared for things to be different from how I expect, and that I must care only that we succeed in our mission. He pleaded once more that we continue our journey. But I would not hear of leaving him alone to die.

Of course I know that the Rinpoche will still be with us, in all the wisdom that he has passed on to us, and that his life will continue elsewhere. Through his actions, through what he has done for me, the whole of Tibet will be strengthened and brought closer to enlightenment, to the benefit of all sentient beings. This I have been taught, and was in my mind constantly as I prayed continuously by the side of my master, until his last laboured breath and all was still.

So I know I shouldn't cry. I should feel calm and relief that my master's suffering is over, and that the Rinpoche now lives on in a baby's scream somewhere on the Amdo plain, maybe, or in the valleys of Kham. It is my own weakness that causes tears to run as I wrap the old man's body in my crimson cowl. In the visions I have been carrying in my mind, I would be crossing the border in this cowl with the snow underfoot, a proud prince walking forth to claim freedom for his people, the Rinpoche at my side, years of worry and doubt about whether he had done the right thing all gloriously vindicated. Whenever I have thought about the garlands of flowers, the smiles, the warmth and joy of welcome we will receive from His Holiness the Dalai Lama, the Rinpoche is always next to me. Now I cannot think of flowers or smiles. Ahead is only more cold, and more stumbling over rocks, and more hunger, and more hiding from the sun. And behind us is only a body slumped high on a stony ledge with birds pecking out its eyes.

The three us pray as we arrange the body, and stand to look on it one more time before turning away. Then we trudge upwards in the dark, each lost in our own world. I lead the way, sobbing silently into the night. The others should not see my grief. I am their leader now. The Rinpoche has bestowed many gifts on so many people and I have no right to claim a greater bond. Any of our group would sacrifice themselves for the cause to which I have been born. I know all of that. But I have never before felt so alone.

Chapter 23

Lying in the back of the pick-up truck with the side of her face resting on its vibrating wooden base, Rose wondered if Fairchild's journey to Lhasa had been more comfortable than hers was. She was wedged in between piles of crates on all sides. Even without the canvas sheeting roped on over the top of the crates she would have been invisible. The smell of diesel from the truck's exhaust made her feel sick. Every time the truck went over a bump, the back of her head hit a crate. And they weren't even off-road yet.

She hadn't had long to wait in the end: they'd set off just after midnight. At the moment they were making, she estimated, about fifty miles an hour. Lhasa was twelve hundred miles from Xining. At this speed it was a twenty-four-hour road trip. Her mind, for some reason, transported her to the armchair in her brother's living room. There she was, sitting in comfort waiting to be served a delicious oversized Sunday lunch, the carpet scattered with her brother's offspring and their ever-multiplying plastic toys, making small talk about schools and house prices with her IT geek brother and his other half who seemed to be gunning for some kind of parenting award. Thank you, brain, she thought, for reminding me why I'd choose a stinking bone-rattling truck journey to the centre of nowhere over settled suburban mind-numbing normality. It's made it all so much more bearable.

Her body slid forwards as the brakes were applied. They were swinging off to the side and continued to slow until the truck was at a halt. Rose checked her watch. They were barely three hours out of Xining. Two slams from the front rocked the truck: before they left Xining, the driver had been joined by another guy who helped him pack up, younger and smaller but muscular. Two sets of footsteps clumped round to the back and she heard the rustling sound of the ropes being released and the canvas rolled back. She sat up but could still see nothing around her but crates. The truck creaked and moved as the men climbed onto the back and shifted some of the crates, revealing more of the night sky. Then the faces of the two men stared down at her as she sat. They didn't look very friendly. She hauled herself to her feet, welcoming the fresh air at least. The truck had pulled in at a sparsely lit makeshift parking area, by a small hut which during the day might sell things, but right now was shut up and dark. Several other vehicles were parked a way off with no lights on. She could see no sign of anyone around or awake. Behind the men the main road hummed every now and then and the beam of a headlight would pass by.

The driver was pointing at her bag and rubbing thumb and fingers together, a hostile look on his face. It was amazing how much could be communicated without a common language.

"You want your money?" asked Rose. "No. Not till we get to Lhasa. I'll give it you then." She shook her head with her palms towards him. Absolutely not. The driver looked amused and repeated the gesture. He was saying something as well. "Lhasa," she repeated. Both men smiled, not in a nice way. So that was their game. They were going to take her money and dump her in the middle of nowhere, poor defenceless female that she was. Well, we'd see about that.

The driver snapped an instruction to the smaller guy who stepped forward. "All right, all right," said Rose. She grabbed her backpack. "Can we at least get off this truck? I wouldn't mind stretching my legs."

She was pointing down as she said this, and they clambered aside to give her space to jump out. It would save them having to throw her off anyway. On the ground she fumbled in her bag for the money while they closed in on her on either side. She carried on fumbling for a while.

"D'you know, I can't find it at all," she said, trying to sound abashed. "It must be in here somewhere."

The younger guy clicked his tongue with impatience and stepped forward to grab the bag out of her hands. It was what she'd been waiting for. She dropped the bag, grabbed his arm and twisted it decisively. He shouted out in pain and surprise. An elbow to the face and a kick to the knee, and his face was pressed down hard on the back of the truck. Rose grabbed the back of his head and slammed it into the wooden base. A couple of punches into the body from each side generated groans. She tightened her grip on his arm, shoved his head once more down onto the truck for good measure, then lifted and threw him to the ground. Straddling him, she pulled his head up by the hair and punched it again, this time with accuracy. His body slumped.

She let him drop and turned to the driver. He was rooted to the spot. Tricky for him. Not feeling inclined to join in, he clearly didn't fancy himself as a fighter. He might have run, but they were in the middle of nowhere and all his stuff was in the truck.

"You want a go? Come on, then, try it!" She took a step towards him, fists up. He backed off hurriedly, jabbering something angrily. "Oh, I see! Two against one, thought it would be easy, did you?" She was shouting at him, her blood coursing with the adrenaline. "Well, your friend's out for the count, I can guarantee that. I don't see anyone else coming to your rescue, and where are you going to run to?"

She was angry enough to do him some damage and wanted him to know that. From the beads of sweat on his forehead he'd got the message. She made an effort to calm down.

"So. Lhasa, then. Lhasa. You and me." She pointed to him and then herself, to make this crystal clear. "And I'll be in the front now with you. Load your friend in the back if you want."

She picked up her backpack and went to sit in the front. It took the driver some time to haul his friend onto the back and pile up the crates again, but she wasn't going to help. It didn't matter to her if he was left here. That's what they were going to do to her. Eventually everything was strapped back down and the driver climbed in behind the steering wheel. He slammed the door shut and looked at her. She held up the two mobile phones she'd retrieved from the glove box.

"Don't think you can call anyone either," she said. "I'll keep hold of these until we're there. You and me, we're inseparable for the next twenty-four hours. You go for a pee, I'll be going with you. We're best buddies, all the way to Lhasa."

She stared at him, wondering how much of the meaning he'd picked up. Most of it, probably. The situation spoke for itself. His eyes wandered as he seemed to consider what the alternatives were. When he realised there weren't any, he started the engine and they set off. Rose settled back in the upholstered seat. It was going to be a long, silent journey but at least she had a more comfortable ride.

Chapter 24

As soon as Fairchild stepped off the train at Lhasa, he knew from Wei Li's body language that something was wrong. The tour guide drew him away from the crowds with an uncharacteristically serious look on his face.

"Shigatse's in lock-down," he said. "Roadblock. Foreigners can't get near the place."

"Why?"

"Trouble at the monastery. Big riot, arrests, all of that. Now the army's crawling all over it. You were lucky to get into Tibet at all. All new permits now cancelled."

"When did this happen?"

"A few days ago."

"A few *days*? Could you not have got a message to me?"

Wei Li shrugged. "You were travelling. No mobile signal."

Fairchild wondered how hard he'd tried. It was no surprise that it hadn't been reported elsewhere: the Chinese government's control of the media meant that insurrections were often barely known about outside the immediate area. Wei Li walked them to his SUV. They spoke quietly, in Mandarin. Fairchild had been watching since the train pulled into the platform. He was pretty sure no one was anticipating his arrival here. Before they got into the vehicle he swept his eyes around the car park.

"Well, we have to get there," he said to Wei Li. "We just can't drive in. Some other way. Overland, by foot if necessary."

He didn't hear the response from Wei Li, muttered while the Chinese man swung into the driver's seat, but had a rough idea of the sentiment. Fairchild climbed in next to him and they joined the queue of traffic over the newly built bridge into central Lhasa. Wei Li crunched the gears with unnecessary force.

"I got a tour arriving in Lhasa tomorrow night. I have to be there."

"Fine. Drop me off tonight. Within a couple of miles of Shigatse. This thing will go off-road, won't it?"

"I don't know how to go cross-country. I only know the roads. We'll end up in a river, or driving off a mountain."

"I can find us a guide."

"What, today? In Lhasa?"

"Yes."

This silenced Wei Li. The traffic started moving freely and they approached the Potala Palace, on its hillock at the centre of the old city of Lhasa. Newer gridlines of wide roads spread outwards across the plain. Wei Li's foot was on the gas then off again, getting right up to the bumper of the car in front then having to brake. Fairchild felt sorry for his customers. If he cared at all about running a decent travel agency, he'd sack the guy. But that wasn't the point of it at all.

"Your boy may not be there, though," said Wei Li, as if he'd only just thought of it. The Chinese man glimpsed across at Fairchild with a sly look. "I heard rumours some dissidents have disappeared from Tashilunpo. Gone missing. On the run."

Wei Li was fishing. He wanted to know if Jinpa was a dissident, whether Fairchild and he were involved in some kind of plot to destabilise China. Fairchild wasn't planning on answering the unasked question. His business with Jinpa was not Wei Li's concern.

"Any idea who they are, these people who've disappeared?" he asked.

"One of them is the Rinpoche. You know, that's the—"

"The abbot. Yes, I know." Wei Li shot him an annoyed glance. "How many?"

"Five, six. They can't hide in the towns for long. Must be going for the border. Or the mountains."

Wei Li pumped the brakes too hard and they jerked to a halt at the broad traffic junction at the foot of the Potala Palace. Fairchild pressed the button to wind down the window. It was mid-afternoon and bright sunshine but the air was thin with a coldness to it. Lhasa was three and a half thousand metres above sea level. It always took him couple of days to adjust to altitude, even though he'd done it so often. He looked up at the towering mass of Potala Palace, a hundred rooms so they said, heavily framed square windows punctuating its massive thick white painted walls. Most of those rooms were empty now. If the Rinpoche had fled Tashilunpo, so had Jinpa. Something had happened as a result of the riot to trigger their escape. There was no point in trying to get to Shigatse. Fairchild was too late.

"When did they leave?" he asked.

Wei Li jerked the vehicle into movement again. "Riot was last week. They left straight after."

"So at least three days ago?"

"Good idea to get out, if you're involved in something, yes?"

"If they were involved, they would have been arrested straight away."

"If they weren't involved, why did they leave? Now they look guilty anyway."

The jeep slowed. They were making their way along the main city centre thoroughfare. Small lanes off to the right led into the old town, the area around the Jokhang temple. Wei Li was taking Fairchild to the hotel he'd booked him into. Fairchild had no intention of staying there but to please the paper-shufflers he needed to check in at the place that was on his permit.

"If they were making for the border," he said to Wei Li, "where do you think they'd go?"

"You think that's what they're doing?" Wei Li was giving him that sly look again. Not for the first time, Fairchild wondered if he could fully trust Wei Li.

"You're the one who said they were making for the border. Could they get through a border check?"

"Some people can bribe a way through, but not if there's a security alert. They may try that if they don't know what people are saying about them. Or if they're stupid."

"And if they're not stupid?" Fairchild knew, as did Wei Li, that Jinpa was not stupid. Neither was the Rinpoche.

"The mountains. Over the top. The border is thousands of miles of snow and ice. Always places to hide, always ways of getting through. That's what they think, these people. The so-called refugees, they try it all the time. They don't all survive, though. Down there."

Wei Li was nodding towards one of the narrow lanes. Like most of the others it was too narrow to drive down. He gave Fairchild brief directions which weren't familiar to him.

"It's not the same place as last time?"

"That one was full. This one is nice. You'll like it." Fairchild grabbed his bag. Wei Li was probably getting a slice for booking him here. He wasn't going to argue with him, not now. Wei Li let the engine run and turned to him. "So, what's the plan?"

"I'll call you. But be ready tonight. Meet here. I'll call you with a time."

"You and a guide?"

"Maybe."

"You're going to Shigatse?"

"Maybe."

"Even if your boy isn't there? Even if he's in the mountains?"

Fairchild opened the jeep door and climbed out. He closed the door and looked back at Wei Li's face through the open window, a face that was putting two and two together.

"You're going after him?" said the Chinese man. "Into the mountains? That's crazy. You'll die."

"I'll call you tonight," said Fairchild. "Don't fall asleep."

"You think you can just walk through the Himalayas? Even you, Fairchild, can't do that. Even with a guide, we're not mountain people. You know how high it is? How cold it gets? You're mad."

"Thank you for your concern," said Fairchild. "Don't worry, Wei Li, you'll still be paid, no matter what happens to me."

Wei Li rolled his eyes. "Seriously. Who is this monk anyway? What could he possibly know that makes you do this?"

Fairchild put his hand to his face in the shape of a phone as he walked away from the jeep. "Tonight!"

Wei Li made a dismissive gesture and the jeep slammed into movement again.

Fairchild navigated the labyrinth of narrow crowded streets following Wei Li's instructions, and found himself at a glass door leading to a very new-looking marble-floored lobby totally out of keeping with the old town. He checked in, dumped his bags, showered and went straight out again, stopping at the check-in desk on his way out to ask a question. His Tibetan was serviceable but a little rusty.

In this part of Lhasa, Chinese soldiers were a constant presence and one was stationed almost opposite his hotel, but Fairchild didn't detect any unusual interest in himself at all. He went to the outdoor shop recommended by the woman on the check-in desk and bought a good solid pair of walking boots, thermals and gloves. He put the boots on straight away to wear them in as much as possible. He also picked up climbing gear, crampons, a large water bottle and high-energy food. It wasn't cheap. He put it on a Dragon Fire credit card. It would go down as a business expense. Molly could figure out how to deal with that.

Using cash, he bought a SIM card at a mobile phone shop and used it to make several calls. Then he went into a local restaurant he hadn't visited before. While ordering, he chatted to the owner, the chef and a friend of theirs. After their initial surprise at his Tibetan, they responded amicably enough. They'd heard something about the trouble at Shigatse but didn't know the detail. Nothing unusual was going on in Lhasa. One of them was acquainted with someone from Fairchild's circle of contacts. They seemed honest people, running things as squarely as possible in difficult circumstances. He told them his name and memorised theirs, for the next time he came this way.

He sat in the window and ate, watching shapes pass by the window as darkness fell. He thought of his last night in Beijing, as he had done repeatedly on the long train journey. Rose Clarke was a British spy. She'd been sent to follow him, and he couldn't have that. He'd been harsh with her, but only because he had so little time. And how could her actions, or more precisely Walter's, be justified anyway? It was a ploy, a tactic to keep him from knowing what sordid events had robbed him of his parents. He was only trying to find out what they should have told him in the first place. He was tired of Walter's shiftiness, his protestations that there was nothing else. That was why he had pushed her. He needed to know what she knew, what they wanted, needed to know that night, before he left the next day. But it turned out she didn't know anything. He closed his eyes and saw her lying on the ground face down, her legs white in the dark of the alleyway. He remembered her faint moan as Zhang's concoction brought her round; the weight and warmth of her body as he supported her, stumbling, to her hotel room; the blankness in her eyes as he closed the door.

This journey was not what he'd been expecting. He never thought the trap would spring here. Tibet was a forgotten land, considered backward-looking or ignored entirely. Jinpa was a chance acquaintance, just a boy at the time, who became a friend nevertheless. Fairchild had seen something different about him and had fathomed his secret, though never saying so, and had passed him secrets of his own. At least with Jinpa he could be sure it wasn't some trick from Walter or one of his people to misdirect him yet again. But he'd have to reach Jinpa before the Chinese discovered who Jinpa really was. If Fairchild failed in this, everything he'd done these past twenty years would be for nothing. He had to do this alone, completely alone, for Jinpa's sake as much as his own. So he knew why he had to get rid of Rose Clarke. He would probably never see the woman again, and just as well. But it turned out he was wrong about that. Because just as he was about to stand and leave the restaurant, Rose Clarke walked in through the door.

Chapter 25

She stood at the doorway and watched as his face registered her presence and reacted with barely concealed shock. It was not dissimilar to what he had done to her at the convenience store in Beijing.

"Surprise!" she said, sitting at his table without asking him. He looked a little pale, she thought. She could feel the anger building up inside at what he did to her last time they met. But she repressed it for now. "Did you enjoy your meal?" She looked at the empty plate in front of him. He didn't respond. "Well, I'll have the same." She signalled to the restauranteur to bring her the same. "It's been a long journey, after all."

It certainly had been. A full day never letting the Xining smuggler out of her sight had taken its toll. She'd had to make a real effort time and time again to stop herself falling asleep. They must have crossed a border somewhere but the roads they were on were so small there was no sign of it whatsoever. As soon as they started seeing road signs for Lhasa the driver had wanted to ditch her, but she made him drive right to the city outskirts before she got out. The bastard had even asked for his money. She'd just looked at him and walked off.

Fairchild hadn't said a word and was simply sitting looking at her. "Last time we met," she said, "you told me not to follow you." Fairchild raised an eyebrow. "What's the matter? Aren't I supposed to remember? Amnesia guaranteed? Is that what it said on the label of whatever little drug you used? Maybe you should have a word with your supplier."

He looked away. That bit of needling had hit home. Interesting. But she hadn't finished. "You drugged me, Fairchild. But you didn't even have to. You already knew I was a spook. I'd already offered to tell you what I wanted. But you still went ahead and drugged me. Why did you do that? Because you like power, that's why. You like control. You tinker in people's lives but resent it when they do the same to you. You think you're superior to people like Walter and me, but you feed off us at the same time. You're all manners and cleverness, but you get your way with filthy secrets and date rape drugs. What a piece of work you are, Fairchild."

He was, if anything, paler, and his mouth was thin. "And yet, here you are," he said.

"You think I followed you here because I like you? Please! I'm doing this to get my job back. Believe me, the sooner this is over, the better."

"You really think they're going to take you back, don't you?" he said.

Rose wasn't playing that one. It didn't work last time and it wouldn't work now. Trying to focus on her position was just a way of distracting her from his. Her food arrived, meat in parcels, like ravioli but with more flavour. "What kind of meat is this?" she asked.

"Meat," he said.

"Okay." She ate. The meat was tough and gristly. "You chose this?"

"It's all they've got."

It was a pretty modest place. Fairchild looked different here. No nicely cut jacket and pressed shirt, just a regular brown t-shirt and dark overshirt. He looked unassuming, toned down, more in keeping here like a seasoned traveller. Not at home exactly – he was clearly a foreigner – but not out of place either. He had a distant look on his face.

"Are you trying to work out how I knew you'd come to Tibet?" she asked.

He focused on her face. "Presumably, you managed to bug my apartment. You must have been listening when the courier dropped off the tickets."

"*Your* apartment? That's not what I've heard." He frowned. "Walter claimed it's his flat and you appropriated it. It all sounds a bit odd to me. But apparently you and he are like family."

Fairchild's face turned sour. "Walter, family? Hardly. And given that you're prepared to invade my privacy in that way, I'm surprised you're claiming the moral high ground."

"I'm doing a job. You're a security risk to my country. As far as I can tell, you're just pleasing yourself."

"Just going about my own business, you mean? Well, that's what I'm trying to do. Without being hounded by you and your erstwhile employers."

"If your business is putting our security operations at risk, it's our business as well."

"And you believe that, do you? That I'm jeopardising lives just to make money?"

"From what I've seen of you, I wouldn't put it past you. What are you doing in Tibet, for example? Quick holiday?"

"Since you're so pally with Walter, why does he think I'm here?"

"He thinks you're working for the Chinese. Identifying dissidents for them to lock up. Or minerals for them to exploit. Whatever, as long as it earns a crust I suppose."

"And you don't approve."

"You're a mercenary. You'll work for anyone. There's nothing to approve, far as I can see."

"So you're in it for queen and country, are you? That's why you do this? Allow them to exploit you? To throw you out then send you on a wild goose chase to have you back?"

"I know who I am and where I'm from. You've got to belong somewhere. My country's not perfect but it's a heck of a lot better than many. I don't have all the answers, but that's good enough for me."

Rose swallowed the last mouthful of the unappetising dish. The restauranteur and his friends were giving them some curious looks. She smiled at them as she forced the food down. "More friends of yours?" she said to Fairchild. "You seem to have willing accomplices in every corner."

"And you just walked in here and found me, did you?" asked Fairchild, "having got to Lhasa?"

"Walter said try the most expensive hotel first. I've been working down a list. I've got down to about fourteen. Then I just caught sight of you here as I was passing. That was a bit of luck, but most hotels are in this little area. And it doesn't look like you're trying to hide, sitting in the window and all. As I say, I guess you thought you'd seen the last of me in Beijing."

"Obviously I was wrong."

"Yes. And you made a mistake, doing what you did. Because now I'm pissed off. And I don't give up when I'm pissed off. Let me ask you a simple question. Do you want to get rid of me?"

"Yes," he said, with feeling.

"I never meant you any harm, Fairchild. My task is to persuade you to meet with Walter. That's it. All this stuff I'm doing, following you around, wanting to know your business, it's all for that. I couldn't care less what you're doing in Tibet. My objective is to please Walter so I get my job back. All you have to do is agree to meet with Walter."

"And why would I suddenly do that? What do I owe you?"

"It's the quickest way to get shot of me, that's why. Once the meet's happened it's over. You'll never see me again. If you don't agree, I'll stay on your tail until you do. More surveillance, more bugging, more dodgy drug orders from your dealer. Why go through the hassle? I'm not interested in you, Fairchild. Agree to do the meet, go through with it and I'll bugger off. It's a promise."

Fairchild looked grave as he considered this. "Okay," he said. "I'll meet with Walter. You can arrange a date and time. And a location. Not China, presumably, given Walter's history with the place."

This guy really seemed to know everything. Rose shook her head. "No. Now that I've found you again I'm not letting you out of my sight until it happens."

"You don't trust me?"

"After you spiked my drink and left me lying in a back street? Why on earth would I trust you? Of course I don't. I'll be sticking to you like glue for as long as it takes. Which means, the sooner the meet happens, the quicker I'm off your back."

Fairchild shrugged. "Okay. Come with me. If you insist. But it's not going to be easy. You'll have to keep up. I can't have you slowing me down."

"I think I preferred you when you were drugging me. But don't worry. I like a good trek."

Fairchild blinked. "And what do you mean by that?"

"You're wearing a pair of heavy-duty mountain boots. Whatever you're up to, it involves walking or climbing. But you weren't expecting it to, which is why your boots are brand new."

"Not bad," he said grudgingly, with something approaching a smile. She hadn't been expecting him to agree to this so quickly. He was being uncharacteristically accommodating. Unless he was just feeling guilty for what he did to her in Beijing. Either way, she was happy to take full advantage.

"You may as well tell me what this is all about. I need this assignment of yours, whatever it is, out of the way as soon as possible, so I can get you to Walter and my job is done. I may even be prepared to help you."

His smile turned into a laugh. She waited solemnly for him to finish. "Fine. Have it your way. I thought you might welcome the offer, but clearly not. As I've just said, I really don't care. Hell, you could make something up if you wanted."

There was a long pause during which she scraped the remnants of meat off her plate. It was looking like she was heading for another long conversation-free journey.

"All right," Fairchild said eventually. "Since you've persuaded me you don't care anyway. Have you heard of the Dalai Lama?"

"Of course I bloody well have."

"Right. Well you probably know then for most of the time since the Chinese invaded and annexed Tibet in 1950, the Dalai Lama has been challenging their occupation from his base in exile."

"Yes, I know. He's in India. Dharamsala, in the Himalayas."

"From where he's served as a phenomenally successful spokesperson, not just for the Tibetan cause but for Tibetan Buddhism and spirituality generally."

"Good for him." Rose started wondering if Fairchild was in fact making something up.

"What a lot of people don't know is that the Dalai Lama isn't the only senior political and senior leader of Tibet. The Panchen Lama is almost as important as he is. They had a dual role for hundreds of years, the Panchen Lama being more of a spiritual leader while the Dalai Lama took on an increasingly political role. Panchen Lama literally means Teacher. The Dalai Lama was based here in Lhasa and the Panchen Lama in a town called Shigatse, in a very wealthy and influential monastery there called Tashilunpo."

"Good for them." She watched Fairchild take a sip of water before resuming.

"Over the years, these two characters haven't always got along in practice and have taken different views, for example on their attitudes to the occupying Chinese Communist government. But they are tied together in one fundamentally important way, which is that they each have a pivotal role in identifying the other's successor."

"Oh. Reincarnation, you mean." He was definitely making this up.

"According to Tibetans, when the Dalai Lama dies, he's immediately reincarnated in a baby which is being born at the same time. But how do you identify which baby it is? Lots of traditions have developed, such as interpreting the reflections in a sacred lake, or looking at what the stars are doing, or the behaviour of animals and such like."

"People still actually believe this?"

"Absolutely. Didn't you see the pilgrims in Jokhang Square on the way here? They've walked hundreds of miles to come here and pray. They have photos of the Dalai Lama hidden in their homes. They've brought coins they've saved for years to scatter on the shrines here. This means everything to them."

Rose had seen them; sombre peasants in heavy coats and brimmed hats with the brown skin and red cheeks of mountain people, falling to their knees, lying fully prostrate on the ground, then getting up again, taking a step forward and doing it all again. It was a rare sight in the West, a person lying face down in the street. It would normally result in an ambulance being called.

"So, in the years following the death of one of these figures," Fairchild was continuing, "a set of senior lamas will read all these signs and draw up a shortlist, if you like, of potential candidates. But they don't decide who's the one. It was the Panchen Lama of the time who identified the boy who became the current Dalai Lama. And it's the Dalai Lama who identifies the next Panchen Lama. That's the tradition."

"So where is he, then, this Panchen Lama? Is he in exile too?"

"Well, that's the question. The previous Panchen Lama, the tenth Panchen Lama, died in 1989 and his successor was identified when the Dalai Lama was in exile. It was a covert cross-border project. The priests inside Tibet did their divining work to draw up the list of possible boys. That was in 1995, so the boys they selected were all six years old. Then they smuggled the list out of the country to Dharamsala where the Dalai Lama made the decision about which one it was."

"And dare I ask how he did this?"

"He looked at the photos and had a good feeling about this particular boy."

"That's it?"

"As far as he's concerned, it's centuries of accumulated wisdom speaking through him. Faith to believe in things you don't fully understand. Not dissimilar to what you were saying earlier about queen and country."

"That's hardly the same, but never mind. So what happened then?"

"The Dalai Lama made public the identity of the boy."

"Oh. And?"

"And the boy hasn't been seen since. It took the Chinese government a year to admit that they had taken him. As soon as the Dalai Lama made the announcement, they showed up at the remote village in Nagchu province where he lived and picked up the boy and his entire immediate family. They've been in custody ever since. No one knows where."

"So what was said at the time? What happened with the priests, the Dalai Lama?"

"The Chinese claimed that the wrong boy had been chosen due to 'outside influence'. They were furious that the Dalai Lama had been given a role because they see him as a threat politically."

"Well, he is, I suppose."

"Really? A Buddhist monk against one of the biggest, richest and most dictatorial governments in the world?"

"But he has a voice, doesn't he? People listen to him. And it must have riled them."

"It did. So they coerced a group of priests to select another boy instead, who's been carrying out the role ever since under the close supervision of the Chinese. He lives in Beijing most of the time and only comes out to Tibet every now and then, with an entourage of Chinese military of course."

"Charming, these taskmasters of yours. So how does this relate to you being here now? Do you know where the boy is?"

"He's not a boy any more. He's in his twenties."

"You do know where he is, don't you?"

Fairchild was looking at her carefully. "I may have a rough idea."

But something was nagging Rose. "But why would the Chinese keep this guy in Tibet where he could be discovered and be the focus for rebellion? It would make a lot more sense to hold him thousands of miles away, in Beijing or just anywhere out east. Not here." Fairchild was still looking at her. Her brain continued to tick over. "Unless he's escaped somehow. Managed to get away from the authorities and come back home. And you're on the hunt for him. You're going to track him down and turn him back in to the Chinese, before word gets out that he's escaped. That's it, isn't it?"

"Maybe. But that's all I can tell you right now."

"Why?"

"Because we're leaving in two hours."

Two hours! Rose was determined not to show her shock. She looked at her watch. "Midnight? Where from?"

"My hotel. It's just down there, the one with the marble lobby. Probably the next one on your list." He got up. "Out of interest, do you have a travel permit for Tibet?"

"Unfortunately not. I entered the area – informally."

He nodded. "I thought as much. Make sure you don't get stopped, then. You'll be sent back to mainland China, best-case scenario."

He left. Rose mulled over his implied threat. It would be easy for him to tip her off to any of the Chinese soldiers patrolling the place, and she would be out of there. For the next two hours she would have to stay out of sight, and play things very carefully when they met after that. It didn't feel right that he had agreed so quickly to her coming with him. On the bright side, at least this time she was in command of all her faculties. Despite her exhausted state, she needed to stay that way.

Chapter 26

Fairchild stepped out of his hotel two minutes late. Rose was already there.

"Been waiting long?" he asked.

"Just arrived."

She'd probably been there at least twenty minutes checking for an ambush. That would certainly have been the quickest way of getting rid of her: by calling the police now and get her carted off as a foreigner without a permit. But Fairchild's idea was better than that. He set off for the main drag, glancing at her as she walked beside him.

"New gear?" Her boots were brand new, strangely similar to his, and her backpack looked heavier. The backpack itself, in fact, looked brand new.

"That's right."

"Find a mountaineering shop?"

"Yes."

"I'm surprised it was still open, at this time of night."

"It wasn't."

"Don't tell me. An open window round the back."

"Something like that."

They got to the main drag. The people-carrier was waiting exactly where Wei Li had dropped him off earlier, and Wei Li was behind the wheel. Fairchild introduced them in English then blanked Wei Li's outraged stare until they were on the move, with Rose in the back. He explained her presence to Wei Li in Mandarin, keeping an eye on the rear view mirror for any signs of understanding. He was pretty sure she didn't speak Mandarin, but in any case he didn't give much of an explanation to Wei Li except that she was coming with them and didn't have paperwork so they'd have to hide her for the checkpoints. His response was predictably forthright.

"Are you mad? We drive south after all kinds of unrest at Shigatse with an illegal foreigner in the back? Dragon Fire will lose its permit to operate if we're caught."

"Well, we need to make sure we're not caught then. Have you still got that load of camping equipment in the back, that I saw earlier?"

"Yes, for the base camp. They need more supplies up there."

"Great. So we rearrange things a little. She can slip underneath."

"What if they search?"

"They won't."

"You cannot know that, Fairchild. Even you."

"They probably won't. Look, both our names are on the permit. This is a work trip, we're dropping some gear off, that's all. We're not going to Shigatse town, just passing through."

"Passing through to where?"

"Tingri."

"Tingri? That's hours away. I have to be in Lhasa tomorrow. A tour arriving tomorrow night. I said."

"You can drop us there then come straight back. There's time."

Wei Li muttered some words of Mandarin Fairchild wasn't familiar with, and smacked the steering wheel.

"Just pull in where we can get out of sight of the road."

Twenty minutes later they came off the main road and drove some way up a side road to be out of sight. Fairchild got out and looked into the back window to find Rose looking back at him expectantly.

"I suppose I need to jam myself into some hidey-hole," she said. "How far's the checkpoint?"

"Not far."

Rose scrambled out and stretched while the men rearranged the equipment, leaving a space for her in the footwell of one of the back seats. "Great," she said when she saw it. "More travelling in the freight department." But she climbed in. He hadn't noticed before how small her frame was: she could curl up easily in the space. They arranged bundles and backpacks around her and positioned the dirty plastic flysheet of a large tent on top.

"Can you breathe okay?" called Fairchild.

"Yes!" She sounded bad-tempered. He exchanged glances with Wei Li and they got back into the front and set off, driving in silence.

He had travelled this route frequently and could picture the landscape: shallow stony rivers, rocky passes topped by chortens festooned with prayer flags, clusters of nomad tents and scattered yaks chewing on the sparse vegetation. But in the darkness the SUV's headlights illuminated only a few metres of rocky land either side of the road: everything beyond was blackness. A dull pain was settling across his forehead. They were ascending again. Tingri was the highest point on the main highway, the closest you could get by main road to the mountain passes themselves.

"So you found a guide?"

"Yes."

"And where is he? Not coming with us?"

"He'll travel separately. I'll meet up with him in Tingri."

He closed his eyes, hoping Wei Li would shut up. But he didn't. "Gives me someone to talk to," he chuntered. "You fall asleep, how I supposed to stay awake all this stupid all-night journey?"

"You don't speak a word of Tibetan," Fairchild pointed out. "Even if he were here, you wouldn't be able to have a conversation."

"Come on, Tibetans learn Mandarin in school. This is China!"

"They don't see it that way. China's the enemy, an occupying force. Does Tibet look like China to you? We're thousands of miles from Beijing. Tibet has more in common with India than it does with China."

"They're fools. China is good for Tibet. They say they want independence but how would they survive? Nothing here!"

He gestured to take in the empty surroundings. He had a point. Even the Dalai Lama recognised that a more practical way forward for this empty, isolated mountain state was as a genuinely autonomous part of China rather than a fully independent state. Fairchild had discussed some of these ideas with Jinpa, planted some seeds perhaps, which might germinate in future years, if Jinpa were to succeed in reaching exile. A political solution was within grasp if only the main players could countenance it and articulate it to their supporters. Jinpa was a truly original thinker, bringing a unique perspective to things. Where did that come from? Not from the diet of Buddhist philosophy he was brought up on. Possibly from the Rinpoche, who seemed to have done what little he could to broaden the young leader's outlook as much as possible. They would both say that Jinpa's intellect stemmed from the Panchen Lama's inherited wisdom, built up over hundreds of years, bringing him and the whole of Tibet closer to full enlightenment. And could anyone prove them wrong?

Wei Li looked across at him. He'd said something that Fairchild hadn't heard. Fairchild was struggling to concentrate. A steady headache had set in like it always did when he didn't acclimatise properly. "Shame the guide not here," Wei Li said balefully. "Better company than you even if we don't speak same language."

"If he were here," said Fairchild, "how would it look having me, a Chinese guide and a Tibetan man all travelling together? We'd get pulled over. You've got the most to lose. If they mark your file as a suspected dissident you'll lose your tour guide licence."

Wei Li shrugged. "He could go in the back as well. Two people, all cosy!" He seemed to find this very amusing. Fairchild stared out of the window.

They drove in silence. Fairchild tried to get comfortable in the seat but couldn't. He turned to stare at the pile of gear in the back where Rose was buried. The image came into his head, yet again, of Rose standing in her Beijing hotel room looking at him uncomprehendingly, just before he shut the door and left. Did she remember that?

He blinked. He needed to stay focused. Rose's backpack was on the back seat. He reached and gently lifted it. Placing it on his lap, he opened it up and had a careful look at the contents. Wei Li eyed him without commenting. A few items of solid mountain gear from her raid of the Lhasa outdoor shop, including a length of rope and an ice axe. Food. What looked like a cosmetics bag. No weapon. A mobile phone. It was switched off. Fairchild wound the window down a crack and tossed it out. He watched in the wing mirror as it bounced on the ground, turned over a few times and came to rest by the side of the road. He zipped up the rucksack and put it back.

"You don't trust her," said Wei Li.

"No. I don't."

"So why bring her? Should have left her in Lhasa."

"She's more dangerous in Lhasa than she is here. In Lhasa she can go straight to the police, the MSS. Out here she'll be isolated, no means of getting about. With no paperwork. Much more difficult for her to cause trouble."

Wei Li's expression was wary. "You think that's what she'll do?"

"I don't know." Rose's assurances in the restaurant that she didn't care what Fairchild was up to in Tibet were credible. She certainly seemed focused on her task above everything else. But he couldn't be sure. Rose could cause problems for Fairchild if she mentioned his name and it got back to the MSS, although she seemed to be under the impression that he was working for the MSS, a useful development. Either way, by the time she was in a position to bandy his name about, he and the guide, Geleg, would be long gone and she'd have no idea where they were or how to catch up with them.

"If you're planning some funny business," said Wei Li, "make sure I've gone first. I'm coming back soon as we get to Tingri."

"Whatever." Fairchild was trying not to think about exactly how he would deal with Rose when the time came.

Wei Li uttered an expletive.

"What?"

"Traffic. Queue for the roadblock. Already!"

The road ahead was illuminated with brake lights. "This is the roadblock at the turning to Shigatse? How far are we from Shigatse?"

"Miles," muttered Wei Li miserably.

They crawled along, Wei Li's jerky stop-start driving making Fairchild's stomach churn. He turned and called out to Rose. No answer came from the back, no movement either. She was either asleep or dead. Dead would be easier. Asleep was more likely. She'd looked tired earlier, and he'd caught the smell of coffee on her breath. She must have gone through some arduous journey to get across western China into Tibet by the back door. He was impressed, he had to admit, that she had caught up with him. Hopefully she wouldn't wake up at a critical moment when they got to the front of the queue.

After two long hours inching forward, Wei Li whistled through his teeth in relief and they drove up to the checkpoint. Fairchild looked up into the torchlight of the soldiers but left Wei Li to do the talking. A young-looking officer looked carefully at their papers and swept a torch around the inside of the vehicle. His beam rested on the pile of camping gear. Wei Li, with a bored voice, reeled off a list of what was in it and offered to unpack it all. The soldier withdrew his torch and waved them on. It was a long night for the officers as well. They accelerated away.

"This journey taking far too long. I won't get back to Lhasa in time," complained Wei Li.

"If you have any suggestions," said Fairchild, "I'd be glad to hear them."

"Give up. Go back to Lhasa. Get on train to Beijing. Forget about this backwards, freezing cold place. Back to civilisation. That's what I suggest."

"Right." Fairchild was only half-listening. He was also worried about the time, and Geleg would have to get through all the same checkpoints. He texted Geleg to tell him about the queue. Geleg replied, saying that he hadn't even left Lhasa. Fairchild sent a strong suggestion that he get moving.

Geleg was known to a contact of his who vouched for him, but Fairchild was uneasy nevertheless. Geleg certainly knew what he was doing: he led groups of refugees over the border all the time, all ages and abilities. But he did it for money, not out of principle, or some high-minded motivation around personal freedom. Fairchild made sure he was paying him well. Even with the added complication that they weren't just making for the border but trying to catch up with another group, this would be one of Geleg's relatively easy jobs: only one client in excellent health, apart from this constant headache. He could only hope that was enough of a motivation.

"Seriously, Fairchild," Wei Li was saying, "your boy's gone now. Up in the mountains. Maybe he'll make it, maybe not. But he's not coming back, is he?"

Fairchild looked across. Wei Li was right. This was a one-way journey for Jinpa regardless of how it ended. "So?" he asked.

"So why you need me any more? No more messages, back and forth. That's why I'm here, isn't it? Doing the Tibet tours. Now though anyone could do this! I could do something else instead. Something in Beijing. When you need someone with my skills. Someone you can trust. Must be things I can do in Beijing. Many things."

His tone sounded a little desperate. Someone you can trust. Meaning, someone who needs to stay on the right side of him to ensure his secrets didn't get out. It was a form of trust, he supposed. There was something in what he said. Did Fairchild really need him, or Dragon Fire or any of the rest of it, once he'd caught up with Jinpa? He could reel in all the ribbons he'd been placing in people's hands across the globe this past twenty years. Anyone who might sympathise or dare to question the things that are done and why, he'd confided in and asked to keep watch. Just let me know, he'd say. I'll do the rest. Just keep listening, keep watching. A security guard at a New York department store; a cafe owner on the Finnish–Estonian border; a hostess in Mexico City; many from the armies of spooks and eavesdroppers; his own employees. Some were cajoled, but others volunteered willingly. While he was waiting he'd set more traps, constantly moving from place to place on the logic he could never bring himself to abandon, that there must be an answer somewhere. Was he supposed to be doing all this? Is it what his parents were expecting of him? Was it all a test? And when would he find out if he'd got it right? After twenty long years, he was still only guessing.

"I'll think about it," he said. "Let's stop here."

Wei Li pulled over. They had just arrived in a one-street town. The sun was about to come up and the pre-dawn light had turned the bare rocky landscape grey. He left Wei Li to wake Rose and strode over to get food from the single restaurant, which was closed but the door was ajar and the kitchen in operation. A cluster of trucks parked outside had given that away, drivers hanging around their cabs smoking or eating fried food out of greasy white serviettes. He came back over with hot round flatbreads and noodle soup in polystyrene cups. Rose was standing in the road, her hair messed up, rubbing her face. They ate standing up. The air was cold and dry. Distant mountains lined the southern horizon, their peaks obscured by cloud. The massive Himalayan plateau. The border with Nepal cutting across it east to west. Ahead somewhere he knew lay the distinctive peak of Cho Oyu. Everest was further away to the east. Somewhere in there was a small group of monks. He thought about what lay between them and him. He turned round and saw that Rose was watching him.

He binned his polystyrene cup and wandered off to the restroom which turned out to be a hole in the ground and a cold water tap on the end of a hose. He walked to the edge of town to try and clear his head. When he got back to the truck, Wei Li was there smoking a cigarette, his elbow on the open driver's door, but not Rose. They looked at each other, then Wei Li nodded over Fairchild's shoulder.

"Don't even think it," said Rose, crossing the street towards them. She climbed into the back. Her hair was wet around her face. She had used the cold water tap as well. "When's the next roadblock?" she asked.

"Less than an hour," said Fairchild. Rose sighed and shuffled back under the camping gear while Wei Li stubbed out his cigarette.

The queue for the next roadblock was as long as the first, and by the time they drove into Tingri, the mid-morning sun was high in the sky. The buildings lining both sides of the road were like those in Lhasa: thick white stone walls faded to a dirty brown; ornate red gable ends; heavy-framed windows with intricately laced panes. Street signs were in Chinese and Tibetan with its Hindi-like script, some in English as well. Ahead and around loomed bare mountains, coming down to rocky scrubland which met the long, straight road.

Wei Li got out and lit up. Fairchild opened the back door of the SUV.

"This is as far as we go."

The pile of canvas stirred. Further up, a group of men in wide straw hats sat on the ground talking and eating, next to two horse-drawn carts standing by the side of the road. Fairchild approached them and asked if they knew of a room. One of them nodded towards a house with no signage and piles of rubble in front of it. They looked curiously at the three of them, particularly Rose as she emerged from the back of the van, smoothing down her hair and glancing about her. He went over to the house and called out. A woman appeared. They did have a room, but only the one. She led him upstairs. Four low beds had been squeezed into the room, each made up with brightly coloured blankets. A large flask for hot water and a plastic bowl sat on a small table in the middle. The key was in the lock on the inside of the door. He asked about the bathroom. She pointed him to another door, behind which was a wooden bench with two holes in it. He nodded. On the way back down he took the key out of the bedroom door and put it in his pocket.

Wei Li had found coffee from somewhere and was trying to drink it while it was still too hot. Rose, bag in hand, was standing and watching him.

"What now?" she asked Fairchild. "Your friend's itching to make himself scarce."

"Wei Li's heading back to Lhasa." Fairchild nodded towards where they had come from. "He's late already."

"And what's the other way?"

"The border with Nepal. The border town, Dram. Not much else."

"I see. And what do we do?"

"We wait here for our guide."

"Who is due when?"

"Whenever. We can't set off until nightfall anyway."

"Oh. So we're going to spend an entire day in this place?"

"That's right. You can go sight-seeing if you want. I'm going to sleep. We'll be walking by night and sleeping by day from now on. May as well get used to it. I've found a room. Only one, I'm afraid."

"I see."

"There's a choice of beds."

"Glad to hear it." She was watching Wei Li as he scrunched up his coffee cup and squeezed himself back behind the wheel. The jeep did a rapid three-point turn. Facing the other way, Wei Li rolled down the window and aimed a torrent of resentful Mandarin at Fairchild. Fairchild kept the response to a minimum and watched blandly as his reluctant employee drove off. Silence descended. They were being watched by the group of men.

"Well," said Rose. "Let's see this room, then."

She dumped her bag on the bed furthest from the door, under the window, and fiddled about to close the shutters which went some way to shutting out the sunlight. "That'll have to do," she muttered. "Is there water in here?" She lifted the flask. The woman had come in while they were outside and filled it. Rose poured some into the bowl and started washing her face and neck. Fairchild hung around in the corridor outside, feeling awkward. It went quiet. When he went back in, she was curled up under some blankets. He washed as well and lay down on the bed facing the wall, not feeling able to sleep at all.

In the end he must have slept because when the phone in his pocket buzzed, it woke him up. The room was dark. Geleg had texted to say he was ten minutes away. He shifted noiselessly. Under the window Rose was still. He could see the side of her face and her mouth, illuminated through a crack in the shutters. It must be a full moon, or as good as. That was a pity but they couldn't delay any longer.

He sat up on the bed. Now was the time to slip away and leave her here. He'd wait until Geleg had arrived. He thought he could handle her but good to have an additional pair of hands if things got ugly. He'd brought heavy-duty duct tape. They could use that to disable her and stop her from crying out. He didn't have any of Zhang Lao's substances with him. Never again would he mess with that stuff. But they'd have a much better chance if they knocked her out for a while. They'd lock her in, of course, but she'd find a way of making a noise, attracting attention. She was resourceful, and this mattered to her. Maybe Geleg could give her a punch. He shook his head. Geleg might go too far. Fairchild would have to do it. He stood up abruptly and turned to face the wall. His headache was no better. The sound of a car engine grew, then petered out, and his phone buzzed again. Geleg was here. He'd go out and speak to him in the street. It wouldn't take long. He felt in his pocket for the room key. He frowned. His head thumped. He felt again. The key wasn't there.

"Looking for something?"

Her voice sounded loud in the dark. He turned. Rose was standing now, fully dressed and booted. Her face was in shadow. "The door's locked," she said. "I presume the vehicle that just pulled up is the guide. Shame it's a full moon, but never mind. It's only a few minutes until we're out of sight of the town." Her words were conversational but her tone solid ice. "Don't try it, Fairchild. You can't disable me without me waking up the whole town. I don't know what your plan is, but it's clear you want a low profile. You want to disappear unseen. Try anything with me and that won't happen."

Her eyes stayed fixed gravely on his face, the room key in her hand. "So," she said. "Get used to the idea. We're all going together."

Chapter 27

Geleg's eyes glittered in the moonlight as he spoke quietly in Tibetan, the three of them standing in rough scrubland behind the main street buildings.

"Extra person means extra cost. More risk. This not what we agreed!"

"Things have changed." Fairchild needed to sort this out swiftly and quietly. They were packed and ready to walk. Rose was watching them both carefully. Geleg's expression when he looked at her was one of unease.

"Fee has changed also."

"How much?"

"Double."

Fairchild held Geleg's gaze. The guide's weathered skin had days of stubble and his eyes were younger than the rest of his face. To him it was simple: risk versus money.

"Okay." Fairchild counted out some dollars and handed them over. "The rest when we find them."

"We may not find them. There are many routes."

"In that case, the rest when we get back, or cross at the border, whichever we decide to do." Fairchild spoke impatiently: they had already negotiated this. "Let's go."

Geleg led the way, a thin figure in a bulky padded jacket and ragged fingerless gloves. He was carrying a knife: Fairchild had seen a glimpse of the handle in an inside pocket. Not unusual for a mountain guide, but it did mean he was the only one of the three of them who had a weapon. He wondered if Rose had also noticed.

They walked in silence. Once away from the town, the moonlight which had made them vulnerable became an asset, lighting up every rock under their feet. Geleg moved swiftly and Fairchild had to lengthen his stride to keep up. Rose was behind but also kept pace, eyes to the ground, a stoical grittiness to her movements.

They started climbing, Geleg's speed hardly diminishing. He could hear Rose's breathing become heavier but she was sure-footed enough. She didn't appear affected by the altitude. As well as the constant ache in his forehead, he was feeling light-headed. They paused after a few minutes, when the town was no longer in sight.

"This is the most common route out of Tingri?" he asked Geleg, who nodded. "There are different routes ahead of us now?"

"Many routes, yes." He swallowed a mouthful of water and continued abruptly. Fairchild's further attempts to engage Geleg about the route met with similar outcomes. The shapes of the looming mountains were continually changing as they walked, and he struggled to form a coherent picture in his mind. They lapsed back into silence and the hours passed.

The sky was starting to lighten when they paused at the top of another ascent. They would have to stop soon. Rose was no more than a few steps behind them. She caught up with Fairchild as he took a drink of water.

"I meant to ask. Whatever happened to my phone, I wonder?"

Fairchild swallowed another mouthful before answering. "There's no signal out here anyway."

"Huh." She took off the backpack and rolled her shoulders. "So what are you going to do, then? When you catch up with them? How are you going to let your Chinese clients know where this poor guy is?"

"That's what I'm going to do, is it?" He managed a smile, though it made his head hurt.

She shrugged. "That's the kind of thing you do, isn't it?"

He stowed the water bottle back on his backpack. "Well, there are such things as satellite phones."

"But you haven't got one."

"Oh, so you've been through my stuff, have you?" He must have been out cold in that guest room earlier.

"Thought I'd return the favour."

Geleg was a few metres ahead of them. They started walking. "I'm curious," said Rose. "If this guy in the mountains is who you say he is, why aren't the Chinese all over the place combing the ground looking for him? Apart from the riot at Shigatse it seems to be business as usual. Are they trying to keep it quiet that he's got away?"

Fairchild considered his answer for a few paces. He'd already told her more than he should have done. Rose spoke as if reading his thoughts.

"You may as well tell me. I can't do you any harm now. No phone, no weapon, we're away from civilisation. Besides, as I said before, I don't really care what you're doing here. I'm just keeping an eye on you, remember? Making sure you don't disappear before I can get you to Walter."

She was right. There was nothing she could do now, out here. The fact that Jinpa was fleeing at all indicated a strong likelihood that the Chinese were going to discover his identity. It was simply a matter of when, and whether he could reach them first.

"They don't know he's gone," he said.

"How can they not know he's gone? They were keeping him in custody somewhere. They can't have just not noticed that he's not there anymore."

"The person they have in custody isn't the Panchen Lama."

"What?"

"He's a substitute. They think he's the Panchen Lama, but he's just an ordinary village boy."

A stunned silence. "How come?"

"Back in 1995, the monks of Tashilunpo knew several weeks in advance that the Dalai Lama was intending to announce the identity of the boy. Rather idealistically, the Dalai Lama thought the Chinese would accept his choice, but the monks had more realism. China would never have accepted the decision of the exiled political leader of Tibet. So the monks took some precautions. They smuggled the boy out by switching him with another boy from a nearby village. When the Chinese arrived to pick up the boy and his family, it was the substitute that they captured. The real Panchen Lama was taken to Tashilunpo and brought up there as an ordinary monk."

Another pause. "This all sounds like nonsense to me. Plotting monks? I mean, really?"

"It's the religious orders in Tibet that have been keeping the resistance going all these years. Being a devout Buddhist doesn't stop you being politically savvy when you have to be."

Another long silence, with only the crunching sound of their boots on the dry ground. "And how come you happen to know all this?"

"I don't, for sure. But it struck me as odd that the abbot of the monastery would go to the trouble of teaching an ordinary monk to speak English, and a whole lot of other things besides. Jinpa never told me as such, but he was being raised in a particular way for a particular purpose. I did some research. All the dates checked out, the region of Tibet that he's from. Over the years he's let a few things slip."

"Over the years? So you and he go back a long way, then?"

"When we first met, he was ten. That was about twelve, fifteen years ago. Since then we've met three, maybe four times."

"In Tibet?"

"Of course in Tibet. He's never been outside Shigatse. He's never even been to Lhasa, for goodness' sake." He knew he was sounding irritable.

Geleg's cry interrupted them. He'd walked further ahead and had stopped, pointing up in front of them. Three or four birds were circling over a ridge in the near distance. They caught up with him.

"Vultures," he said to Fairchild, More precisely, he used a word in Tibetan that Fairchild didn't recognise, but the birds wheeling in the air were definitely vultures.

"Is there a dead animal up there?"

"Maybe, but it's too high for grazing up here. Nothing for them to eat."

The sky was getting brighter. "How far away is that? About an hour?"

"An hour, maybe more."

"Let's take a look. Then we stop."

Geleg glanced warily upwards at the growing light, but resumed walking.

"What are we looking at?" Rose was right behind him, closer than he realised.

"Vultures, up there, above those rocks."

"So?"

"It could be a sky burial."

"A sky burial?"

"Tibetans don't bury their dead. The rock's too hard and dry. They leave them out for the birds to eat. Once life has passed, a body is just flesh and blood. It may as well be put to some use."

"You think there's a body up there?"

"We should look. To attract that many birds it must be something substantial, and it seems too high for a grazing animal." She was rubbing her eyes. "Then we'll stop."

"Fine." She started walking again without looking at him.

They all trudged on. It was an hour and a half before they reached the stone ledge and the sun was up, causing Geleg to look round questioningly several times. Each time, Fairchild pointed him onwards. It was worth the risk to see if anything was of interest here. As soon as he had scrambled up the steep rock face to the ledge, he knew that he'd been right. The ledge was not a pretty sight: the vultures had picked through clothing and pulled out large chunks of flesh, including most of the face. Rose followed him up, eyeing the mess of remains without expression.

"It's a monk," he said. "This red robe is very distinctive. His vest is yellow."

"What's left of it," said Rose.

"He's been here a day or two, not much more. It's the right colours for Tashilunpo."

"Is it your friend?"

"No, it's not Jinpa."

"How can you tell? His face is missing."

"The skin on his arms. This is an older man." He looked up into the mountains.

"They're not that far away from us, then."

She was right. From what Wei Li had said about the timing of the riot and their departure from Tashilunpo, they should have been much further ahead than this. Something had gone wrong.

"Let's rest and get out of the light."

He turned to Geleg.

"Nomad hut. We passed it earlier. That way." They started descending. "That body is definitely the people you are looking for?"

This was the first question Geleg had asked him since they set out. "Yes, for sure. I'm looking for Tashilunpo monks. They must have come this way."

"Tashilunpo?"

"Yes."

Geleg considered this. "Others still alive, you think?"

It was a stark question, but valid. "That body was put there by someone. They carried it there and wrapped it in a monk's robe, like a shroud. Not an easy job for one person on their own. I think they're still out there, more than one of them anyway."

"If they came this way, I know which route they took." Geleg's face had lightened and he almost skipped down the rocky slope. "Only one route this way. Nangpa La. They go up to Nangpa La glacier." His animation suggested relief. Maybe he'd been more worried than he'd let on about finding the group.

Fairchild had heard of Nangpa La. As they walked he took advantage of Geleg's surge of energy to encourage him to say more about the route. It was arduous and provided no water supply beyond a certain point. But Geleg was certain that they had gone that way.

The hut was small and square with a corrugated-iron roof weighed down with rocks and no windows, just a simple shelter for nomad herders. Inside, the dirt floor was dry and clean enough. Rose sat, her back to the wall, and drank water. Her face was covered in a sheen of sweat. Fairchild's fatigue had built as well, and he was struggling to stay focused. Geleg wandered off outside. Fairchild stayed at the door of the hut. He looked at Rose, her head resting on the back of the wall and her eyes closed. She only wanted one thing from this whole escapade, and that was to please Walter. This far from the town, if she were restrained here, Geleg and he could disappear before she were able to call the alarm.

The thought didn't appeal to him, but he needed to consider it. He mulled it over while Geleg came into view, emerging from scrubby bush in the distance a good way off. As he came towards the hut, he straightened his padded down jacket and zipped it up. Fairchild watched as he walked back towards him. Everyone knew some Tashilunpo monks were on the run from Shigatse. Including Geleg. If Geleg had realised that this courier job involved enemies of the Chinese state, he ought to be nervous. He ought to have questioned Fairchild about it, asked for more money at the very least. But he hadn't. In fact, he'd seemed quite chipper after they'd seen the body, chatting away out of character. Right now, he looked rather pleased with himself. His look became sterner, though, as he approached the hut, self-consciously so. Fairchild watched Geleg getting closer and keeping his eyes away from the hut itself, his hands nonchalantly in his pockets, his step light. He watched him straighten his jacket again.

Rose was still sitting behind him next to the wall. Fairchild stepped in front of her to let Geleg into the hut. Then he swung round, grabbed the front of Geleg's jacket with both hands and slammed him hard into the wall.

"What were you doing all the way out there?" Geleg's eyes bulged as Fairchild grabbed his throat. One hand was pressing on his neck, the other felt for the object inside his jacket, whatever he'd been trying to disguise earlier. He pulled it out.

"Satellite phone. You little shit. What did you tell them?" He threw the phone against the stone wall. It clattered to the floor.

Geleg was wheezing. "Nothing!" he managed. "I said nothing!"

"Don't lie to me!" Fairchild punched him in the jaw, knocking his head back against the wall. "You take my money, and you take theirs as well, you greedy little toad!" He punched him again and gripped Geleg's throat harder.

"I didn't call!" Geleg hissed. "Not yet! Check phone if you don't believe me."

He was aware of movement behind him. Rose had picked up the phone. Fairchild switched to English. "Check the call log," he said. "When was the last call?"

He kept his eyes fully on Geleg while Rose checked. "No outgoing calls today," she said. "He must have been waiting until we were asleep. The knife!"

He pulled back sharply. Metal flashed as Geleg swept the knife across, missing him by inches. He took two steps back as Geleg advanced, eyes glinting. In one fast movement Rose stepped forward and grabbed Geleg's hand in a simultaneous grip and knock, propelling the knife across the floor. Rose readied to punch him in the stomach but Geleg was fast. He lunged down after the knife and Rose threw herself on top of him, her hand closing on top of his. Fairchild could not see where her other hand went, but whatever it did caused a shout of pain from Geleg. Rose's grasp on the knife hand tightened, and he stepped forward to deal with it. The knife, held in competing grips, shot out sideways and sliced, cutting deep into his lower leg. A line of red appeared instantly. The pain hit him and he staggered sideways into the wall. The room lurched as a wave of dizziness came over him. Arms and legs flailed on the floor. Geleg gave another moan of pain and his body contracted sharply. The struggling gradually ceased. Fairchild realised his face was on the floor. His leg was wet and felt like it was on fire. Then someone was standing in front of him. He turned his head to look up.

"He's dead," said a voice above him. Something was odd about her hand, how it shined in the light. A spasm of pain made him double up. Everything started to go black. The body standing in front of him seemed to hover. He turned his face and retched. The body didn't react. It just stood there. All he could hear was his own shallow breathing. Two hands gripped his shoulders and pulled him sideways away from the wall.

"Put your leg up against the wall," the voice said curtly. By now he was lying on his back. He tried to lift his leg but couldn't. He felt pressure under his shin as she lifted it. The sole of his boot made contact with the wall and his ankle exploded with pain. She rolled his trouser leg up away from the wound. Then a hand grabbed the wound and pressed the two sides of the gash together. The pain tore a noise out of his throat.

"It's a deep wound. You're bleeding a lot. Keep pressing it. Sit up."

The pressure released. He sat up and reached out but fell back again as the room swam. She came back and he heard a light tearing sound repeated several times. Surgical tape, duct tape maybe. Possibly from his own bag. Her fingers were on his skin, fastening and pulling the wound together. He gritted his teeth and closed his eyes in an effort not to scream.

The fingers withdrew. "That should hold if you don't put any weight on it."

The grinding pain was replaced by a throbbing. The dizziness was receding. He could hear her moving around behind him. Then the noise stopped. He tried to breathe normally, live with the pain.

"So," she said eventually. "What now?"

The voice was further away – she must have sat down against the wall again. He made an effort to think. "He's definitely dead?" he asked.

"Oh yes." The voice was unemotional. "Straight to the heart. It was a messy little struggle. It could easily have been me."

"Or me," said Fairchild, wincing as he tried experimentally to flex his foot.

"That was an accident," said Rose. "You got in the way. Don't move." Fairchild tried to turn onto his side. "I said, don't move," she repeated.

"I need some water," he said. Rose got up slowly and passed him a flask. He got onto his elbow and drank a little, spilling most of it.

"It's over," said Rose. "You can't go on like that. The guide's dead. The only thing to do is wait here until you can walk and go back to Tingri."

Fairchild looked up at the ceiling of the hut, flexing his leg slowly, exploring the pain. "Is that phone still operational?"

"Yes, I think so." He heard her pick it up. "You want me to call for a doctor? Do they do house calls out here?" Fairchild gingerly lifted his foot from the wall, swivelled round and placed it on the floor. Another jolt of pain. He twisted her body so that he could see her. She had the phone in her hand and was looking at him curiously. "You really don't want people knowing where this guy is, do you?" she said.

He glanced at Geleg's body, uncomfortably close to both of them. "I wasn't going to kill him."

"Neither was I. But he had a knife. It was self-defence. If anyone asks. But who's going to? No one's coming. We're in the middle of nowhere."

"Can I look at the phone?" he asked. She pushed it over the ground towards him. Repositioning himself to free his hands, he opened it up, removed the battery and the SIM card.

"What are you doing? We could use that to get out of here!"

Rose lunged forward to try to grab it back from him. Fairchild folded the keypad and broke it in half.

"Oh, great!" Rose grabbed the pieces and examined them briefly before flinging them into the corner. He forced himself to sit up more so that he could look round the hut at the belongings scattered about.

"Can you pass me that scarf?" he asked.

She didn't move. "It's over, Fairchild. You can't seriously be thinking of going anywhere on foot in the state you're in."

He moved his leg and couldn't stop himself gasping at the spasm of pain. Recovering, he pulled himself along the floor towards where the scarf was. She watched as he wrapped it round and round the wound, tying it off.

"You cut off the circulation, that's a good way of losing your whole foot," she said. She was right, but stopping the bleeding quickly was the most important thing. He gently put some weight on his foot. A red-hot bolt shot up his leg.

"Are you listening to me? You're not going anywhere."

He rolled himself over onto his front then put his weight back onto his knees. Slowly he manoeuvred himself into a standing position, balancing himself with one hand against the wall of the hut, the toe of his injured leg barely touching the ground.

"That's madness." The voice was more subdued. "You'll never reach him like that. You'll bleed to death, or die of exhaustion."

He took a step towards the doorway and leaned heavily on the frame. Outside, the sun was fully up and the rocky landscape was bathed in a golden light.

"You know the way back, I take it," he said.

"No, I don't."

"You'll figure something out." Gritting his teeth against the pain, he stepped outside. He heard her get up to follow him. Along the side of the hut lay some lengths of cut wood. He leaned with difficulty to pick one of them up, that looked about the right length and had some breadth to it. It fit well under his armpit. She was standing in the doorway, two blue eyes accusing and hard.

"I'll need my pack from in there," he said.

"Fine." She stepped aside. Using the plank as a crutch, he hobbled into the hut and stooped over it to pick up his backpack. He strapped it on, balancing awkwardly while she watched.

"This is practically suicide, Fairchild. What's this really about? This isn't a job. You're not working for the Chinese. What's so important that you'd do something as crazy as this?"

He turned away from her to look upwards at the mountains in front of them, and set off.

The smallest weight on his foot shot pain up his leg. He knew he should rest but he had to make some headway now while the adrenaline was still coursing. He was a fool. This close to finding the monks and he'd made such a mistake. It was more difficult than he thought to keep moving across the rough ground, but he made an effort to smooth out his movements as much as possible, at least until she was out of sight.

"It's cold up there," she called after him. "You'll freeze, going at that pace." She was probably right. He wasn't thinking straight. Maybe the altitude was affecting him. But he couldn't turn back. The rocky terrain stretched away in front of him. He focused on establishing some kind of rhythm and not wincing with every footstep.

"You don't even know where you're going."

He didn't want to think about that. He started counting paces to himself. Ten, eleven, twelve.

"You're crazy."

Fourteen, fifteen. Don't stop until thirty. Keep going until thirty.

She had stopped calling after him long before then.

Chapter 28

Rose watched as he limped into the distance. He was struggling to find a comfortable grip on the wooden plank, shifting its position several times as he inched forward. Above and around him loomed the sharp-edged icy mountains, like teeth in an open mouth waiting to swallow him, a tiny morsel which grew ever smaller as he edged further and further into the open jaw. When his shape started to become indistinct from the rocks surrounding him, Rose turned and went back into the hut.

She looked at Geleg's body on the floor in front of her, hunched forward over the knife. Where his face was in contact with the floor, a pool of blood was forming as it slowly seeped through his mouth. A metallic smell hung in the air. His legs lay apart with his feet splayed. His elbow stuck out to one side, hand underneath the body, its fingers probably still gripping the weapon directed by her into his own chest. It had been a messy little fight and it could have gone either way. She didn't regret it.

She listened. No sound reached her at all, no wind, no animals, no sign of life. Should she set off back to Tingri? There was no point staying here. What would she do then? Going home seemed the only option, once her lack of paperwork was overcome. While watching Fairchild hobble away, she was convinced that he would realise the sheer stupidity of what he was trying to do and come back. The risks of venturing into the highest mountain range in the world without a guide, adequate food or water, and with a badly injured leg, were obvious. He was clearly desperate enough to put his own life on the line. Why? For something much more important to him than work, a mere task in exchange for money. What would happen if he never materialised again? Would Walter blame her? He shouldn't. It was Fairchild's decision. But Fairchild was clearly of great importance to Walter. And if Fairchild was important to Walter, that unfortunately meant that Fairchild was important to her as well, suicidal though he seemed to be.

The inside of the hut was starting to smell like a butcher's shop. She went outside and walked slowly once round the outside of the hut. A bird was wheeling in the distance. She thought of the body up there on the stone ledge, wrapped in crimson, its face pecked away, and felt sudden disgust. She was surrounded by death. Back at the door of the hut, the sight of the hunched body made her start. Calm down, she said to herself. It's a dead body. Just flesh and blood. It hasn't moved.

She stood still and listened for the rasp of a tyre on rock, the beat of a helicopter blade, a distant voice in the wind. Nothing. Could she make her way back to Tingri on her own? Eventually she'd have to try. She looked down at her rucksack, picturing the contents and calculating how long it might keep her alive. She thought again about the body in the crimson robe, the bones of its face exposed where the vultures had torn away eyeballs and flesh. She shuddered.

She went into the hut, only glancing at the body, packed her bag and lifted it onto her back. She went through Geleg's bag and salvaged what little food and water he'd brought. Outside, she laid out the lengths of wood and picked two that were a similar length to the one Fairchild had taken, but lighter and narrower. She stood for a moment, listening to the silence, then turned and walked away briskly without looking back.

It didn't take long to catch up with him. He was resting, leaning against a rock, head bowed. He looked up at the sound of her approaching. His face was pale and he was breathing rapidly through his mouth.

"I didn't like the company," she said. "You have the advantage over Geleg of not actually being dead yet."

"I'm not sure I'll be any more entertaining." Fairchild's voice was hoarse.

She sat by his side. "It's something to do with your parents, isn't it?" she asked. "Why you need to catch up with this monk so badly. He knows something. About what happened. Walter told me."

Fairchild took his time. "Walter told you something. He didn't tell you everything. He's never told me everything."

"You'd really risk death to know what happened to them? It's that important?"

He looked at her. His eyes were bloodshot. "And what's your excuse? Why are you here? You could turn back now, tell Walter you lost me, carry on with your life."

Rose considered. He was probably right. But she wasn't turning back. She picked up his bag and weighed it in her hand. She could carry it on her shoulders on top of her own. She pulled out a water bottle, unscrewed it and passed it to him.

"How much did Geleg tell you about the route?"

Fairchild raised his hand lethargically to indicate the ascent in front of them.

"Over that saddle, along the valley on the other side then up again."

"We can't wait till nightfall now. We'll just have to hope we're not seen."

"There's no more water after the next valley. From where we were it was three days, up and down again."

"What you're saying is that if we haven't found them within the next twenty-four hours, we have to turn round and come back down, or we'll run out of water."

"Assuming we don't lose our way and that we haven't been shot by border police or died of exposure or exhaustion first."

"I see what you mean about the company," said Rose. "What's the time now?"

Fairchild looked at his watch. "Eight am."

"So eight am tomorrow is our deadline. At eight am, regardless of what's up there, regardless of how close we think we are, we turn round and come back down. Agreed?"

Fairchild's eyes were hollow. "Agreed," he said flatly.

He stood up, with difficulty. Rose held out the two planks of wood she had brought.

"One for each side will give you more support. You were lurching around before. It's wasted energy."

He took them from her with a look on his face she couldn't interpret. They set off.

Chapter 29

It began well enough, despite the uneven ground, the boulders and the thorny scrub. Fairchild established some kind of rhythm with the makeshift crutches, though his pace was still slow. With the weight of two packs across her shoulders and chest, Rose's feet become sluggish and she had to focus to avoid tripping or catching on the scrub. When directly in the sun, she felt it burning her face. But the air was so thin that as soon as they were in shadow the temperature plummeted.

They climbed gradually to the top of the ridge then clambered down the other side. The descent was steep. Rose went first, stopping when she felt Fairchild hesitate behind her as he tried to find a way down without putting weight on his injured leg. A few times she offered her arm to steady him, if there was nothing else. His breath was laboured and uneven and she could sense his frustration although they barely spoke a word. At the bottom they crossed a wide valley with a shallow stream and just enough grass and moss to graze yaks. They looked out for herders but saw no people, animals or tents. The valley had a desolate beauty to it. At the stream they drank liberally and filled up every container they had. They also washed the blood off their hands and arms. It had congealed and hardened, and they had to scratch it off with their nails. Rose's hands were pink and numb by the time she was clean.

The next ascent was ten times more difficult. It didn't help that they could not be sure they were going the right way. Fairchild knew the approximate direction Geleg had indicated, but with the mountains' shifting perspectives it could only be a best guess. Not being sure made the packs heavier, the slope steeper, the muscles in her legs more painful. They were getting higher all the time and the heat of the sun was greater mid-afternoon. Rose tried to drink only a little despite her perpetual thirst. Further up, they had to use hands and knees to climb. Fairchild abandoned the crutches and repeatedly sucked in air through gritted teeth every time he put weight on his slashed leg. Then she lost her own footing and swung backwards wildly into the rock as she kicked out for a foothold. The water bottle strapped to the outside of one of the packs shot out and bounced down the hillside. They watched it tumble out of sight. Fairchild suggested that they rest. They sat and ate some fruit and dried biscuits, but it wasn't enough to fill the emptiness of her stomach.

They had to go on again because now they felt cold as soon as they stopped. Fairchild picked up his own bag again as they stood. Rose didn't try to stop him. They continued as the sun went down and the mountains morphed into gloomy shadows looming above them. Even with gloves, Rose couldn't feel her fingers. With no moon she had to concentrate to avoid tripping, staring at every patch of darkness, unsure if it was a rock or a shadow. Her muscles throbbed and her hands and legs stung with scratches from thorns and rocks. Every now and then she would sway with dizziness and have to stop and wait for it to pass.

Each time it looked as though they were reaching the top, the land opened out above them again. It felt as though they had been walking forever. The landscape gradually changed from dusty brown rocks to immense clefted granite boulders towering above them. It was even more difficult to keep a sense of direction as they were constantly working around these giant masses. She had long since stopped asking him how sure he was that they were going in the right direction. Earlier, there had been signs that they were on an established path, the dirt ground slightly more impacted, the rocks slightly worn from other feet. But the ground was more difficult to see in the dark and those signs could easily have been the result of an optimistic imagination.

She was so tired that she felt as though she were walking in a dream, sleeping as she trudged. Not looking where she was going she stumbled and fell to her knees. She did not have the energy to get up again and asked for five minutes to rest. She curled up on the ground where she had fallen. The next thing she knew Fairchild was shaking her arm. She opened her eyes. He was kneeling in front of her and the sky behind him was beginning to lighten. She didn't ask how long she had been sleeping.

Rose watched carefully as Fairchild drank. It looked to her as though they had less than half of their water supply left, not even counting the bottle they had lost down the mountainside. She ate most of the rest of her food, fed up of the weight of carrying it and hoping for an energy boost. But she was no less tired than before, and her feet smarted with tenderness when they started walking again.

Finally they reached the top of a plateau which gave them a view. Fairchild pointed to an asymmetric peak next to a rounded dip in the far distance.

"Cho Oyu. One of the highest points of the Himalayan range. The Nangpa La pass runs below it. You walk up the glacier to get onto the pass to cross to Nepal. That's where they're going."

He scanned the distant view as if trying to see them. Rose said nothing, feeling only despair.

Up on the ridge, the wind was stronger, blowing grains of dust into their faces. Rose had on all the clothing she had but it still seemed to penetrate. The sun came up but she felt no warmth from it. They did not have the energy or capability to move quickly enough to generate heat. Everywhere she looked was rock: no plants, no animals, no water. It was a vast expanse of emptiness. You could walk here for days and not see a living thing.

They topped another ridge and suddenly the ground was white with thin powdery snow. This time it was Fairchild who asked for a stop. He seemed disheartened at reaching the snow line. He sank into a patch of dry ground in the shadow of a rock and curled up. Rose looked at her watch. It was seven am. Their twenty-four hours were almost up. They were going to have to descend again. The whole journey would have been for nothing. And they still had to make it down.

If she lay down too, she was not sure if she could get up again but she was too cold to stand still. The ground rose gently ahead of where they were, and it looked as though there might be a vantage point at the top. She put her bag down next to Fairchild and walked on a few steps. Perhaps she would be able to see the distinctive peak of Cho Oyu. The snow was soft underfoot and covered everything in a uniform white. She crossed her arms and put her hands into her armpits. She felt light without her pack on. The snow deadened all sound, making the landscape seem even emptier. The ground fell away on either side of the wide ridge they were on. Beyond, the mountains looked down on her silently, as if poised, waiting to claim them. Rose put one foot in front of the other, the squeaking sound of compacting snow the only noise, wondering what it would be like to freeze to death, feeling each part of her flesh lose all feeling, her body gradually becoming absorbed by this quiet, frozen wilderness.

The moment her ankle gave way seemed to interrupt the passage of time. She felt her weight falling slowly backwards while her arms wheeled wildly and ineffectively. It felt like several seconds between her feet losing contact with the ground and the back of her shoulder hitting the earth with a juddering thump some way below. She was sliding down head first, rocks rising on either side of her. Some unseen force caused her legs to rise and flip her over so that her face was pressed into the earth and her feet were leading the way. Under her was earth and rock, nothing to grab hold of. Dirt spewed up into her face.

The gully opened out and flattened. Rose's slide forked sideways and came to a halt. She lay still for a moment, her heart thudding madly. She sat up and coughed, clearing dust from her mouth and nose. She felt her legs, convinced something must be broken or twisted. She got to her feet, testing her weight. She peered upwards, looking for the snow line, trying to work out how to get back up there. But she had got up too fast. The sky went black and she swayed. She thought she heard something behind her, footsteps approaching. It must be her imagination. But then something cold and metallic touched the back of her neck. She recognised it. It was the barrel of a gun. The last thing she remembered was the ground coming towards her.

Chapter 30

"You are a long way from home," said an unfamiliar voice. Rose opened her eyes. In front of her was a thin young face lit by a flickering yellow light. Black eyes were looking at her curiously. Beyond his bald head was darkness. She was lying on dry earth.

"Are you lost?" said the boy. He had Tibetan looks but was addressing her in English, in a soft, light tone. The air was different. She could hear a rasping, sucking sound and smelled something bitter that she recognised from somewhere.

"You are safe here. This is a place for rest and recovery. I fear my friend Yonten may have given you a shock." His voice held disapproval. Rose half sat up. Rough black rock arched over her head. Wide square candles like those outside the Jokhang temple were giving off the distinctive rancid yak butter smell. A small metal stove was burning noisily. She realised that it was the first time in hours that she was not cold. Behind the boy, an older man sat cross-legged with his back to the wall eyeing her cautiously. Hovering in the shadows, a well-built broad-shouldered man stooped awkwardly, his face sullen. Her brain was gradually starting to work again.

"Fairchild," she said.

The boy's eyes widened. He scrambled to his feet. "John Fairchild? He is with you? But you were alone!"

"I fell. We were higher up, at the snow line. Fairchild was resting. He's injured. I went walking off and fell down the slope. How long have I been here?"

The young man's face had transformed into a combination of delight and concern. He turned to his companions and muttered urgently. The older man got to his feet and both the men wrapped heavy coats around themselves, stepped through a gap in the rock and disappeared.

"They will find him," he said. He was looking at her more keenly now.

"How long have I been here?" she repeated.

"Not long. You were very weak."

"Well, I'm in a better state than Fairchild."

His face clouded. "I fear, if you were travelling with him, then it was me that you were looking for. We were not making ourselves easy to find."

Rose looked more carefully at the young man in front of her, perched on his knees, rocking slightly as he observed her.

"My name is Jinpa. I wonder how much my friend told you about me."

"More than he should, probably," said Rose. "I know who you are."

Jinpa nodded slowly, not seeming surprised.

"What is this place?" she asked.

"The mountains are full of caves. Just a few know of this one. Those who know about it can always find food here, water, a stove, medical supplies. The nomads and the guides look after it, for all who are passing through. A very precious secret, yes?"

"Yes, very."

"Do you like caves?"

She struggled with what seemed like a strange question. "I haven't been in enough to know."

"I don't like caves. They remind me of a time before, a bad time. I was kept imprisoned for many years. Then I was released, in later life. But the bad feelings remain. This cave has saved many lives, though, I think. What is your name?"

"Rose."

"Rose." It seemed strange to him. "Please, have some water. We have a little to spare." Jinpa rose to a crouch, poured water from a large flask into a solid plastic cup, and offered it to her. She drained it, remembering how thirsty she was. He filled it again and she made an effort to drink only some of it. All the time, he was watching every movement with his curious little smile. She was trying to process what he had just said. According to Fairchild, this man hadn't been imprisoned at all. And what was "later life" when he could not be older than early twenties? For the sake of simplicity she decided to let it pass.

"How did you know about the cave?" she asked.

A distant look came over Jinpa's face. "My master, the Rinpoche, took a lot of trouble preparing for this journey."

Rose noted the use of the past tense. "We found a body further down," she said gently.

Jinpa nodded sadly, then seemed to come back to the present. "Please, have some food."

Rose sat up slowly. Jinpa passed her wrapped plastic packages from a large wooden crate behind him. They contained dried meat and a dry flat bread. He watched her eat, rocking back on his heels.

"The mountains are wild and dangerous," he said at last. "I understand why my friend Fairchild is here. He has a desperation that would lead him to such a place. It surprises me that he brings a companion."

The food and warmth were making Rose feel half human again. "It wasn't his choice that I'm with him, and in some ways it wasn't really mine either. Some things happened on the journey." She hesitated to share the details.

"Do you know him well?" asked Jinpa.

"I hardly know him at all," said Rose. "Do you?"

Jinpa smiled broadly. "The first time we met, I was running away from the monastery. He was with a group of foreigners leading a tour of my home town. He called out to me as I was running past and asked where I was going. I had never heard a foreigner speak Tibetan before. I was amazed. I said I was running away because the Rinpoche made me do the worst chores, like carrying the morning tea, and that he didn't let me eat as much as the other boys.

"Fairchild said that he'd once heard about a boy just like me who ran away from the monastery. He stayed in the mountains, then he got bored of being by himself. But when he returned to the monastery no one was there. No Rinpoche, no chores, no tea. Everyone was gone. I asked what the boy did then. He said that the boy is still out there, wandering in the mountains all alone, a little lost boy, always looking." He contemplated her.

"He was talking about himself," she said. "The way he lost his parents."

"I only realised that years later."

"You know he's looking for you because he thinks he'll get answers from you."

Jinpa shook his head wistfully. "I fear that it will not help as much as he thinks. I find in him such a strong need for information and answers. But what will this change? If we could only accept the mysteries of being, the great expanse of darkness and shadow outside our own small experiences, we could truly be at peace with ourselves. Of course I have many times tried to persuade Fairchild of this, but he takes as little notice of me as I do of him." He spoke with the humour of old friends who have got used to their differences.

"And why do you take little notice of him?" asked Rose.

Jinpa sighed. "He has a lot of anger. He says that outside of Tibet people will not welcome me. That it would be more convenient for them if I were imprisoned or dead. That some will accuse me of being a fraud. That others will say good words and greet me as a friend, but never do what they have promised. That they will waste time and make excuses while my country is on its knees begging for its life."

"Fairchild said that?"

Jinpa reacted blandly to her surprise. "You said you do not know him very well. I choose not to believe him. It's easy to overpower and force people to do what you want them to do. But a person who has no weapon or strength can shame their oppressors with the wholeness of their hearts. You know of the Dalai Lama?"

"Of course. Everyone does."

"Exactly. Millions listen to his words and have let him bring them closer to peace and enlightenment. But does he have wealth, or an army?"

"I suppose not."

Jinpa suddenly reached into a bag he was carrying across the front of his body and took out a bundle of photographs and papers.

"Look." He offered them to Rose. "This is who I am."

Rose flicked through them – group photographs of monks in a monastery. They looked like the same people at different ages in their lives but it was difficult to be sure. She struggled to recognise Jinpa in all of them.

"I am to give that to His Holiness when we meet. It will persuade the world. But he will not need persuading. He will recognise me straight away, like he always has. These photographs are for an unbelieving world, a world without faith. That is the world in Fairchild's eyes."

"You're going to the Dalai Lama?"

"Of course." Jinpa's face took on a dreamlike expression. "It makes me very happy that soon I will be seeing him again."

"Again?"

"Yes, of course. The Panchen Lama and the Dalai Lama have supported each other for hundreds of years. In India we will be reunited, to the blessing of all humankind. That is my mission, my journey. And what is yours, I wonder? Why did your destiny bring you to this place?" He put his head on one side, appraising her.

"I don't really believe in destiny. We make our own decisions."

"But you said earlier you had no choice but to be here."

She looked at him. He was sharp, but seemed kind as well. "I suppose I'm here because I made a mistake and I want to correct it. I want things to be back how they were before. I want that – a lot."

Jinpa nodded slowly. "And Fairchild can help you with that."

"In an indirect way, yes. In the short term."

"You feel your dealings with Fairchild will be short term?"

"I have a job to do that involves him. Once it's done I don't suppose we'll have any further business with each other."

He narrowed his eyes. "You do not feel, somehow, that you and he will share a path for a long while?"

"Oh, no. Him and me, it's not what you might be thinking."

"Of course. I know so little of such things. I am a monk, after all." Jinpa's eyes were twinkling. He stopped at the noise of boots scraping on rock. They both tensed, ready to move. But it was Yonten's large form which appeared between the rocks. He made a short remark and pointed behind him. Jinpa frowned and replied. Yonten shrugged.

"Have they found him?" asked Rose.

"Yes. He has come as far as he can. It seems that we need to bring help to him. Please, rest here where it's warm. We have blankets and bedding. I will go out."

He picked up the flask of water and some food, and slipped out. Rose didn't welcome the idea of going back outside just yet. She felt safe in here with these people. With the food and warmth, her body was already starting to shut down. Jinpa had pointed out a pile of thin mattresses and blankets. She positioned a mattress next to the wall near the stove and pulled a blanket over herself. Her muscles gratefully relaxed. Just before she fell asleep, an image came into her head of a small shaven-headed boy wandering alone through the harsh rocks and ice outside, lost for ever, looking for something that could never be found.

Chapter 31

These worn black walls are cold to the touch. I feel in the darkness as I turn my back on our unexpected visitor and clamber through the narrow cleft between two stones. On the other side but not yet outside, light penetrates more freely through an oblique entranceway, nothing more than a space behind a rock, almost invisible from outside. I think of this as an antechamber. I wrap my cloak more tightly, missing the warmth from the stove. The light is bright after the gloom inside and I have to blink and wait for the indiscriminate glare to recede back to shades of grey. When shapes start to form in front of me, I can hardly believe what I am seeing.

The person sitting on the ground with his back against the rock is a battle-worn ghost of my old friend. His face is white and his hair hangs in lank strands. His eyes are glassy and his expression pinched. He breathes heavily. His clothes are dusty and dirty with brown stains across the front of his body and his arms. His leg, extended awkwardly out before him, is wrapped in a scarf which is soaked with blood. As I approach he raises an arm slowly off the ground. We shake hands wordlessly. I crouch on the ground beside him.

"You have suffered to find me here. I am sorry for that."

Fairchild smiles, clearly with some effort. "And you're in some trouble because of me, I think. Wei Li said as much."

I sit down next to my friend. "You would say that we have met by chance. You only found us because your travelling companion fell. You would have walked on above our heads otherwise. But I do not believe in chance. If we cannot understand the reasons why things happen, that does not mean there is no reason."

At the mention of Rose, Fairchild seems wary. "Is she inside?"

"She is resting where it's warm. We have a stove. Come. You need to rest also."

Fairchild doesn't move. "You're still planning to cross at the glacier?" he asks.

I suddenly feel very tired. "We cannot do anything different now. We are too close."

Fairchild is looking at me. "We saw someone on the mountainside. Your companions. I haven't seen the Rinpoche." I look down at the ground, unable to speak. "I'm sorry. He was a good man. He did everything for you."

My friend is kind. My friend knows what the Rinpoche meant to me. I must not cry. I want it all to be over. "We will lose no more people to the mountains," I say. "We will go to the pass tomorrow. If it is clear, we will cross, all three of us."

"Remember to watch out for crevasses."

"I will remember, my friend. You have warned me before."

"You're going tomorrow?"

"We leave tonight. Maybe by sunrise we will be in Nepal. Please, I have water and food. You need them." I offer them to him. He drinks the water thirstily. "Will you not come inside? It is warmer."

Fairchild's jaw is set hard. I notice a sheen of sweat below his hairline. I hear a stifled grunt behind me. Palden has scrambled out carrying a small wooden box.

"So. You can eat here while Palden looks at your injury. No, No." I wave aside Fairchild's attempt to protest. "We do not have much but maybe it will help a little."

Palden gently unwraps the scarf around Fairchild's outstretched leg, muttering about the amount of blood. I do not ask about the cause of the great gash. It is not a wound made by nature. I watch the Englishman drink and eat and wince as Palden dabs at his leg trying to clean it up. When he has finished, Fairchild's eyes are livelier but his skin is still white, and he rests his head back on the rock behind.

"Are you armed?" he asks. He speaks English so Palden does not react.

I sigh. "My young friend Yonten has a Chinese weapon stolen from somewhere years ago. You know what I think about it."

"If they discover who you are and find you, they won't hesitate to shoot you."

"They tell me that in my previous life, the bullets from the Chinese guns bounced off me when they tried to shoot me in prison."

"That's a nice story."

"You don't think it's true."

"You think it is true?"

"Of course. Can you prove that it's not?"

"Give me a gun and I could."

We both smile. The skin on Fairchild's face is pulled taut. The old Fairchild is here, though. The one who used to watch me and seemed to know who I was without being told. The one who only cares about one thing. The one who does so many desperate things.

"Wei Li told me what happened at Tashilunpo," he says, serious now.

I know what he is asking. "My brother Sonam was taken into custody," I say. I am suddenly overwhelmed by the losses we have already suffered. "I pray for him." My voice trembles.

He speaks gently about something so difficult to countenance. "So, it may be that he has been forced to say more than he wanted to. They could know about you already. What will you do if you go to the pass and the Chinese are waiting for you? Do you have another plan?"

I flex my feet. I do not want to think about that. There will be no one on the pass. The snow will be smooth and white, just as I have imagined it. We will walk to freedom together, the three of us. No soldiers will be waiting with rifles at the ready. We will be in Nepal as the sun rises tomorrow.

"You worry about me, my friend," I say, patting his arm. "And I worry about you also. I am hoping you will rest before I give you my news. Your body needs it, I can see."

A flash of emotion passes his face at the mention of the news. Maybe hope, maybe fear. I delay still more. Now that I am to tell him, I feel an apprehension about it, a feeling that it will not really help him. "Will this news give you what you want, do you think, Fairchild?"

He looks at me evenly. "I'm grateful that you thought of me, and for the efforts you made to get it." His answer seems very formal.

"You know, I cannot make sense of your philosophy that a single life means something on its own. The fire makes sparks that dance above the flame before they disappear. Yet you think that there is no fire, only the sparks themselves, coming from nowhere, rising into nothing. Little flashes of light, flying around, crashing into one another, and then gone. How stressful it must be, trying to take meaning out of such a short and random journey."

"That's not my philosophy." His tone is polite.

"I have never been able to comprehend what your philosophy is, my good friend, despite our conversations over the years."

"Perhaps I don't have a philosophy. The understanding I seek is factual."

"Will knowing make you happier? Will it change who you are or what you could do in the world?"

"I honestly don't know. And I don't care. I just need to know."

Fairchild's voice has hardened and the corners of his mouth are tense. Suddenly I feel like a torturer in front of a captive. Palden is finishing with the leg, methodically wrapping a bandage around it. I wait for him to finish and we both thank him for his care and diligence and wait for him to return to the cave. This information I have, scant though it is, seems too precious to discuss in front of someone else, even in a tongue they will not understand.

"I met a Russian," I say. "His name is Dimitri. He is a Buddhist monk. He lives in a remote part of Russia, in a monastery in the forest, where no roads go. He became a Buddhist after seeing His Holiness the Dalai Lama visit his home town." I can hear the eagerness in my voice. "He was inspired to become a monk, and then many years later he came on a pilgrimage to Tibet, to Tashilunpo. So you see, it was all meant to be, that he and I would meet. His path led him to my home."

Fairchild rests his head on the rock again and closes his eyes. He is sceptical. But there is more. "He is an old man," I continue. "He moved to Moscow when he was young. Before that, he lived in Georgia. He left home after an accident. The accident left him with two fingers missing from his right hand." Fairchild opens his eyes and looks at me. "The third and the fourth," I say, "just like you told me."

The eyes don't waver. "In Moscow he kept company with some rough people. They did some things he is now ashamed of. One day they were sent on a special mission to Vienna. He remembers it well. It was his first time across the border to the West. He was excited about all the Western cars. He was the driver. He remembers the street where he had to wait. He remembers a boy with brown hair and big eyes, who came to the apartment where he and his colleagues had business. He remembers you, Fairchild. He is the one you saw. He was there."

Around us all is quiet. Fairchild is perfectly still, not even breathing. Then he says in a low voice, "What happened? Did he see my parents? Who was he with? Did they take them? Did they kill them? Who were they working for?"

I shake my head. "He could not tell me these things. We had so little time. You must go to him. He told me where you could find him. He will tell you everything. That's all we had time for. It is dangerous, my friend. People are always watching."

He nods. "Of course. I'm sorry. You've already taken too big a risk for me. I'm grateful." He rests his head again and his eyes close. He is exhausted.

I stand. "I feel you want to be alone for a while. But inside is warmer. When you are ready, join us."

I look back before climbing inside. Fairchild's face is stark and white. In the dingy inner chamber one candle remains lit, casting immense shadows across the walls. The Englishwoman Rose and Yonten are asleep on opposite sides of the stove, two breathing shapes, one large, one small. The stove is no longer lit but some of its heat remains. Palden slowly lets himself down between them, looking like a man far older than his years. I sit apart from them and face the wall. I close my eyes and chant silently to myself, my lips forming the sacred words. I picture the five of us here in this cave perched on a mountain on top of the world, tiny beings placed within the vastness of existence. I pray for Sonam and Choden. I pray for the Rinpoche. I pray for Yonten and Palden and picture the three of us topping the crest of the white pass tomorrow, looking down the other side into another country, another life. I pray for Rose, a stranger so distant but still so human, that she will somehow feel fulfilled. And I pray for Fairchild, the lost boy in the mountains, that he might find some way to come home. When my soul is composed, I join the circle round the stove to sleep for a while.

When I awake, the others are still asleep. Only the four of us are in the cavern. I pull my cloak tighter, shivering. Fairchild will be even colder. Why has he not come in? I get up and clamber out into the antechamber to persuade him. But Fairchild is gone.

Chapter 32

When Rose woke, the cave was cold. Several candles were sputtering to their end, casting an inconstant light between moments of total blackness. For the last few hours she had slept fitfully, aware that others were sleeping nearby. But now no one else was sleeping. Jinpa sat cross-legged across from her, staring at nothing. She sat up and he turned to her and spoke.

"It's time for us to leave. If we do not go soon, we will not reach the pass before daylight."

"Where's Fairchild?"

"He's gone."

"Gone? Gone where?"

"I gave him my news, and now he's gone." Jinpa sounded angry.

"The news about his parents?"

A guarded look entered his face. "The news he came for."

It didn't sound like Rose was going to find out more about what the news was. "How long ago was that?"

"I don't know, hours maybe." Jinpa seemed on the point of crying. "We cannot wait any longer. Already we've been here too long. It will be too dangerous for us, and for others who use this place if we stay. You must come with us. Otherwise you will be alone here."

"We're leaving without him? Shouldn't we go and look for him?" Rose was struggling to make sense of the situation. She was stiff and bruised all over, and still felt groggy. The cave was airless and she had no sense of time. The thought of walking again sickened her.

"We must go now," said Jinpa. "We must cross tonight."

Behind Jinpa, Yonten's large form emerged as he squeezed into the chamber and approached. His face was black with fury. Glaring at Rose as he passed, he took several packages of food out of the crate and climbed up out again.

"What's wrong?" asked Rose.

"His gun is missing."

She remembered the touch of metal on her neck just before she passed out after falling. "I have to say I'm quite surprised you have a gun."

"I never liked it. It was more likely to bring us trouble than save us from it."

"So why are you worried that it's missing?"

Jinpa appraised her with large, dark eyes.

"Fairchild must have it," he said. "He must have come in here when we were all asleep."

"Why would he need a gun?"

"I don't know," said Jinpa quietly.

Chapter 33

Fairchild stopped and sank down next to a boulder which shielded him from the wind. He could only think when he stopped. He'd been walking all afternoon and all night, off and on. A couple of times he'd dropped to the ground, hugging himself against the cold, unable to countenance the idea of taking another step. He must have slept like that, although he didn't understand how. Now he was close, but not close enough. He needed to get moving. Just as soon as he could bear the grinding pain again.

He pulled out the gun and looked at it. The barrel glinted as he turned the weapon over in his hand. It was a small revolver with a limited range. To make any difference, you'd need to be near.

The first gun he'd ever fired looked something like this. When he was seventeen, Walter in loco parentis had packed him off to summer camp in Colorado. Once there, Fairchild had faked a message from Walter calling him home. The camp had put him on a long-distance bus which he'd left at the first opportunity and backtracked to a small village in the next county. He'd asked around discreetly and hiked into the woods. He knew he'd found what he was looking for when he came straight up against two bores of a shotgun and a hostile bearded face. Fairchild had needed to talk very fast to make his offer, and produce evidence of its sincerity in the form of dollar bills, but in the end it was accepted. And so he spent the summer in the company of a troubled Vietnam vet named Nate and his extensive firearms collection.

He flipped the barrel. It was freezing to the touch, but moved smoothly. Six chambers and five bullets. He wondered idly where the sixth bullet had ended up. At the cave, he had sat and stared for a long while: exhaustion alone must have sent him to sleep. But he woke before the others. He'd looked inside where the four of them were peacefully asleep. It was afternoon then, three or four hours from darkness, when Jinpa would need to set off. They would insist that Fairchild go with them. Jinpa would refuse to leave him there, he realised that. But Fairchild would slow them down impossibly. At Fairchild's pace they would never make it over the pass before daybreak. It was then that he had caught sight of the pistol, on the ground near the big monk's hand. If they were putting their faith in that little thing against the might of the Chinese border police, they were doomed. Jinpa didn't even want that. He thought the bullets would just fall off him.

Not from a long-range assault rifle, they wouldn't. And if by now they had any idea who Jinpa was, they wouldn't hesitate. Fairchild had silently lifted the gun, and left straight away.

He turned the revolver towards himself and squinted up the barrel. The first time he had fired a gun, the noise and the recoil had startled him. It was like having a live animal in his hands. Nate had roared with laughter as the shot had gone stupidly wide into the trees. Ready for the kickback, he had tried again and hit two Coke bottles and a soda can before the chamber was empty. Nate had stopped laughing. Fairchild kept practising, learned how to anticipate and react, gently squeeze the trigger, be ready for the deafening crack, see the chamber advance and be ready for the next shot. That summer had a purpose. He liked learning things and could see the value in it.

He was sixteen when he'd tried to interest Walter in his discovery about Dimitri's cigarettes. Walter's reaction made him realise that the time would come when he would have to demand answers, not ask nicely. And the answers he needed were from people with skills and resources, provided by organisations that did not give up their secrets lightly. He needed some skills of his own. What a lifetime of foolery, he had often thought, chasing shadows round the world. Some of the things he had done to further his cause were unforgiveable: callous, manipulative, betrayals, some of them. But he had been betrayed too. And now, finally, he had a piece of real information from a real person who was there in the flesh on that Vienna night. He thought back to the way they had looked at each other in the empty street thirty years ago, him with indifference, Dimitri with shock and concern. Dimitri remembered him. Dimitri could tell him everything. How much of Dimitri's story did Walter already know? All of it, probably.

It was getting lighter by the minute. Hopefully they had crossed by now. He needed to get moving again. He would, in just a few moments, when his leg stopped throbbing.

Something moved in the corner of his eye, something dark and small, almost out of sight. He lowered the gun and stared, but could see only white snow and grey rock. He pitched forward on hands and knees and crawled forward. The ground below the ridge came into view. From its peak at the border next to Cho Oyu, the glacier descended and swept round almost beneath where he was. The pass rose up from the glacier where it curved. Spread across the width of the glacier below him was a line of men dressed identically in bulky bulletproof green moving swiftly upwards. The border police were converging on the pass.

He squinted up at the pass further ahead. Almost impossible to see against the harsh white of Nangpa La, he could make out four figures. One was large and the others were smaller. Two of them were leading the way with one slightly behind and one a little off to one side. He measured their pace against the paramilitary line below. The tiny figures nearing the pass seemed to move so slowly they were hardly progressing at all. The soldiers were racing up, almost at running pace.

As he stared at this scene before him, a faint sound carried to his ears from some distance behind and above him. It was a sound which made his blood run cold and a heaviness settle in the pit of his stomach. It was a rhythmic, slapping beat which meant that twenty years of a precious secret kept safe were over, that he would never see his young friend again, that all was lost.

It was the rotary blade of a helicopter.

Chapter 34

It is not how I imagined it. What looked like smooth whiteness from below is rough and uneven, soft snow coating hard ridged ice with hidden contours to make us trip and twist at every step. For what feels like hours we have been struggling upwards, the pass above us refusing to come any closer. My throat is bone dry and my limbs exhausted. No prayers for now: my cracked lips can do no more than draw essential breath. Yonten ploughs relentlessly on, making a pathway for me in the deep snow. If it weren't for this ox of a man, I would have foundered long ago. The ascent has become steeper. I know without even looking behind me that Palden has dropped further back. The woman, Rose, is beside us somewhere, her head down as she paces along in a world of her own.

It is too light. Anyone can see us against the snow. It was much slower than I thought, stumbling our way up here in the dark. Now we are stuck in this moment, climbing towards the pass forever while the sky gets lighter and lighter.

Yonten hears it first. He stops and turns to look back the way we have come. It is only then that I hear it myself – a steady mechanised beating, so faint that it comes and goes. I stop next to Yonten and turn to follow his gaze. I see nothing, but Yonten points downwards. Around the curve of the glacier figures in green have appeared, crawling up towards us like insects. As we watch, more appear, like ants emerging from a hole. I gaze, horrified. Palden, below us, stops and turns. As if he has no capacity to register what it means, he turns and continues up towards us like a man in a trance. His face is grey and his eyes are empty. Off to the side, Rose has seen the men also, and is looking at us.

Yonten urges me to hurry. I turn and follow him. We can do nothing except continue forwards, keep carrying out our plan. What is meant to happen will happen. I know I should be prepared for death, prepared to accept whatever will take place on this mountainside today. But I cannot help myself. As the distant noise grows stronger, what I feel clutching at my heart, making me hurry and trip over the rough ground, is sheer cold terror.

Chapter 35

Rose had the feeling something bad would happen, but didn't know what or when. The glacier surface was rough and lumpy, waves of a sea frozen into shape then cracked apart. They were so high. Blood was pounding in her head, her muscles ached and she gasped to take in the insubstantial air. They were wading through thick soft snow, up to the knees, the thighs, the hips, as if in a dream, never making any progress. Still the glacier curved up and away from them in front, still they had to keep ascending.

They were vulnerable: slow-moving dark objects on a white landscape, working their way up towards the horizon. Jinpa and Yonten were out in front. They had made it onto the pass. Palden was behind them, struggling. Rose was also behind and to one side. Where was Fairchild? She made an effort to focus on where her feet were landing.

Out of the corner of her eye, she saw the others stop and turn. When she did the same, she finally understood how it was going to happen. Racing up towards them, spread right across the width of the glacier, was a line of green-clad military, standing out against the white, padded, armed and climbing quickly. It wouldn't be long before they were in range.

They had serious business with these monks, and were going about it very seriously indeed. This had nothing to do with her, but what would they care about that? She was caught up in something that wasn't her fight, unarmed, with no cover or reasonable defence. She was only here because of Fairchild. And where was he? Gone somewhere, together with the only weapon these monks had between them.

As her anger grew, it reflected back at her in a new sound which she couldn't make sense of, a low-pitched hum emanating from everywhere. The others had heard it too. They all did the only thing they could do, turn and try to stumble upwards a little faster. They were stuck in a moment in time, their legs moving but not taking them anywhere, while the sound in their ears grew louder and louder.

The hum magnified into a roar. Rose turned back again. Over a ridge behind them a helicopter had risen into view and advanced towards them up the glacier, whipping up snow as it turned. The situation seemed hopeless. No way could they make it over now.

A fountain of snow erupted just behind the Tibetans. Rose's struggling brain could not make sense of it at first. She looked around to see one of the soldiers on his knee, aiming. The Tibetans continued upwards, Yonten tugging at the smaller man's coat in impatience. The helicopter was almost above them. Its drumming vibrated through her and she could feel downdraft from the rotor blade on her skin. She tried to run. Jinpa and Yonten were approaching the top of the pass. Palden was behind. The thundering rhythm of the helicopter drowned out all other sounds.

The ground beneath Rose's feet gave way and she pitched forwards towards the ice. A sharp stab of pain on her forehead was followed by nothing.

Chapter 36

The best Fairchild could manage was a lopsided limping gait, using his hands as much as his feet. His head was buzzing. Altitude. He had forgotten how high he was, with insufficient acclimatisation. That explained the lapses of judgement, time wasted staring down a gun. Idiot, idiot. Now he was half immobilised with cold. He should never have let himself get into this state. His leg felt huge, like an elephant's foot. He struggled to control it, knocking it sideways into rocks, a spasm of pain shooting up his leg each time. It was getting lighter. The black shape of the helicopter had materialised in the far distance and was approaching the glacier, its sound building all the time. The line of police was steadily ascending below him. They moved quickly over the surface of the glacier while he struggled over the rocks above, some slippery with ice, others with pools of gathered snow much deeper than they looked, causing him to land heavily and almost cry out in pain each time. At the closest point he could get without breaking cover he stopped and lay on the icy ground. The pass was wide and flat beyond the ridge of rocks concealing him from the approaching soldiers. They would cross below him as they closed in on the four escapees.

Now he could see the reason for Jinpa and his party making such slow progress: the snow was up to their knees or even their thighs in places. They were wading through it, approaching the crest of the pass, the border with Nepal. The pursuing police were in combat gear with rifles slung over their shoulders. The Tibetans glanced backwards occasionally. But they could do nothing except struggle on and hope they could make it over the border before they were within range. Fairchild pulled out the pistol and flipped the cartridge, needlessly noting again the five bullets inside. Five bullets in a tiny handgun against an advancing line of paramilitaries with airborne backup. The most he could hope to do was buy Jinpa's group some time and draw fire away from them.

A soldier in the centre rank dropped to his knee, aimed his rifle and fired at the group. The shot echoed in the air. Snow spewed up like a geyser a few feet short of the Tibetans. All of them turned to look, then turned back and pushed forward with more effort. Yonten and Jinpa were in front, Palden, struggling more, was just behind them. But where was Rose? He stared. Only three figures were on the pass. Had she been shot? He could see nobody on the ground. The slope was getting progressively steeper as they approached the brow. Slow-moving and visible, they were easy targets for anyone close enough.

The helicopter loomed above the soldiers' heads, its insistent beating steadying to a drone as it hovered. The shooter strode forward a few steps and repositioned himself. This time the snow spurted up in between the walkers. Another shot from somewhere underneath Fairchild's position hit snow to the right of the group. Two shooters within range. Fairchild crawled forward as far as he could while retaining the cover of the rocks. He rubbed his hands to try to bring some life to the ends of his fingers. The first shooter was closer again still and was aiming another shot. Fairchild steadied his hands as much as possible, aimed, and pulled the trigger.

The sound bounced off the rocks around him. *Five*. The shot fell short of the rifleman and some way in front, but it was enough to make the soldier abandon the shot and stare up in Fairchild's direction.

The helicopter's noise changed tone as it swung round above them. The shooter below was now aiming up at the summit again. Fairchild repositioned and fired towards him. *Four*. It hit the snow in front of him and to the left. Another soldier was running towards the second shooter. He stopped and fired at Fairchild's position, letting off several rounds. Fairchild ducked and pulled himself back below the edge of the ridge, cursing as his foot jabbed into a prominent rock.

The volley ended and Fairchild moved forward again, tentatively lifting his head. The first shooter had moved up again even closer to the walkers and the helicopter had dropped several feet, sending eddies of snow out around it. A gap had opened up between Yonten and Jinpa in front, and Palden behind. Yonten had a grip on Jinpa's arm and was pulling him along. They were almost at the highest point. The soldier below Fairchild was aiming again. Fairchild steadied his hands and fired at him. *Three*. A scream reverberated and the shooter clutched his hand. Red droplets sprayed onto the snow around him. Once more the soldier nearest him turned towards Fairchild and fired repeatedly, forcing Fairchild back again away from the edge of the rock. Bullets smashed into the rock face in front of him, inches away from his head. The noise from the helicopter intensified as its rotor dipped towards him.

The firing ceased and the noise lessened again. He crawled back. Jinpa was right on the brow with Yonten next to him, the big man's arm around his waist, projecting him forwards. Palden was a few paces behind the other two. The first shooter had moved up with the advancing line, now directly between Fairchild and the Tibetans. The gunman was on his knee and aiming straight at Jinpa. He had a good shot and was well within range. He was ready to fire. Fairchild raised the pistol and pointed straight at him. *Two*.

The bullet landed off by the shooter's side, too late to prevent the shot but the soldier had flinched as he fired, sending it off course. At the top, a body crumpled. It was Palden. Jinpa and Yonten looked round. Jinpa turned and took a step towards him but Yonten had him by the arm. Jinpa was trying to break free. While the struggle was going on, the shooter was aiming again. And others were now in range, preparing to take aim from positions spread across the pass. More soldiers were approaching, fanning in on the two remaining standing figures on the highest point. The helicopter was so close that the sleeves of the uniformed soldiers were flapping in the downdraft. Jinpa broke away and took two steps towards the fallen body. Yonten, behind him, put his arms around the smaller man's waist and lifted him off the ground. Jinpa's legs were kicking out beneath him, sending snow in all directions. Yonten turned his back on the shooters and walked, hauling his precious load, struggling to break free, mouth open in a scream, over the brow and across the border into Nepal.

The helicopter dipped, closing in on them. On the ground, one of them shouldered his weapon and aimed. He had a good shot, square into Yonten's back. Fairchild aimed and fired. *One*. The gunman jerked. His weapon swung into the air, emptying into the base of the helicopter as the soldier fell sideways to the ground. A clang of metal on metal reached Fairchild, and the droning of the copter altered but continued. That was it. His five shots were up. He'd done what he could. He could no longer see the Tibetans but it didn't look promising. Too little, too late.

Fairchild's only warning of the soldier behind him was the soft sound of rubber on rock. He turned on his back to see the muzzle of a pistol aimed straight at him. The khaki-clad Chinese soldier did a double-take. Surprised to see a Westerner, no doubt. He nodded at the pistol in Fairchild's hand. Fairchild dropped it and climbed to his feet, arms raised. The soldier beckoned with his head. Fairchild kicked the gun along the ground towards him. But not quite far enough. As the man bent to pick it up, Fairchild took one step forward and kicked upwards sharply, hitting him under the chin with such force that he flew backwards into the rock behind. Ignoring the shooting pain in his leg, Fairchild propelled himself forward, landing with his knee in the man's stomach, and bent the soldier's wrist back against the rock, causing him to shout with pain and loosen his grip on his gun. The soldier kicked up, unseating him, and they rolled onto the ground, each scrambling to get on top. From somewhere between them came a muffled bang. Fairchild's right side exploded with a burning pain. He couldn't breathe. Black shapes appeared before his eyes. The soldier pulled away from him and he heard footsteps running off. Then the blackness covered everything and the juddering noise overhead faded.

Chapter 37

The noise is thunderous, the sound of destruction itself. I fight the grip encircling me. Palden is lying down there on the snow, unmoving. I have to reach him and help him but Yonten's thick arms are around my waist and all I can do is kick out, scattering snow in all directions. My mouth is open wide and I am probably screaming but there is no sound except the ear-splitting roar above us. Yonten turns and walks like a machine, holding me up in front of him, indifferent to my resistance. All I can see is more snow and ice and rocks stretching out in front.

Yonten stumbles slightly then recovers and resumes. The ground is falling away beneath us. The realisation comes to me. The border must be at the highest point. If we are descending, we have crossed. We have made it. We are in Nepal.

I am turning my head, about to shout in Yonten's ear when a burst of sound takes my breath away. Snow is swirling up around us and Yonten staggers sideways as the helicopter, almost above us now, tilts towards us. A violent vibration and judder passes through Yonten's body and his grip loosens. Then another, and his huge form pitches forwards onto the snow with me underneath. We slide and come to rest. I am pinned onto the ice by his weight.

I feel oddly enlightened as I lie here struggling for breath, hearing the sound of the helicopter recede. It makes perfect sense. Now I feel I know my enemy. The moment of defeat is also the moment of realisation. Of course they do not respect the border. Of course they do not hesitate to open fire, even after their targets have reached the sanctuary of another country. Why did I ever think that they would? Fairchild was right after all.

The beating sound fades to a muffled silence as I lie, eyes closed, on the blood-soaked snow.

Chapter 38

When Rose opened her eyes, all she could see was blue light. She was lying awkwardly on her side, shivering. Her upper arm and back were numb, pressed against ice. She shifted her weight and lifted her head up. That small movement triggered a wave of nausea and a sharp shooting pain above her right eye. She closed her eyes and kept still while the nausea passed.

She moved her leg, and her foot fell and swung: there was nothing beneath it. Tentatively she raised her head and felt around with her hands. She was on a tiny ledge of ice.

She sat up and knocked something with her elbow. She lunged and managed to grab her backpack before it hurtled down into the gap beneath her. Below the dangling backpack, swinging by the one strap in her hand, was empty space. She pulled the bag back onto the ledge and waited for her racing heart to slow down. She touched her temple. She could feel a graze from the impact but no lump. The cold must have limited any swelling. Everything around her was blue. Light was coming from above, a thin strip above her head no more than a metre wide between two walls of ice. She was in a crevasse, but not far from the top. She had been lucky: the ledge had broken her fall.

The sheer sides of the crevasse, ice ridged with vertical lines, shot up around her towards the light. She could see no other ledges or handholds. She looked down again over the edge. The steep sides continued downwards into darkness below her, getting narrower and narrower. The bottom was lost in blackness. Slowly, she manoeuvred herself into a standing position, the backpack safely stowed by her feet. She reached up above her as far as she could. The top of the crevasse was about half a metre above the tips of her fingers.

Standing with her arms outstretched brought back the shooting pain and nausea. She crouched on the spot, waiting for it to recede. Should she shout? If anyone was up there to hear, would they save her or shoot her? How long had she been down here? It was still daylight, that was all she could tell. She listened. She could hear no sound above her at all. Thinking about what was happening when she fell, maybe the crevasse had saved her from a more violent end – but only if she could get out of it.

She sat, opened the backpack and felt around for the ice axe and the length of rope that she had looted from the outdoor shop in Lhasa. She tied the rope round the eye at the bottom of the ice axe handle. She stood again, raising herself up carefully on the narrow ledge and keeping her feet planted still. Holding a generous length in her hand, she weighed the ice axe in the palm of her other hand, lowered it then tossed it straight upwards. The long arm of the axe hit the edge of the rim on the way up, dislodging a chunk of ice which disintegrated and showered down on her. The axe fell past her down into the crevasse, almost yanking the rope out of her hand when it stopped.

She pulled the axe up and tried again. It was an awkward, long shape to throw directly upwards through a narrow gap. She couldn't move her feet at all on the ledge. Given how easily the ice at the rim had come away, she wondered how secure her ledge was. She tried again and again, working out a twisted over-arm throw that sent the axe flying at an angle out of the rim. She slipped and almost lost her footing twice. Each time when the axe landed outside, she pulled slowly on the rope until it reappeared at the top and fell back down towards her. She had to shield her face with her arms to avoid the rough curved edge of the axe falling into her face.

Eventually she pulled the rope and it stuck. She pulled harder. With both hands on the rope she tentatively tested it with her full bodyweight, lifting her feet off the ground. She tugged gently and then harder. She shouldered the backpack and pulled herself up entirely onto the rope. It was only a short length to climb, but once she was hanging on the rope, the full depth of the crevasse was below her. She had to hope the axe would hold on to whatever it was caught on, a rough piece of ice or a furrow in the glacier's surface. Cautiously she put one hand above the other and managed to grip the rope between the soles of her boots. As she reached out to grab the rope above the rim, a large piece of the crevasse edge shattered into shards with a crunch, and she lurched into the side, her shoulder taking the impact. She looked down for one terrifying moment into the darkness below, her legs thrashing wildly.

She reached for the rope with her feet and eventually got some traction between her soles again. She pushed herself up one more handgrip. The tension in the rope was easing: the ice axe was slipping. With her legs she levered herself up and got a higher grip. Her head was above the rim. Another hand found the rope as it lay tensed along the surface of the glacier. The ice was creaking. She repositioned her feet and pushed out again. Her waist was now above the level of the rim and she was leaning out, gripping the rope. The ice in front of her exploded and the axe came hurtling towards her. She heaved herself forward as the rope went slack, and rolled over. The axe skidded to a halt and she lay panting, facing the sky.

It took her a few moments to recover and come back to the present. She raised her head then sat up and looked about her. She could see no one. No sound, no shouting or gunfire, no droning helicopter. No bodies. Slowly she got up and shook shards of ice off her clothes. She rubbed her hands which were red and sore from the rope and the cold, and dug out her gloves from her backpack. She needed to start moving quickly to get some warmth back.

She tried to get her bearings. The sun was higher but still near the horizon on the top of the pass so she probably hadn't been in the crevasse for very long. She pictured the three figures making their laboured way up the pass. She walked up towards that spot. In front of her she found an elongated deep red stain in the snow. Somebody fell here. They must have dragged the body over the snow. Did they take it in the helicopter? She waded on slowly to the top of the pass, feeling light-headed. The sharp pain in her forehead was back. At the top, a pile of stones decorated with ragged white katas marked the border. In front of her, another patch of red stained the snow. Beyond that the pass descended with no signs of life.

She was alone at a scene of death for the second time in as many days. She looked out at the horizon, unable to avoid thinking how beautiful it all was, a long vista of white peaks gleaming in the sunshine, threads of white cloud clinging to the tops like Christmas decorations. She looked back down the glacier, which she had ascended with Jinpa, Palden and Yonten, after they had realised that Fairchild had disappeared. All those people were now gone. She looked down the route into Nepal, which should have been freedom and a kind of homecoming for Jinpa. She was a long way from anyone, alive by the skin of her teeth, dangerously, exhilaratingly alone. She turned in a full circle, gazing at the view in all directions. Then she stamped her feet to get the blood circulating, shouldered her pack, and set off.

Chapter 39

Fairchild woke with a jolt. He was shivering. His right side throbbed as if being gripped by a vice. He moved his arm from under his body and felt around tentatively, gasping when his fingers caught raw flesh. His skin was wet. He forced himself onto his side and pulled his jacket away to look. His clothes were soaked with blood, heavy with the weight of it. He zipped up his jacket, a shock of pain making him ball his fists.

He looked around. The soldier had taken his own gun with him, and left the bulletless revolver by his side. He crawled slowly and painfully over to the rock edge to look down. No one was on the glacier. For how long had he blacked out? The only thing to see was a dark spot of red and, evidence of what he had realised was almost a certainty, another bloodstain in the snow several yards further away, beyond the brow of the pass.

They had taken the bodies. Why did they not come up here to find him? Maybe the soldier thought he would be in trouble for shooting a Westerner. Maybe they were coming back. If they did, he could do little about it, in this state with nothing but an unloaded gun. The blackness was returning. He was not sure he could stand, let alone fight. He may as well just wait for them to arrive. He lay on his back and closed his eyes.

He opened his eyes. His teeth were chattering. There was a sickening ache in his side. The blood on his body had congealed. He rolled over and looked at the sun. It was well above the horizon now.

He rose on one knee and a choir of humming voices filled his ears. His forehead knocked against his kneecap. Oxygen, he thought, trying to fight back. Loss of blood will worsen the effects of altitude. He was weaker and needed to compensate. No sudden movements. Slowly he lifted his head and rose to his feet, the humming choir advancing and retreating. He felt his way slowly down the rock face. The pain stabbed whenever he moved. His hand on his jacket felt wetter than before. He limped slowly.

His instincts led him down. He had no plan. It didn't really matter where he went, or whether he made it. He thought of Jinpa, eyes shining, their last conversation, his belief in the future, his faith. All to finish here, mown down on a glacier and squirrelled off somewhere, so that the Chinese could re-invent a more palatable version of what happened, if they even needed to bother. Extinguish life and then extinguish truth. His plucky, clever, unique, eccentric friend with his bizarre upbringing, he and his band of brothers never had more than a whisker of a chance. And it was Fairchild's fault that chance was lost. Jinpa had said as little as he could about his encounter with the Russian, but that in itself told Fairchild that Jinpa had taken an unacceptable risk to speak to the stranger. That was enough to prompt the security services into high alert, enough to increase surveillance, get people's backs up, provoke a riot. It was Fairchild's doing, his silly stories about events long gone, that had done for his friend. And Fairchild hadn't even been there with him at the end. He'd snuck away while they were all asleep.

He stumbled on a rock and fell to his knees, the pain of the impact drawing a long groan. He doubled up, his forehead on the icy ground. Then there was Rose. She was only here because of him. Even after what he'd done to her in Beijing, she'd felt compelled to follow him to Tibet. He hadn't wanted her to come with him into the mountains. She'd insisted on that. But without her he'd never have reached Jinpa. She'd joined him on this foolhardy journey, and now she was gone, too. If it weren't for her he wouldn't even know about the Russian.

The Russian. He lifted his head. Was it worth one more effort, to try to get to him? After all that had been done to deliver this secret to him? It was enough to get him to his feet to try one more time. Down, downwards, it didn't matter which direction. He'd lost all sense of direction anyway. From here he could see a long way, out of the snow line to the rocky terrain and the valleys below. No sign of life. It was a dead world. In frustration he lifted his head and shouted at the sky. The sound echoed and faded.

Something moved in the distance, far away. He stared, but holes appeared in his vision. A figure, something in his brain was telling him, had turned to look up towards him. Not a soldier. Not a monk. A tiny figure in a long coat. Maybe a nomad, journeying between pastures. Maybe nobody, just a figment of his imagination. He blinked, opened his eyes wide and looked again. The figure was gone.

He stepped out to continue downwards, but the ground wasn't where he expected it to be and he fell, sliding forwards and then backwards, slamming to a halt as the pain made him scream out loud.

Chapter 40

Eventually, the groaning, shaking bone-rattling motion subsided, then ceased altogether as the engine died. Rose stumbled out of the jeep and recognised the street straight away. She was back in Tingri. It seemed symbolic of the massive great full circle she'd just travelled on.

She'd been lucky to get back at all. Her instinct to head east towards Everest had been right. It had taken a day and a night of walking, resting in whatever shelter she could find, and she had got through all the supplies the monks had given her from the cave, but she had eventually reached a road of sorts. One of the jeeps servicing the tourist base camp at Everest had stopped for her and brought her here. She had paid them, realising how suspicious she must look wandering around alone on the Himalayan plateau. They had given her food and water and she had slept in the jeep, but was still hungry and beyond exhaustion.

The town was quiet this late in the evening, with no lights visible through any of the shuttered windows. She paced slowly in the road, flexing her feet to stay warm, and wondered what next. Maybe she could get the room back that she'd shared briefly with Fairchild. A few hours of proper sleep would be more than welcome. Ultimately she needed to get somewhere with internet and an airport, either back to Lhasa or on to the border. The border made more sense. She had little reason to remain in Tibet. Fairchild's friends were all dead, and Fairchild could be the same. If he wasn't, he had nothing to keep him in this part of the world. She really was back to square one.

As she stood and stretched her muscles, a small high-sided van drove into the town and pulled in near the jeep. Two men got out. The guys who had given her a lift were standing smoking. The men all started talking to each other. Their voices carried and caught Rose's attention. They were speaking more loudly than if they were just passing the time. There was an urgency about their movements, worry or even fear in their faces. One of them opened up the back of the van and another man jumped out. Now they were pointing to the inside of the van, discussing something that was inside. Then one of the jeep guys nodded back in her direction as he talked. He was telling the others something about her, where they'd picked her up, probably. They turned and looked at her. Then their attention went back to whatever it was that was in the van. It was clear from the body language that they had a problem and didn't know what to do about it. The conversation came to a halt. One or two of the group turned and looked at her. She stared back at them, then went over.

"What's in here?" She pointed. The men exchanged glances but didn't say anything. If she was going to find out what was happening she would need to see it for herself. She put one foot on the tailgate to climb in. One of the van passengers stepped forward to stop her, but another one put his hand up to hold him back. She climbed up and peered inside.

In the gloom, the back of the truck seemed empty except for a pile of blankets along the front. She edged forwards, got a torch out and shined it on the blankets. She drew a sharp breath: a human arm was sticking out. It was a body. She knelt and peeled back the blankets. She was looking at a face, almost buried beneath blankets. A very recognisable face.

"Fairchild!" He was a pallid grey colour and his eyes were closed. But he was alive: she could hear his ragged breathing. She touched his cheek with the back of her hand. It was cold. She peeled back the blankets and pulled open his coat. He moaned and moved his head. She gasped as she directed the torch at his body. The whole of his torso was shiny with blood. She scrambled back to the men outside.

"What happened? Where did you find him?" They watched her with large eyes. It was hopeless. She suddenly envied Fairchild's easy way with languages. Even without Tibetan, Mandarin might have worked, but she had nothing, no means of finding out from these people what had happened. The sheer amount of blood suggested a gunshot wound. Her best guess was that Fairchild was up at the pass and had got caught up in the firefight in some way. He was lucky to have got help thus far, but that kind of blood loss at high altitudes was serious.

They were muttering to each other. If they knew of any medical resources in Tingri to call in, they would have done it by now. "Is there a hospital in Dram?" she asked.

"Dram!" One of the jeep drivers picked up on the word and nodded, animated. They discussed this between them and the others nodded too.

"So can you take us both to Dram?" She pointed at Fairchild and herself and addressed this to the van driver. He looked non-committal. She reached into her bag for a bundle of money. It was understandable: getting involved in something like this was a big risk for an ordinary Tibetan. Lesser people might have decided to dump him somewhere remote and have nothing further to do with it, but these men had done what they could for him. Some finger-waving and gestures with the money settled a price, and Rose climbed in the back along with one of the men.

The other two men slammed the door shut from the outside, plunging them into darkness. They set off, lurching over the potholed road. Rose tucked the blankets around Fairchild as much as she could, then sat back against the wooden side of the van. The Tibetan did the same on the opposite side. The floor of the van amplified every bump on the road surface. There was a strong smell of rotting food. She sighed and closed her eyes. She should be used to this style of travelling by now.

Somehow she managed to doze off, and when she woke she felt the change in the air, warmer and clammier. They were descending, swerving their way down a switchback road, round corner after corner. She checked up on Fairchild. His breathing was hardly detectable now but she found a slow pulse in his neck. She had no idea how much further it was and no way of finding out. It started to rain. The drumming reverberated noisily on the roof. Water dripped through a corner and started pooling on the floor. She moved to avoid getting slowly soaked. A thin light made its way in somehow.

She awoke from another light sleep as the van came to a stop. The doors opened and the back flap fell with a bang. The men jumped out and produced smokes from their pockets. They stood by the roadside talking and pulling on their cigarettes. Rose checked on Fairchild again: still a very slow pulse. She emerged and stretched. They were in a lush steep valley, green trees growing densely right up to the roadside. The van had pulled in just before a sharp bend, no buildings in sight. The sun hadn't yet risen. She felt the rain on her face. Not being cold made a welcome change. She walked a few paces into the undergrowth to relieve herself. When she returned, they had carried Fairchild out and were setting him carefully down by the side of the road.

"Hey!" she called to the men's backs as they returned to the van. "What are you doing? This isn't Dram."

One of them turned and pointed down the road.

"Dram," he said, and make a walking gesture with his fingers. He pointed at Rose. "Dram."

"He can't walk," said Rose, pointing at Fairchild. The man pointed at Rose again.

"Dram," he said finally. One of the men climbed out with Rose's backpack and placed it on the ground next to Fairchild. They turned and got into the van, which performed an awkward three-point turn and drove off, leaving a cloud of diesel fumes.

Rose pulled Fairchild so that he was slightly sheltered under the trees, but could not stop the rain dripping onto him altogether. The men had left one of the blankets wrapped around him. His breathing was now rough and uneven. Rose knelt and went through his pockets. He had his passport in the false name that matched his permit, and a wallet with a large wad of cash. Rose left the ID and took most of the cash from the wallet, leaving some of it on him. She stood looking down at him for a while, thinking. Then she buttoned herself up against the rain, put her hood up, and set off down the road.

Chapter 41

It was still raining some considerable time later when Rose woke and realised that someone was in her hotel room.

She came to this conclusion slowly and groggily, gradually emerging from the long and deep sleep her body had been yearning for days. Entering consciousness, she first recognised the yellowed walls, the sound of rain on glass and the smell of wet paper and mildew. The air was solid, warm and clammy. Her sheets felt damp. She blinked a few times and half sat up. The chain of events leading from the roadside in Dram to her being in this room returned to her mind. Through bleary eyes she realised her instinct was right. Someone was indeed sitting in the chair, watching her.

Large eyes stared intensely from an angular mid-brown face through glasses with severe black rims. The woman was sitting forward in the chair actively observing her, hands clasped together on her lap, slender fingers intertwined. A worn bulky leather bag was sitting by her feet. Her soft black shoes were ringed with damp. Resting against the wall behind her was a large folded umbrella.

"Don't be alarmed," the woman said. "If I were intending to harm you, I would have done it by now." Rose could hear a British note in her English.

"How did you get in?"

"I used a key."

"The hotel gave you a key to my room?"

"They came up to let me in. I told them it was a house call. That you'd summoned me. That you were too weak to get out of bed."

"You're a doctor?"

"That's right. I am useful to them, you see. I can help them to avoid the trouble they sometimes attract. This is one of the few hotels in Dram where they don't ask too many questions of foreigners who don't have the right permits."

Rose had noticed the lack of a chain on the room door. She'd already identified that the heaviest item within reach was the table lamp next to the bed. She could do some damage with that if need be. She looked around the room. Everything was how it had been before, as far as she could tell. She remembered the grimy ceiling, the unwashed windows, the cobwebs in the corners. Behind her own stale sweat was a smell of frying food, the vent from a kitchen somewhere. "I didn't think it was the best place in town. You're from the hospital?"

The hospital was where Fairchild was. After leaving him by the roadside, she'd walked into the town and bribed a taxi driver to help her pick him up, manhandle him into the cab and drop him off outside the hospital. To avoid any contact with the authorities, she'd stayed only long enough to ensure he'd been noticed, then returned to Dram to check into the least reputable-looking hotel she could find. She wasn't about to reveal any of that, though, to someone who'd been calmly watching her sleeping a moment ago.

"I've come from the hospital," the woman confirmed.

Rose rearranged the pillows behind her and sat back on them. "May I ask who you are?" she said. "And what you're doing here?"

"Of course. My name is Parajuli. As I said, I'm a doctor. Born and trained in Kathmandu. Studied in London, for a while. At first I worked in rural areas. As you probably know, Nepal is not a rich country and medical services in the countryside are in great demand."

"What are you doing here, I mean?" This Parajuli clearly liked to give a detailed response.

"Well, I'm not sure Dram is the kind of place where anyone intends to end up. I realised I could be of use here, and we all want to be of use, don't we? Of course this is not Nepal, as we are still on the Chinese side. But Dram is not very Chinese, is it? A mixture of all identities and none. Border towns really are fascinating places. I can come back and forth as I wish here. Being a doctor has some advantages."

This wasn't what Rose meant either, but there was something restful and melodious about Parajuli's voice which dispelled some of her impatience. "And how exactly are you of use in Dram?"

"Well, in addition to my medical practice, I like to keep an eye on things."

"I see." This was more useful. "And who do you keep an eye on things for?"

"My friends are – compatriots of yours. One of them is a Walter Tomlinson."

"You work for Walter?"

"We are in contact from time to time. He dropped me a line recently. He'd been wondering when you might make an appearance. And, indeed, whether." She let this sink in, watching her intensely. Rose stared back at her. If Parajuli wanted her to believe she was working for Walter, it was incumbent on her to gain Rose's trust. Until then, she was just another potential hostile with insufficient respect for personal privacy.

"Walter and I go back a long way," continued Parajuli, sensing Rose's guardedness. "I met him in London. I also met your current travelling companion. John Fairchild. He was a young man then, in his teens. He's looking very different now."

"And when did you last see John Fairchild?"

"Yesterday." She waited for Rose's response. There was a restfulness to her silences, as if each were a mini-meditation. Rose kept her face neutral.

"Yesterday?"

"In the hospital. Of course that was not the name on his travel documents. But I recognised him. And Walter said he might pass this way. With you. I am assuming you are Rose Clarke. The hotel staff didn't seem entirely sure."

If that was yesterday, Rose must have slept an entire night and most of the following day. Another restful pause followed. The rain drummed away on the window pane. Rose was thinking. "Why," she asked, "did Walter think that John Fairchild and I would come here?"

"Because of the monks from Shigatse. The fugitives, from Tashilunpo. One of them came through here, you know."

Rose didn't know. "Really?"

"A few days ago, a Tashilunpo monk arrived here on his own, asking some really quite indiscreet questions about how he and his friends might manage to get themselves across the border into Nepal. The poor man unfortunately triggered a few alarms and disappeared shortly afterwards. Since then, security on the border has become rather tight. They are checking every vehicle. It is taking a long time to pass through. You will see when you go down there yourself."

The monk must have been known to Jinpa. Was it ever Jinpa's intention to come here? She hadn't got that impression. "And why did Walter think that this monk had any connection with John Fairchild or me?"

"Well, that relates to another piece of intelligence which came to light." Parajuli shifted in her chair. Behind her through the window the overcast sky was darkening and lights were starting to come on up and down the slope. It must be early evening already. "After a security incident in Shigatse, a number of monks were taken into custody. They were interrogated, and it came out that these fugitives from Tashilunpo, one of whom came here, may be of considerable interest to the Chinese. So much so that China would go to enormous lengths to track these people down and prevent them from leaving the country."

"But again, how does that relate to Fairchild or me?"

"John Fairchild is working for the Chinese, is he not, the MSS? That is certainly Walter's view. Walter feels sure that Fairchild knew about these dissidents and undertook to track them down for the Chinese. Walter feels that this explains Fairchild's presence in Tibet. If the dissidents were planning to exit through Dram, it is likely that Fairchild would appear here at some point. Although, I have to say I have not seen or heard any sign of any other Tashilunpo monks coming here. Perhaps they learned of the increased security and have revised their plans."

"And how," asked Rose, "does Walter explain how Fairchild knew about these so-called dissidents?"

"It's the kind of thing he knows about," said Parajuli. "Fairchild has grown up to be rather prescient, as I understand it. When something of significance happens and Fairchild is nearby, it often seems that he has some knowledge of it. Walter finds this quite troublesome, I gather."

More than anything else, Parajuli's description of the unique relationship between Fairchild and Walter gave Rose confidence that Parajuli was genuine. Besides, there was no point worrying about Jinpa and his crew: it was already too late for them. "The other monks didn't come here," she said. "They tried to cross through the mountains, at the Nangpa La pass. But they didn't make it." She thought about that moment on the glacier, the bloodstains on the snow, the solitude. "We followed them up there. Well, Fairchild went after them, and I went after him. It all got a bit messy."

"You appear to be in a much better state than your travelling companion." Parajuli was observing her carefully.

"So how is he?"

"As of yesterday, stable but weak."

"And today?"

"Today I don't know. He's not there any more."

"Where's he gone?"

"I'm told he was removed from the hospital by a unit operating for the MSS. He could not have walked out on his own, we can be sure about that. He appears to have sustained a number of injuries."

"He was stabbed in the leg. And then shot, I suppose."

"You suppose?"

"I wasn't there at the time."

"And the stabbing?"

"I was there when he was stabbed. Actually, it was me that stabbed him." Parajuli's eyes widened. "It was an accident," she said reassuringly.

Parajuli continued to regard her. "The leg injury will impact on his movement for some time, but is not life-threatening. My assessment of the other injury was a gunshot wound at close range. While he lost a lot of blood, he did not sustain major internal injuries. He should make a full recovery, if he receives medical care."

"I'm afraid I don't think we can count on that. Not if he's been taken by the Chinese. It must have been them that shot him."

"He wasn't working for them?"

"I thought he was, to begin with. But his business with the monks was personal." She thought about Fairchild's treatment of Geleg's satellite phone. "He really didn't want anyone to know where he was going. He went to great lengths to try and prevent me from following him. I had to work very hard to keep up with him. And now it seems he's disappeared again. I have the feeling Walter will be disappointed."

"You will find out, I expect, when you meet him in Kathmandu."

"Walter's in Kathmandu?"

"He was travelling to meet you. And, he hoped, John Fairchild."

"Well, first I need to get over the border without a travel permit."

"And did you have a plan in mind to overcome this?"

"I was assuming there would be people in this town who could help with that."

Parajuli paused, again as if in a meditative state. Then she reached down to her bag and retrieved a passport and some papers, which she passed to Rose.

"You may find these helpful. A replacement identity to get into Nepal. You were with a legitimate group but were held up in Dram due to illness. It's all been pre-arranged. As I said, being a doctor in these parts has advantages. Once you get across, any of the jeeps on the other side of the river will take you down to Kathmandu. If you check into the Annapurna Hotel, Walter will find you."

Rose scanned her replacement papers. There was her face next to a completely different name. She could have done with this kind of support a lot earlier. "Looks like you've been busy."

Parajuli stood. "I like to be prepared," she said. "You should rest. You took a big knock on your forehead. Other than that, you seem fine. You will have an interesting story to tell Walter, I think. If you do see John Fairchild again, give him my regards."

She picked up her bag and umbrella, gave her one last thoughtful look and let herself out.

Rose wondered if she'd been so out of it that Parajuli had managed to give her a complete medical examination while she was here. Making a mental note not to be so careless again, she threw the bed clothes aside and got up. It was fully dark outside now and the lights of Dram extended vertically up the slope. Her clothes were hanging up in a cupboard with the door open, but they were still wet. They hadn't dried out, in fact, since she'd walked into Dram, past the long procession of trucks that wound tightly round its dog-leg corners down to the border, rainwater spraying off their wheels. Where was Fairchild now? How annoyingly elusive the man was. Even when half-dead he managed to disappear somehow. Despite their paths crossing again at Tingri, she had ultimately failed to keep up with him. Walter would not be pleased.

She stood at the window and watched the rain cascade. Dram clung onto Tibet's southernmost slope as if it had been washed down from the icy plateau above. After the sleep she'd just had, she should have started to feel normal again. Instead, a curtain of unreality had fallen. She was encased inside a rain cloud, suspended in mid-air, surrounded by mist and fog. Fairchild was gone. And so was Jinpa, the extraordinary young man she had met so briefly but who had such an energy and purpose about him. Now everything he and his friends had devoted their lives to was lost. In this sodden little town, hanging on grimly to its steep slope, she had a sense that everything was slipping and sliding away.

Chapter 42

The pain made Fairchild more alert. The nurse worked silently, focused on completing the task as soon as possible, busy with his fingers, not slowing if Fairchild drew breath or flinched. As he worked, the tiny room filled with the smell of disinfectant. The two guards who accompanied the nurse were positioned as usual, one at the foot of the bed, the other by the door. They were armed.

Whenever Fairchild asked something, one of the guards would tell him to shut up. They all spoke Mandarin. He had been on a drip, but now the tubes had been taken away and they were bringing him solid food, which was edible. Whatever they wanted, they didn't want him dead. He had not been out of this tiny cell, out of this bed. Wherever this was that he was being held, it was warm and the air thick and humid.

He couldn't remember coming here. He was gradually piecing together the snatches of images and feelings he had of the last few days. The pain from his leg, still a constant presence. Looking down onto the glacier, seeing fountains of snow spurting up. Blood patches on a deserted glacier. Moments of tortuous awareness during a long rumbling journey in the dark with this gash in his side. Rose was there. At least he thought she was, but perhaps he was imagining it. Then he was in a hospital bed, a soothing voice he somehow recognised addressing him in English. Then here.

He looked at the ceiling, the plain painted walls. He had to get out of this cell, out of this place. The nurse worked quickly. The tubes had been taken away. Under this grey blanket, they had dressed him in a generic hospital gown. They were building his strength before interrogating him, but he was already stronger than they realised.

The nurse never looked up while he worked on the dressing. Fairchild silently readied himself. The nurse's hands came to a halt. At that precise moment he shoved him violently backwards into the guard who was standing by the door. With his feet he pushed the blanket into the path of the second guard, who grabbed him and they fell to the floor grappling. He felt for the man's ID card and pulled it off him, disabling him with a heavy kick in the groin. The other guard had pulled his gun and was aiming at straight at him, screaming. Fairchild looked at him blandly, turned, and swiped open the door. The guard didn't shoot. Of course not. They were keeping him alive.

He tore barefoot down the corridor, the guard five paces behind. He made it through the next set of doors before the alarm sounded. He held the door and kicked it shut as the guard came through, throwing him backwards. He ran on, scanning for clues, indicators of where he should go. He needed to be outside.

He could smell food, meat and something sweet. He turned sharply towards it and launched himself through another set of doors. A dozen men in drab prison uniform were seated at long plastic tables. They looked up and stared. None intervened: it wasn't their business. He leaped over the serving counter, scattering food trays onto the floor. More guards were now close behind him. Through the kitchen, staff and prisoners quietly got out of his way as he crashed his way to the door at the back. He had been running for about a minute and the wound was already bleeding.

A wave of heat hit him as he pelted through the doorway. Outside, the ground was dry under his feet and the sun almost blinded him. It was hot, tropical, a glimpse of green jungle visible beyond the fencing. Swerving into the middle of the compound he saw four or five guards on the perimeter wall aiming their weapons at him. His pace slowed. Pain shot up his leg with every step he took. His mouth was dry and he couldn't draw enough breath. The fence stretched before him with no sign of a gate. He had no hope of getting out. The guards were right behind him now. Still no one fired. One of them threw themselves forward and grabbed his waist. He pitched forwards onto the ground. The pain became intense as the other guards piled on top of him. Then he blacked out.

Chapter 43

I feel the helicopter blades beat, their drumming vibration penetrating my body. A huge weight presses my bones into the snow and stops me from breathing. The panic begins to build inside me, that old panic I recognise from long ago, a horror of being enclosed. I am straining against the mass on top of me but my legs and arms are locked and I cannot move.

"Yonten! Yonten!" I am shouting but can only produce a whisper. Finally the weight rolls back and cold air floods my lungs. I am looking at bright blue sky. I clamber to my feet and turn. The body is there, lying face down, encircled by an aura of red in the snow. I put a hand on its shoulder and pull it over. When I see the face I gasp. It isn't Palden at all, but the Rinpoche, his eyes empty sockets where the vultures have picked at them.

Suddenly I am awake, gasping in the darkness. Wooden rafters loom high above. I sit up, my heart hammering. The barn is silent, except for Yonten lying next to me on his back, his face composed, his breathing regular and deep. I wish I could sleep like that.

The blankets covering us smell of unwashed bodies. Other refugees have slept here in this safe house on their journey to Kathmandu, the capital of Nepal, where Tibetans can find support. They would have lived through their own stories too, and been jolted awake by nightmares just as I am. It is the first time we have been able to rest, but as soon as I closed my eyes, the memories crowded in, mixed up and wrong. That was not what happened on the glacier. My heart starts to beat harder as I think about it yet again. It felt like forever that I was pinned to the ice under Yonten's unmoving weight while the helicopter roared and circled around. Then it retreated, its sound distorting as it tipped and moved off. Eventually it faded into the distance. Yonten, clutching his body and bleeding, had rolled over on the snow groaning. Then I stood up, dizzy and disorientated. Palden's body was gone. Only a patch of blood remained where he had been lying. I wanted to see my old friend's face again, to pray for him. Where had he gone? Yonten was on his feet by then, his hand on my arm as solid as steel. We had to run, he said: it was our only chance. I knew that he was right. So we abandoned Palden just as we had the Rinpoche, and set off clumsily over the snow and ice down into Nepal. We ran and ran, expecting the thundering helicopter to return, expecting the snow to explode all around us as it had before. We ran until we could run no more, collapsing in the shelter of rocks, Yonten pale with gritted teeth, me sobbing through shallow breaths.

We had no chance to sit and talk. Onward we had to go, to the places we had been told about where help is available. And onward we went, without stopping or speaking except for the things that were utterly necessary for our survival.

Yonten shielded me from the Chinese bullets and took their force. I was lucky not to have been injured also. It is a miracle, I suppose, but I am too tired and too shocked to find wonder or even optimism. Too sad, thinking about what has been lost, to feel gratitude for what has been saved. Maybe that will come later.

I lie flat on the mattress looking up, my lips forming a mantra but my mind not connecting with it. What happened to Fairchild and his reluctant companion? I cannot say. We just turned and ran. All I can do is hope that they evaded the shots and that the mountains were kind to them. I listen to Yonten's steady breathing. Yonten has hardly let his own wounds slow us down. His wounds have been treated and he has a strong body, but for my sake he has tried to hide how much pain he is suffering. We both need to rest: we have a long way to go before we are really in safety. I turn onto my side and close my eyes, praying that the dreams will not come back.

Chapter 44

Chu gave Fairchild no greeting, just a dead stare as he was shown into the interview room. This was another tiny windowless cell, empty except for a table and two plastic chairs, one occupied by Chu, dressed for business today in a black silk shirt and smart trousers. Dark red lipstick defined her mouth and her face was translucent and pale. The fluorescent light was harsh and bright. Three guards stood facing forwards, giving the place the feel of a service elevator. All the faces in the room were damp in the stale humidity, even Chu showing some shininess on her cheekbones. He noticed another two guards hovering outside the door, before it slammed shut.

Chu had caught Fairchild's glance around the room. "You won't be able to attempt another break-out," she said as he sat. "I don't know what you were thinking of anyway. This is a high-security centre and you are in no state to be running anywhere. You should be grateful we are taking such care of you."

Fairchild smiled faintly. It hadn't really been a break-out attempt. He just wanted to make sure he'd been seen. All kinds of people might be interested in a Westerner being held in a high-security Chinese prison. The food had become sparser since his supposed escape bid, and his wounds were receiving only a cursory schedule of treatment. He was struggling to recover his strength, but his memories were fitting together more coherently.

In typical fashion, Chu got straight to the point. "You knew who this person was. Claims to be. This supposed Panchen Lama. But you said nothing."

"You didn't ask."

"Don't play games. We had an agreement."

"Did we?"

"You weren't arrested, were you? You were free to do as you wished."

"I seem to remember going to great lengths to shake off your surveillance. Do you think that might have had something to do with it?"

"That was unnecessary. I kept my side, Fairchild. But you used your time in our country to work against us. You should have told me about this plot."

"It seems that you found out anyway, without needing my help."

"The imposter's Tashilunpo co-conspirator came to his senses while in our custody."

"After you'd given him adequate persuasion."

"It was still too late."

This was an interesting admission from Chu. "Oh, really? So he made it across?"

Chu continued regardless. "You were supposed to give them up, your dissident friends. But instead you disappeared. You even changed identity. We wouldn't have found you at all if you hadn't ended up at the hospital."

"Ended up? You make it sound like some kind of accident. It was your people who shot me, Chu. They left me for dead."

Chu's usual placidity was in danger of evaporating. "You carried out an attack on border guards as they tried to prevent known criminals from making an illegal exit."

"Known criminals? What crimes were those, exactly? And what do you mean, *tried* to prevent?"

Chu looked a little peevish. "Because of your deliberate attempt to distract the unit, the helicopter sustained damage and had to retreat before recovering all the bodies. When another unit returned shortly afterwards, two of the bodies were gone. As was yours."

"Well, I do apologise for surviving. So the border guard only managed to murder one citizen and injure the other two, as opposed to killing all three of them outright? Four, if you count me. How disappointing."

Chu's expression was thunderous. If she'd been directing operations on the pass personally, Fairchild was in no doubt that no one would have got away. He had to admire her self-control as she continued in a muted tone.

"I'm told there may have been someone else. Another person attempting to cross the border. The reports are conflicted about that."

"If you're expecting information, you're asking the wrong person, Chu. I've been in a hospital bed for a while now."

"The result of your own actions. You were firing on border police as they did their job. They were defending themselves."

"They were shooting unarmed civilians in the back."

"Not just civilians. Subversives determined to destabilise this regime and cause chaos and bloodshed."

"A small group of monks, Chu! Buddhist monks. Seriously. Do you not think the Chinese regime overestimates the threat that Tibet poses? Is the Dalai Lama really going to invade? Look at them, Chu. Look at you. Who has the power? Really? Let them go, if that's what they want. They're no threat to you."

Chu's eyes narrowed. "This charlatan lama was planning to gather Tibet behind him and defy China. And you were helping him! Distracting our border police with your pathetic little pistol shots. Two of them were injured! What are you doing, Fairchild? What do you expect to gain from this? Whose side are you on?"

Fairchild just stared at her. Her colour had risen a little.

"Why were you meeting them anyway?" she continued. "Was it part of the escape plan?"

"No," said Fairchild after a pause. "I found out about that when I arrived in Tibet. Their decision to leave was prompted by the riot in Tashilunpo and the arrests. But you know all about that."

"So why, then?"

"Personal reasons." Chu's eyes swivelled upwards. "You can't blame me," said Fairchild pleasantly, "for a riot that happened before I even arrived in the region."

"Can't I? I never know what strings you can pull, over what kinds of distance. It's very hard to believe your visit was just a coincidence."

"It's the truth, whether you find it believable or not. It would have been far better for me if I'd been able to meet him in Shigatse rather than trekking all the way into the Himalayas to catch up with him."

Chu was looking at him again. "And what was so important that you had to do that?"

"As I said, personal."

Chu sat back and looked thoughtful.

"We will need to consider your future," she said. "This has all been very disappointing. In the meantime, you'll be staying here. Certainly for the next few days. No more trouble, no more Fairchild, at least until we are sure the threat has been eliminated. We are looking for these traitors, waiting for them to appear, and we will deal with them. Then we will deal with you."

With an inclination of her head the guards stepped forward and pulled Fairchild to his feet. Chu's face returned to a dead stare as the prisoner was led away.

Chapter 45

Rose was at the border an hour before it opened the next morning, but it took another two long hours to pass through and cross the bridge into Nepal. The journey by jeep down through the mountains to the capital was as straightforward as Parajuli had described, the lush green scenery breathtakingly beautiful. Kathmandu reminded her of India, with women in colourful saris, grinning toothless old men, makeshift shrines on street corners, and the smell of rubbish from the gutters. The streets seemed narrow and everything felt closer in on itself. Messy multi-lingual signage festooned the sides of the buildings. Jumbles of power cables criss-crossed overhead against the heavy grey sky. The first downpour came as she arrived at the Annapurna Hotel. A volume of water dropped from above, instantly soaking everything in its path. Then it stopped, just as suddenly.

A message from Walter had already arrived at the hotel, directing her to a nearby coffee house. She set out straight away. Walter was sunk down on a low black sofa at the back of the first floor, overlooking a four-lane highway. He jumped up and came forward to kiss her on both cheeks as if they were old friends. She got a waft of fragrant aftershave as she leaned in. This was an expat haunt, with gingerbread latte promotions, lemon drizzle muffins and copies of the Kathmandu Daily on the counter. Rose got herself a cappuccino, looking forward to the first decent coffee she'd had in weeks. She updated Walter with the events of the past few days.

Walter stirred his tea. "Well, my dear, this all says something about the quality of Fairchild's network, does it not? How many people anywhere in the world had advance knowledge about this Panchen Lama boy being at large? No more than five or six at the very outside. But Fairchild knew."

"He didn't really know," said Rose. "He guessed. He put two and two together."

"Exactly! He has a way of making connections, like his father."

"Well, you can't always get it right making assumptions like that. He must be completely off target sometimes."

"Maybe. But the Service will be facing some chastisement about why we didn't have a heads-up about this ourselves, I have to tell you."

"That seems unreasonable."

"It often is, but nevertheless. Fairchild was removed from the hospital by the Chinese authorities, you're sure about that?"

"That was Parajuli's information. I don't see who else could have done it."

Walter looked thoughtful. "I really had assumed Fairchild was working for the Chinese."

"Definitely not. He didn't want anyone knowing where he was going. Including me. He needed to speak to Jinpa because Jinpa had found something out about his parents."

Walter's alertness intensified into a watchfulness. "And what was that?"

"No idea. He wouldn't trust me enough to tell me that."

"But you spoke to the monk as well?"

"Jinpa wouldn't have revealed anything to me. He would only tell Fairchild himself. That's why Fairchild had to trek into the Himalayas to find him. It was too important to entrust to anyone else. And now Jinpa's dead."

"Is he?" Walter stirred his tea casually.

"They're all dead. The Chinese border police opened fire on them."

"Did you see three dead bodies?"

Rose pictured the scene in her mind. "No. I saw them come under fire, that's all. By the time I'd got out of the crevasse all the bodies had been removed." Walter tapped the teaspoon delicately on the side of the cup, his mouth pursed. "What are you saying, Walter?"

"The head of station here in Kathmandu has heard that China has made tentative enquiries with the Nepali government for the return of two Tibetan dissidents which they believe are in the country. Nepal isn't generally keen to help with such matters, but they are being put under pressure."

"But how could they have survived? They were unarmed. The border police sent in a helicopter, for goodness' sake."

"Well, maybe all three went down but two were only injured. Could Fairchild have played a role?"

"Fairchild had a gun with him. He could have used it to try and draw their fire, but I wouldn't have thought on his own he would have had much effect."

"Well, whatever happened up there, two of them seem to be unaccounted for, and one of them must be this Panchen Lama chap, otherwise the Chinese government wouldn't be quite so worked up about it. We must assume they're on their way here. Kathmandu has help centres for Tibetan refugees, and their sympathisers have set up a network of safe houses from the mountains all the way to the capital."

"And what will China do if they don't have any joy with the Nepali government?"

"I doubt they'll just give up. Our Tibetans would be wise to stay as unobtrusive as they can until they get themselves to India. They'll be safe enough in the company of the Dalai Lama and his entourage, in the glare of his public profile, but until then they're pretty vulnerable I'd say, with or without the cooperation of the Nepali authorities."

Rose thought of Jinpa in the cave, candlelight reflected in his wide eyes, his disarming faith, his words that had a depth and wisdom far older than the piping voice that spoke them. What would become of him, assuming he had even survived this far? She pictured again the blood stains on the snow. "None of this helps us find Fairchild, though," she said.

Walter took a sip of tea. "We've had a report that a Western prisoner matching John's description is being held at a remote detention facility in the jungle west of Chengdu. If we're sure he was taken from the hospital by the authorities, it seems to add up."

"What kind of facility?"

"The unofficial kind. For prisoners they don't want anyone to know about. We like to keep an eye on places like that. One of the guards is in our pay. He caught a glimpse of this Western prisoner during some kind of failed escape attempt, and reported it to us. If it is him, and if Fairchild intervened at the border in support of these Tibetans, I doubt he'll be receiving the five-star treatment there."

"So you'd like him out?"

"Well, yes, but it's tricky of course."

"We could get him out, couldn't we? We've done extractions before from places like that."

Walter looked regretful. "The problem is, that kind of operation would need very senior sign-off. I'm sorry to say that too many people within the Service would happily see John Fairchild incarcerated in a secret prison for the foreseeable. As I've said, he isn't universally popular."

"In other words, Marcus Salisbury wouldn't particularly mind if Fairchild didn't make it out?"

"I think we might say, quite rightly in fact, that MI6 doesn't really owe Fairchild anything and getting him out is beyond our remit. An operation like that puts our own Special Forces at risk. If we were to lose someone in the process of an attempted rescue, questions would be asked. And there's the cost, of course."

"Of course. Reassuring to know that the Service has our backs, as long as it doesn't cost too much."

"Fairchild isn't one of us. That's the whole point here."

"You still want him out, though, Walter?"

He held her gaze. "Absolutely."

"Are you suggesting that *I* might be able to get him out?"

"I'm hoping you can."

"But you can't provide any help with it?"

"None whatsoever, I'm afraid."

She sat back on the sofa. "So you're saying that I could single-handedly find a way of breaking into a secret Chinese prison in the middle of a jungle and rescue someone?"

"I didn't say you could do it single-handedly," said Walter.

"So you're suggesting I get help from elsewhere."

"I'm not suggesting anything. All I'm saying is that I can't help. If I haven't said so already, you've really done terribly well, Rose. All things considered. It was never going to be easy."

Rose sighed. He was making it sound like she'd won the egg and spoon race at the school fête. Walter seemed much more interested than MI6 senior management did in Fairchild's survival, to the extent that he was all but advising her to go behind their backs. "Well, it's good to know you've got confidence in me, I suppose."

Walter finished his tea and placed the cup back on the saucer. "Yes, my dear," he said, looking up at her, "I do."

Chapter 46

I wake up to the sound of a rushing stream and children playing. This village is our final resting point before Kathmandu. I have been charmed by its worn red-brick houses and uneven roofs, its weed-tangled paths. The warmth of welcome these people have given us, the shy but curious smiles of the children who stop and stare, have made me believe I could live here and feel some measure of peace. Today, however, we must continue our journey. I turn to wake Yonten so that we can make our preparations. But he is not there.

I go out to look for him. I walk all round the village, then I do the same again. He is not in the village. I sit on a stone wall and look out at the sloping green fields and the hills above, and I breathe in the animal dung smell of straw bales. Where is he?

I try not to feel disappointment or anger. Yonten has been even more taciturn than usual since we crossed the border. I thought that it was due to his wounds and the shock of events on the glacier. But he was recovering well from his injuries. Maybe he has a secret resentment for everything he has endured. He was not given a choice about his role in my deliverance. He was very young, like me, when he learned the secret, and since then was forced to give me his full support, including an expectation of willingness to sacrifice himself. He saw, one by one, his other comrades imprisoned or killed. Now, across the border and with the abbot gone and me free, perhaps he finally felt under no further compulsion to stay.

Yonten and I have been together every step, passing from one quiet outhouse to another along this route that so many of our fellow countrymen have taken. I do not want to continue without him. Despite the difficult silences we shared, I feel very solitary now. Perhaps he will change his mind and return.

I pack and prepare for the journey, taking longer than necessary in the hope that he will reappear. But then I discover something else, something even more troubling. The bundle of photographs in my bag which proves my identity is missing. Why would Yonten take those? I was not even aware that he knew about them. Why would he want to make my task more difficult now? I am confident that His Holiness will recognise me without the aid of mere photographs. But they would have made it easier to gain support amongst those who have less faith. I tell myself that Yonten has been my loyal friend, that he saved my life on the pass and that he must have a charitable reason for this, even though I cannot fathom what it could be. Nevertheless, I am uneasy.

The journey through Nepal has not been how I imagined it. I am still not free. My task is yet to begin. I am compelled to reach Dharamsala and be recognised. The Rinpoche told me I should not reveal my identity until I have been reunited with the Dalai Lama. But I am tired of hiding away. I wish to greet the world in honesty, now that we have escaped our tyranny. The feeling is growing stronger inside me, like the ever-louder clanging of a bell, that the time for secrecy is over and that I should embark on my life's purpose.

I must move on. I cannot wait any longer for Yonten, much as I would like to welcome him back. I bid goodbye to my hosts and thank them for their hospitality and kindness. The children come with me to the edge of the village and wave as I trudge off. Despite their smiles, my heart is heavy. Maybe Kathmandu will look and feel how I have imagined. Maybe there I will feel the elation I have been expecting, walking through the city streets without needing to hide my face. Maybe in Kathmandu I will wear garlands of flowers, and live amid celebration and smiles and welcome. Maybe there I can be free.

Chapter 47

Zack was standing in the exact same place as last time. It was, after all, a Friday night. He was again making inane small talk with some attractive young women. Americans this time. And waving a cocktail around. But his smile became a little less wide when he saw Rose approaching.

"Oh, you," he said, when Rose had finally shouldered her way close enough to be in earshot.

"Yes, me. Sorry about that." Rose squeezed through his immediate audience. "Mind if we have a word?" The girls seemed fine about moving on. Relieved, in fact. Zack sucked his straw noisily.

"What do you want now?"

"That's not very friendly, Zack."

She wasn't too pleased about having to do this herself. It was a four-and-a-half hour flight from Kathmandu to Hong Kong. She'd spent most of it fuming with Walter and his colleagues. They'd got her chasing round the world after this guy, and couldn't seem to agree between themselves whether he was with them or against. Once again she found herself wondering if this elaborate goose chase was going to get her anywhere.

"You're a friend, are you?" Zack muttered.

"Brits and Americans? We're on the same side, aren't we?"

"You're not part of them. I know all the team up at the embassy. You may be MI6 but you're up to something else and I don't know what. Don't much care either. Long as it doesn't involve me."

"Well it does, I'm afraid. Or at least it involves your buddy."

Zack gave a weary sigh at the mention of Fairchild. Rose was picking up a wide variety of responses when she mentioned Fairchild's name. Positive or negative, there always seemed to be one. "What's he up to now?"

"He's been shot. And stabbed."

Zack gave her a long look, or at least she assumed he was, because he was still wearing his sunglasses. "He's dead?"

"No. At least he wasn't a couple of days ago. He was in hospital."

"Great. I'll send flowers."

"But he disappeared from hospital. We think he's now in a secret detention facility to the west of Chengdu."

"Cheng what?"

"You heard me. I bet you even know about this place."

"Nope."

"Really? Well, now's your opportunity to find out."

Zack shook his glass to make the remains of the ice chink. "I don't think it is."

"We need to get Fairchild out of there."

"Well get him out of there, then!" he said with sudden energy. Rose merely looked at him. "Come on, if you're short of ideas, how about trading him for something? Or someone. Or you could try a break. Late-night raid, helicopters, quick in-and-out?" Rose kept staring at him. Zack made a pretence of realisation. "Oh, I see! I get it! You're the British! So of course you aren't going to do anything for Fairchild! Why would he expect that? Being British and all? Silly me."

"He's rubbed a lot of people up the wrong way over the years. So I'm led to believe."

"Yeah. I guess. Doing really inconvenient things like trying to find out why his parents disappeared into thin air. That must be pretty annoying."

"Look, I've only just found out about that myself. I didn't know about his history. I get it, it explains a lot, it really does. But the fact remains that I can't get British clearance for a rescue. He's injured and we have no idea how he's being treated in there. We can't expect the guy to get himself out and survive a long trek through a jungle. So, if he's going to make it, someone else is going to have to step in."

"Someone else. Huh."

"Someone who values him. Someone who's made use of him and may want to do so again. Someone who owes him."

"Hey! It's your fault I owe him anyway."

"That's as may be. But it was you who came in before, with your speedboat and everything, to save him getting arrested. So he must be worth something to you."

"Christ." Zack's voice had reduced to a growl. "Always the same. When it's tricky or expensive, you Brits come running to us."

"Nonsense. I can just see some mutual goals here. It makes sense to work together. We've got eyes inside the place, we can get schematics, an idea of where he's held. You provide the extraction team. You said yourself, a quick in-and-out. Easy, right? So what do you say? I mean, you and he are friends, aren't you? You wouldn't just leave him in there? Would you?"

"Christ," was what Zack said.

Chapter 48

I walk into Kathmandu alone. My host has given me directions. I have never seen anything like this place. But it is also in a strange way like coming home. I recognise something in these streets, some element of Shigatse or maybe something I experienced in a former incarnation, but so much is exotic and different too. It feels more alive, more spontaneous. Even the weather is its own master. As I walk along, spots appear on the ground and dark grey clouds send down a heavy soaking rain. I stand in the shelter of a doorway and stare up at the cascade. Then the clouds sweep away leaving white wisps and fleeting sunlight and patches of blue sky. The wet road glows in the light.

I see no soldiers in the streets. People here have no need to look over their shoulder or avoid each other's gaze in case they see too much. I look at everyone and everything. I find myself at the bottom of a long series of steps lined with fluttering prayer flags drying out from the rain. Something calls to my soul from up there. I climb the steps to the top of the hill and find a huge Buddhist temple. It is a mass of odd-shaped monuments blackened by moisture set amongst thick trees with the sprawl of the city below. As I slowly walk the kora, everything I gaze on is familiar yet different. Elaborate layered gold decorates aged red-brick walls stuck with colourful statues and frescos. Green mildew spreads over the curves of the huge white stupas. So much life is here, bursting forth.

Back down the steps I continue on my way. The streets narrow, squeezing people and traffic closer together. I see garlands of marigolds dangling from the awnings of street stalls, curtains of yellow. They are just as bright and heart-lifting as in my dreams. My host gave me some money, just enough to live on for a few days. I offer the stallholder a handful of unfamiliar change. She takes two coins and lifts a garland over my head, smiling. Her eyes are big and brown.

I find the square that my host described. Scooters and carts fill the space with noise and fumes, squeezing round each other in every direction like a herd of unruly animals. In the centre I stop to peer inside a concrete hut at the top of some steps. I believe it is a Hindu shrine. A statue of an animal is sprinkled with powders and petals, deep red, bright blue, indigo and green. I smell a deep woody smell. On the steps a woman in a red headscarf sits next to a plastic crate full of oranges. Everywhere I go is full of colour and sound and smell.

My eye is caught by a sign on the wall of an office building in my own language. It says that here I can find advice and support for Tibetan refugees wanting to reach Dharamsala. This is the place I have been told about. Inside and up the stairs, I go into a tiny waiting area. A young man behind a desk asks me my name and my situation. I speak English to him. I think he is surprised that I can speak so fluently. To me, it is a joy to be able to speak English without worrying about being overheard.

Sitting in a chair is a girl. I sit next to her to wait. Like me she is wearing the rough, dirty clothes of the Tibetan villages. She has short hair that has started to grow back all over her head, like me. She is probably a nun. I think she is perhaps thirteen or fourteen. "Are you going to Dharamsala too?" I ask. She looks at me and nods, but doesn't say anything. Her eyes are large and sad. I wonder what has happened that she is here on her own. My heart feels heavy with love and anger. My people have suffered so much. I am suddenly proud that I have been given a role which will help and strengthen my country, and give hope to people like this girl that their suffering can end.

The girl is called through to another room and I wait alone. I read all the dog-eared notices that are on the walls, offering support and food and shelter and advice. This tiny place is brimming with a gentle generosity. I close my eyes and whisper thanks, sending mantras up into the rain-laden sky.

A woman calls my name and I follow her into a small office. She tells me her name is Veronica. She wears bangles on her arms and has a tattoo on her neck in the shape of a swan. She asks me questions and writes down what I say. She compliments me on my English. I tell her that the Rinpoche wanted me to learn languages for my future role. I tell her what happened to the Rinpoche. She says she is sorry. She scribbles everything down. She says that it is important to document the experiences of Tibetan refugees. I feel a wave of empathy coming from her. She asks me why it was so important to flee Tibet, to risk our lives as we did. I promised the Rinpoche not to tell anyone who I really am until I reach His Holiness, but right now in this moment everything feels right, that this woman is asking these questions at this time. The wisdom in me prompts me to act.

"I am the reincarnate of the Panchen Lama," I say. "That is who I am. In my previous life I was the spiritual leader of my monastery."

"That's wonderful," says Veronica. She smiles warmly at me. Her pen hovers over the page.

"That is why I had to flee from the Chinese, before they discovered my secret. Before they discover that the boy that they took is not the real Panchen Lama. He is a substitute."

Veronica nods slowly. She writes down the word "Reincarnate".

I say, "In the monastery I was just an ordinary monk. But the Rinpoche knew my secret. This is why he took special care of me, why he spent time with me. To prepare me for the future." Veronica is looking at me carefully. I wish I had my bundle of photographs with me. I have so much I need to say. I start to tell her about the riot in the monastery, the protest. Veronica's pen starts to move again. I tell her about the arrests, and my friend Sonam, and about how our small group fled in the middle of the night. Her writing gradually fills the page as I tell her about how we left Choden and walked up into the mountains, and how the Rinpoche got sick and how we said our goodbyes to him and had to carry on. I tell her about the cold, and the aching feet and the hunger. But I don't tell her about the cave in the mountains. That is for my people only. And I don't tell her about Fairchild or his companion. That is Fairchild's business.

I describe the long walk up the glacier to the pass, the thick snow that we had to wade through, the stumbling upwards that lasted forever. "When they shot at us, they made fountains in the snow," I said. "I didn't know what it was at first. But then my old friend Palden fell."

Veronica suddenly stops writing and looks up. "You mean," she says, "that someone was shooting at you as you crossed the border?"

"Yes. Indeed. You see, I fear that my friend Sonam may have given away my identity. He is brave and loyal but it is hard to understand the pressure put on people when they are being held out of sight of anybody."

She frowns and looks back down at her notes. "So – on the glacier. They came up behind you?"

"Yes. They were fast, faster than us although we tried to run. Then they started shooting."

"From behind?"

"Yes. And from above." She stops writing again. "From the helicopter," I explain.

"There was a helicopter?"

"It was so noisy." It upsets me just to think about it. "Palden was just lying there. I wanted to get to him. But Yonten held onto me. Then he fell too, on top of me."

Veronica is staring. "You mean that two of you were shot on the glacier? Two unarmed monks?"

"Yes." She doesn't hear my slight hesitation. Besides, we were unarmed because Yonten's gun was not with us. And I do not know where the gun is now, or where Fairchild is, or the woman Rose, though I often wonder what happened to them. "Yonten was injured only. He and I ran from that place and got away. But now Yonten is gone too."

I can see that Veronica is thinking. She says, "You know, this is something that might be of interest to the media. I mean, exposing the harshness of the Chinese state. Do you think, Jinpa," she has to check on the page what my name is, "that before you go to Dharamsala you might agree to talk to a journalist about your experiences?"

"Of course." I give her a wide smile. I was right to share all this with her. I can feel that now my work is beginning, that there is no time to lose.

Chapter 49

The sheets were soaking wet. He shifted position but knew he wouldn't find comfort. He had lost track of how long he had spent in this narrow bed, this concrete cell. The harsh fluorescent lights were on all the time. He couldn't sleep. He could only drift in and out of a feverish dreaming state. He was either too hot or too cold. Right now he was shivering, his hospital robe insubstantial. He tried to curl up but it didn't help. The pain in his side felt as though someone were gripping his skin and pulling on it. He hadn't seen the nurse for a long time, since before his interview with Chu. He had been recovering, but not any more. Twice a day they brought water and food, stale rolls or watery soup. Whenever he stood, pain stabbed his side and his vision went black.

"Haven't you figured it out yet?" The voice sounded as though it were in the room, close and quiet. It was his father's voice, almost real. A wave of anger and frustration came over him. Suddenly he was sitting at a table in an apartment, a hand of cards in front of him. On a mahogany sideboard, the pendulum of an antique clock swung steadily. Beyond that, the sky through the window was dark. His mother and father were on either side of him, sitting, watching, waiting for him to respond. They had asked him something. Some riddle, some question, some reference, something he was supposed to know. But he didn't know it.

"You've got to figure it out, John. It's important." His father's voice again, a little more insistent. He'd had this dream so many times. It was a test. Everything was a test. Every family outing turned into a game of challenge, every letter his mother wrote was in a language he had to decipher. Why did they have to do this to him? He was sick of it. He threw his cards onto the table and stormed out, down the stairs, into the quiet street where he paced aimlessly, furiously. Then he came back and the cards were in a mess on the table. His parents were gone. He searched the place, trying to figure out what he was supposed to do. What was the test? What was the challenge? What puzzle did they want him to solve? He sat in silence, watching the pendulum on the clock swinging back and forth.

"Still no idea?" His father sounded irritated now. "After all this time? You're going to just lie there?" Fairchild turned away from the voice and raised the sheet over his head, but it didn't make any difference.

"You put your friends in danger." It was his mother's voice now. She was more distant, somewhere in the corner of the room, in the shadows. Her voice was hard. She was looking down on him, judging. "People died because of you. And now you're giving up, John. Are you never going to find us?"

The lights went off. Fairchild opened his eyes. For a few seconds he could see nothing, but he could hear; shouting, running, a distant alarm. Then the slamming of doors. Was this real, or another dream? He sat up, and the dizziness kicked in. He put his bare feet on the cold floor.

Footsteps pounded in the corridor outside, getting louder. They stopped outside the door. A harsh grinding sound filled the room, unbearably loud. The door crashed open with a shattering bang.

Chapter 50

Bursts of automatic gunfire punctured the air. Strapped to her seat inside one of the copters, Rose peered down at the figures running amid flashes of fire. She hardly dared to breathe as they hovered over the complex, quiet and dark a few minutes ago but lit up now like a Christmas tree. She heard herself gasp when Fairchild appeared on the roof of the prison complex, a skinny figure shrouded in white. One of the unit was supporting him as he stumbled barefoot towards them.

They had to lift him inside while the gunfire below intensified. She lurched as both helicopters dipped forward in unison, whining as they powered up. They rose above the dense jungle and the compound it encircled, taking both crews beyond range.

Opposite her, Zack filled the seat with his square frame. Next to him, Fairchild sat stiffly with his face taut. Zack turned to his neighbour and punched him amicably on the shoulder. His action caused Fairchild to suck in air.

"Pretty cool, huh?"

"What?" Fairchild's shout was barely audible above the roar of the copter. His skin was the same colour as his gown.

"How's that for in and out?" Seeing Zack in this context without a cocktail in his hand you could see his background was military. Ten, twenty years ago he would have been part of this extraction team. His bearing, the way he moved easily around inside the copter, held a certain authority. The expression on his face as the figures in black dropped onto the roof below then melted away was one of envy.

Fairchild nodded to the American in faint assent but said nothing further. Zack sat back, crestfallen at his friend's half-hearted response, like a child trying to impress with the sandcastle he'd just built. It was a pretty impressive operation to be fair: precise, fast and effective. The Chinese would have little idea who was behind the raid, and in any case were unlikely to make a scene and draw international eyes to the existence of this kind of facility. It would hardly improve their human rights record. Rose tried to catch Fairchild's eye but couldn't. He seemed confused, not with it at all. Besides, it was futile to try and communicate over the noise. Meaningful conversation would have to wait until they were back at the Bangladeshi air base they'd scrambled from, and possibly after some medical treatment. Rose had expected to wait at the base for their return and was surprised when Zack suggested she came along. It felt good to be present for an operation in which she'd played such a critical role. As well as her additional approach to Zack, she'd provided the schematics of the base, which she'd managed to persuade out of Walter, without which there wouldn't have been an operation at all.

Zack's headphones crackled and he said something into his mouthpiece she couldn't hear. The engine vibration intensified. The copter was changing direction, slowing. Rose twisted to look out behind her. The other helicopter was continuing. The distance between them was growing.

"What's going on?" she shouted to Zack.

"Refuelling," he shouted. In the dense forest below, the searchlight picked out the shine of a meandering river with wide banks. It didn't make any sense. Why did one copter need refuelling and not the other? Surely the complex was within range of the base. It seemed messy. They were descending fast, into a tiny gap between trees and water. In the darkness around them Rose could see nothing, no lights, no buildings, no vehicles. As they levelled with the trees she turned back to Zack with a welter of questions, to find herself looking into the barrel of his gun.

Zack's eyes, unshaded, held not one whit of uncertainty. She took a quick glance around. The soldiers were staring straight-necked and Fairchild was watching listlessly. Yep, as she'd thought. She was the only person here who had a gun pointed at her head.

"Up!" said Zack. His broad form stood solidly in front of her. Behind him, soldiers were on the doors. Through the open air as the doors slid aside, the hammering blades trebled in volume. They landed with a jolt. Two of the crew lined up on either side of Zack, facing her. Fairchild had disappeared behind this wall of military beef. It really wasn't very fair. Rose brazened it out for a few seconds and stared petulantly at Zack, but when he nodded two of his team forward to help her with her seat straps, she waved them off.

"All right, all right!" The end of Zack's gun followed her as she climbed out of the machine. He motioned her to keep moving, over the flattened grass beyond the range of the blades that were still going full throttle. She ducked and headed forward toward the trees. When the downdraft eased she turned. Zack had followed her and still had the gun pointing at her.

"What the fuck is this?" she shouted. "You're just going to leave me here? Without me, you wouldn't have found him!"

"You had your own reasons," said Zack, his voice granite. "You've been on his case right from the start and you're not doing this for his benefit. So you can make yourself scarce. Whatever he does next, he'll do it without you."

"But it was me who came to you! I'm the one that got him out!"

His eyes didn't move. "You're the one that put him in."

"No! That's not true. He made his own choices. You ask him."

"Lady, I've known this guy a long time. We go way back. And I know you're bad news. You and your kind latch onto him every now and then. It never goes well. So this is what's going to happen. You're going to stay here, and we're going to take off without you."

"I've got no idea where we are!"

"Follow the river. You're no more than a hundred miles from Chengdu."

"A hundred miles? Look, Zack. You've got the wrong idea about me. I don't mean Fairchild any harm. And I don't think the people I'm working for do either."

She took a step towards him. He tilted his head. Two soldiers stepped up on either side of him and raised weapons. "If that's what you think," he said, "you're a fool."

She looked at the array in front of her. "Seriously, Zack. Five guns? Who do you think I am?" No response. The rotor carried on roaring above them. Her voice was growing hoarse from shouting. "Ask him how he would have found his friend in the mountains without my help. Ask him how he got to the hospital."

"Sure thing." Zack's expression didn't change. "Gives us something to talk about on the way."

She held his gaze and gave it five seconds. It was a long five seconds. She lifted her hands in defeat and stepped backwards. They filed neatly back into the copter. Zack was the last to turn away, his eyes and his gun on her right up until the doors slid shut.

As she stood on the grass in the darkness listening to the drumming rotor gradually recede into the distance, it seemed that her life was following a certain pattern. She'd manage a fleeting few moments with the guy before he removed himself, or someone else did. But it didn't matter this time. Zack's little stunt was a pain and would delay her, but that was all. This time she knew exactly where Fairchild was heading next.

Chapter 51

The studio is very small. I thought it would be as huge as a palace, but it only has space for two chairs and a camera. Veronica brought me here and she introduces me to the presenter, Duncan. She has already told me what questions he will ask. She sits down to wait and smiles encouragingly.

The background is just a plain bright green. Duncan says that on television it will be a panorama of Kathmandu. He is amused by how impressed I am. They have found me a robe to wear. It is not a Tashilunpo robe, but I am pleased to have it. It smells musty. I wonder whose it is and what story it would tell.

I sit in one chair and Duncan sits in the other. Duncan is very friendly. His accent is quite strange. He keeps talking to himself then nodding as if he's heard an answer. When I stare at him he explains that he has a microphone in his ear.

A woman brings a microphone on a wire and attaches it to my robe. It does not stay in place and she keeps having to come back to adjust it. The lights shine straight in my face. I feel very warm. I whisper a mantra. The woman thinks I was asking her something. I shake my head and smile.

"Don't stare at the camera," says Duncan. "Look at me. As if we're having a conversation, that's all. You've been through the questions I'm going to ask?"

I nod. My heart is thumping. This is all so strange.

"You ready?" asks Duncan.

I nod again.

He turns to the camera. "Good morning and welcome to *Faces of Kathmandu*! Today we have a very special visitor with us who has an incredible and tragic story to tell about how he got here. Jinpa, welcome, and thanks for coming to talk to us."

I try to say something but the words do not form in my mouth, so I just smile.

"So, first, why don't you tell us something about where you're from in Tibet?"

"Well," I say, "I'm from a monastery called Tashilunpo. I lived there almost my whole life. It's a very beautiful place." I describe it a little and thinking about my home relaxes me. Talking becomes much easier. I describe some of the daily chores in the monastery and Duncan nods and smiles and says that it's fascinating.

"And what made you decide to leave Tibet?" he asks.

"Well, in the end I had to leave, because I was in danger."

"And why were you in danger?"

What I am about to say has been a secret for as long as I can remember. But now it feels right to be saying it aloud. This is the moment I start to fulfil the destiny that we had planned for so long, the entire purpose of our terrible journey. I try not to think about the camera and all the people who might be watching me. I focus instead on Duncan's interested face. I lean forward.

"Because of who I am," I say.

Chapter 52

In exchange for a full report of his experiences at a later date, Zack obligingly dropped Fairchild off in Kathmandu. Fairchild tracked down one of his contacts and got himself patched up and dulled with dubious local painkillers until the fever relented, although he still felt hot and light-headed. His contact went searching while Fairchild slept on a mattress in someone's cousin's upstairs room. They shook him with difficulty out of sleep and directed him to a four-storey office block in a ramshackle city square. A plaque by the main door identified it as the office of the TRAC, an organisation offering advice and support to Tibetan refugees. Of all the places in the city, Jinpa would surely come here at some point.

It was difficult for a foreigner to hang around discreetly for any length of time on a Kathmandu street, particularly a Westerner. When he paused to lean against a wall, ostensibly for a cigarette, he was approached by a steady stream of people offering him everything from white water rafting to shoe shining and night clubs. The square had no cafe or restaurants. Fortunately, the advice centre was not open all the time, only for an hour and a half some mornings and afternoons. As well as being present for those times, he started passing through at different times of the day and evening, altering his appearance and manner, getting to know its rhythm and flow, people who were passing through, people who seemed to hang around. He often feigned the movements of someone much older, walking slowly and deliberately to avoid limping.

His mind was focused on recognition, figuring out if any of these faces were familiar, if anyone seemed to get stuck in the square instead of moving through as people do who are just going about their business. It was a task that could play with your mind. He thought he saw Rose one time, a fleeting glimpse of her face under a wide-brimmed hat before she disappeared into the crowd. But his mind could have been playing tricks. She was still in his head, whatever else was going on. Why was she in the helicopter, and where did she go? Zack hadn't exactly said, or if he had, Fairchild hadn't been in a fit state to understand it.

There'd been no sign of Jinpa or any of his group. Fairchild's people were still out looking as well. Sitting at a desk in a travel agency, he wondered if the Tibetans hadn't made it after all. Maybe they'd already passed through and were on their way to India already. He slowly reviewed details of a coach tour itinerary in the western mountains. He wasn't even slightly interested in taking it. Descriptions of remote snow-clad landscapes had no appeal for him after the last few days. The reason for his visit to the tour operator was that from where he sat in their office, he could see out of the window straight across the square to the entrance of the TRAC building opposite.

He had by now got to know this square very well, the chaotic mass of motorcycles, the squat concrete cubicle of a shrine, the woman selling oranges on the steps, the forest of satellite dishes and mobile phone masts on the roofs. He glanced up from his itinerary into the square where something caught his attention. A round-faced man in a blue baseball cap and a track suit top wandered up to the steps and casually picked up an orange to examine. Then another one. He looked up, as if contemplating the meaning of orange, during which philosophical moment his glance swept around the square. Then he leaned across and spoke to the orange seller. She said something back. Something passed between them, from his pocket to his hand then to her hand. Then, after another glance around he wandered off, having picked up an orange as an afterthought. The woman kept watching him as he walked away, her gaze eventually returning to the square in general, including the TRAC office building, of which, from her habitual spot, she had a clear but inconspicuous view.

As Fairchild played the role of a nervous tourist asking detailed questions about flights and food, most of which were already explained in the itineraries he had just read, he observed this interaction and gave the orange seller some thought. Maybe he'd merely observed a man in a baseball cap buying an orange. Maybe not. Maybe this little transaction related in some way to a woman with a smooth pale face, red lips and a black silk shirt. Fairchild didn't think he was the only person with an interest in the four-storey building opposite. Invisible though the Tibetan refugee flow was to many, someone other than him was paying very close attention.

Chapter 53

Rose had sore feet. This was not from walking a hundred miles to Chengdu. The riverbank where Zack had so rudely ejected her turned out to be less than a mile away from a main road. She'd heard the faint sound of traffic as soon as the helicopter's beating rotary had faded away. It was just a matter of walking upriver to the road bridge. And it wasn't a hundred miles to Chengdu. More like twenty. There was even a bus. Zack obviously liked to mess with people on occasion. It was something she would have to remember if their paths were ever to cross again.

She was back in Kathmandu looking for Jinpa and his friend, who were either here somewhere, or about to arrive, or hadn't made it at all. She'd done a tour of hostels, outreach centres and charities, using a great deal of creativity to invent credible stories for why she'd be looking for two Tibetan monks, but had no joy at all. Even when people didn't buy into her fabrications and refused to tell her anything, the signals they unintentionally gave off showed her that the people she sought were not ringing any bells.

As well as the Tibetans, she was also mindful of Walter's comments about the Chinese, that they might well take the matter into their own hands without cooperation from the Nepali authorities. It was, after all, probably what the British would do if the situation demanded it. Wherever she went to look, others might also be searching. The Chinese had resources and could be in several places at once. She needed to work harder than that. She did not want, she had decided, to be noticed by them. While she had no issue with them and in theory they none with her, it would be easy for her to become associated with Jinpa and seen as an ally of his. So she was careful, took some pains to vary her appearance, allowed extra journey time to stop and double-back. It didn't help the sore feet. What helped a little more was her insistence that Walter provide her with a gun, courtesy of the Kathmandu head of station he seemed so pally with. The weight of the weapon in her bag gave her some comfort but she hoped not to have need of it.

And then of course there was Fairchild, her real target here. Fairchild would go where he thought he'd find Jinpa. Of that she was sure, assuming he'd heard the same rumours as Walter, that two of the monks might still be alive. What happened in Beijing still troubled her, that he was able so easily to tail her and evade her notice. It would be easier, instead of trying to find

Fairchild, to find Fairchild's friend and stick to him like glue, even if that meant being exposed to the Chinese. That was a risk she would have to take.

She'd returned to her hotel room after another fruitless search and was sitting on her bed reviewing all of this yet again. Days had passed since the prison break in China. The obvious places weren't working. Arriving in a city like this, what would Jinpa do? Where would he go? Cross-legged, she rubbed her arches and replayed the conversation she'd had with the young monk in the cave. Then she got up, put her worn canvas shoes back on, stuck a straw hat on her head and went out.

This time she turned off the busy streets and took the three hundred steps up to the Swayambunath Temple. She wandered around the mouldy stupas admiring hazy views of polluted Kathmandu, trying to see it all through Jinpa's eyes. She visited the temples that were part of the extensive red and brown Durbar Square complex. She went to the Pashupatinath Temple, the Budhanilkantha Temple and numerous other places listed in the tourist guides. She went down to the Bagmati river itself, to the ghats. And that was where she saw him.

It was unmistakeably Jinpa strolling slowly up the riverside: the shaven head, the poised posture and the thoughtful expression she remembered from the cave. He paused on the steps for a second, looking up into the sky, his lips moving as if he were talking to himself. She watched him for a while as he meandered along. It started to rain and he held his hands out as if celebrating the end of a drought. He had a garland of flowers around his neck and was, oddly, wearing a monk's robe. He must have picked it up at one of the refugee help centres. He looked exactly like what he was, a Tibetan monk in the modern world proudly living by beliefs thousands of years old. He looked at everything around him with good-natured wonderment, unaware that passers-by often turned to stare, struck by something about his appearance, the vivacity and curiosity on his face. He was noticeable without realising it. This was not, Rose thought, a good thing.

Jinpa stopped and stared at a cloud of black smoke billowing off a cremation platform. His face took on a melancholy look. She wondered what his journey had been like. He was on his own: maybe something had happened to the other monk since they came down from the mountains. This particular cremation had no audience other than the person who tended the remains, bundles of flesh and bone wrapped in plain cloth within piles of wood and straw. Whoever that person had been, they were not much missed. After gazing into the smoke as it slowly drifted up and away, Jinpa started ambling up the riverside, halting every few steps and watching the slow brown swirl of the full water past sloping banks of scrub and junk. Dark-skinned people in brightly coloured robes waded patiently, shuffling and picking through the garbage with hands and feet. Rose followed at a distance, above. At no time did Jinpa look round. Clearly he didn't feel under threat. Rose took careful notice of who else moved in Jinpa's slow wake as he sauntered upriver. When finally she was satisfied that nobody was on his tail or hers, at a moment when no one else was standing near, she stepped up to him and softly said his name.

He turned and his face lit up with delight. "My friend from the cave! I am so pleased to see you again! How miraculous that we meet like this!"

Rose's heart lifted seeing Jinpa's joy. "Well, I don't know about that, but I'm glad you made it over the pass."

"But that is the miracle! The Chinese bullets did not stop us as they intended. We were meant to succeed. But you... I have tried to remember exactly what happened but it's so confused in my head." Jinpa's expression was a combination of puzzlement and pain.

Rose told him about the crevasse and how she got out.

"So that was a miracle also!" cried the monk.

"Well, I was lucky. By the time I got out there was no one there. I saw blood on the snow. I have to say I feared the worst."

"And Fairchild?" Jinpa's face became serious.

"He was shot. I don't know how, or what he was doing. He must have been there. He was badly injured, but he's alive. As far as I know."

"He is here also?"

"Well, I think so."

"You are not together?"

"No. I – don't know for sure where he is."

Jinpa tried to mask the disappointment in his face. "I will pray for him," he said brightly.

"Are you also on your own here?"

Jinpa's melancholy look came back. "My friend Yonten and I ran from the mountain together. But now he has gone." He seemed close to tears and his gaze shifted out to the river. He blinked and took a breath. "But look! What a wonderful city this is. I have seen nothing like this place. Have you? Let us walk together."

They trudged along the river towards the old city. Their journey was stop-start, dictated by Jinpa's general fascination with everything. They turned into the old town away from the river and he pointed out one of the many small shrines that were dotted throughout the city showing images of all kinds of creatures, elephants with colossal trunks and wide-mouthed monsters with many arms. Jinpa had made a study of the Hindu religion, its many gods, each with their own characteristics. All the bodhisattvas he knew so well were manifestations of the Buddha, all part of the oneness of existence. The Hindu religion was full of diverse characters all acting out a great everlasting play. Jinpa was amazed by this discovery.

While he pointed and enthused, Rose discreetly observed. While before she was sure that the city around them was just going about its business, something now was making the skin prickle on her arms. She couldn't pinpoint what it was. A face turning away, perhaps, just as she looked up, a figure which was there then suddenly gone. She was glad the street around them was so busy.

Something Jinpa said made her realise she'd lost the thread. "Jinpa, did you just say something about a journalist?"

"Yes, indeed. That's why they gave me this robe. They said on television it's important."

"You've been on television?"

"To speak about my experiences. Crossing the border. The shootings, my friends who didn't survive. It is important, is it not, to bear witness to these things? Otherwise they could be lost for ever."

The prickling on Rose's skin worsened. "And did you tell them who you were?"

"Of course!" Jinpa's smile was irresistible. "That was the reason I escaped from China. To tell people who I am."

"But would it not be best to get to India first and have your identity confirmed? That's your plan, isn't it?"

"Yes indeed. But it feels right to be talking about it now. Since I came to this city I have felt such enormous reassurance and joy. I have a strong sense that speaking aloud now is the right thing to do."

Rose slowed. Her pulse was racing. She'd seen the same T-shirt twice. Two people wearing similar T-shirts, maybe. Or the same person who happened to be going the same way as them. When she tried to look for it again, she could see no sign. Everything looked normal. But something was wrong.

Chapter 54

Fairchild was already on the move. His contact had phoned him an hour ago while he was sitting uselessly, wasting precious time staking out the refugee centre. Jinpa had been on television, for Christ's sake. Some obscure news channel, but nevertheless it would have been monitored. What was he thinking of?

His phone rang again. A breathless voice delivered a third-hand report of the same man wandering along by the Bagmati ghats in full monastic gear with a garland round his neck. In the company of a Western woman, a fair-haired woman. Fairchild broke into a run, making his leg bleed again, until he spotted them. He hung back as they meandered through the old city lanes. Jinpa was oblivious, but a couple of times Rose almost made him. She was watching as much as she could while keeping Jinpa close. Fairchild maintained his distance. It was while doing this that he realised they had another shadow.

If it weren't for his persistence, he would easily have passed for a regular East Asian tourist, this man, with his T-shirt and shorts, his sneakers and his backpack. But he was focused, manoeuvring closer then dropping back, looking up and round, eyeing the context as well as the target. He wasn't here merely to observe. While the streets were busy he would find it difficult to close in. He was biding his time, waiting for a chance. Then a chance presented itself. Jinpa wandered off into a side street.

Fairchild had a glimpse of Rose's face, preoccupied, glancing up and down before she turned to follow the Tibetan. From out of sight their shadow appeared and slipped through a gap between buildings. Fairchild followed. Within a messy courtyard, iron steps vibrated: the Chinese man was almost at the top. Fairchild paused in shadow and watched him mount. He was athletic, fast, nimble as he lifted himself onto the flat roof which would give him a clear view down into the street Jinpa and Rose had taken.

Fairchild climbed clumsily, sweating with the pain, using his arms as much as his legs. But he could not match the other man's pace. By the time he reached the top, he already knew he was too slow, too feeble, too late.

Chapter 55

Rose hurried after Jinpa up the narrow street. Something had attracted his attention this way, but she didn't know what.

"Jinpa, are you saying it's been on Nepali television that you're here, in Kathmandu?"

Jinpa looked a little blank. "I suppose so. Is it not amazing how fast the weather changes?"

The sun had just emerged from the thick grey cloudscape that had been drizzling on the city. Jinpa was walking purposefully in the middle of the road, his lifted face bathing in the sunlight. Buildings on either side rose above their heads, the gap between them a brilliant blue, the sun blazing down the middle. With a shock Rose realised that nobody else was around.

"Jinpa." Rose caught up with him and placed her hand on his shoulder. He turned and looked down at it, puzzled. It was inappropriate for a woman to touch a monk, Rose realised. She also realised that she was trying to stop him. She was only here to catch up with Fairchild. That was her priority. But this likeable young man had no idea of the danger he was in. She kept her voice low and urgent. "I think it would be an idea to stay out of sight for a while. And get out of Kathmandu as quickly as you can."

"Why? This is not China. Here people are free."

"Yes. But they could come to find you. They could track you down here."

"And do what? In the middle of a city?" Jinpa smiled indulgently. "You are too afraid, Rose. You should have faith. I know that I have already succeeded. My mission has already begun. There's no time to waste being afraid and hiding. It's a time to be free."

"It wouldn't be for very long," Rose insisted. "You're planning to travel to Dharamsala anyway, aren't you? I'll help you with that. I'll help arrange the coach or whatever it is. I could even come with you."

She hadn't meant to offer that. Jinpa looked at her and laughed, a happy, spontaneous laugh. "You have a kind heart. Maybe you don't always like to admit it, but you do. I am touched by that."

She needed to get him away from here, to somewhere less public. How could she persuade him? Now he was looking up towards the top of the street. He turned away from Rose and started walking. "Oh, look, do you see? Do you not feel it, the significance of this moment? Everything has come together just as it should. It is for us! Now we can really be sure, deep in ourselves, that we are on the right path. All our suffering and loss, it was all to bring us closer, to be shown this! Do you not feel it? It is – overwhelming!"

He talked, maybe to her, maybe to himself, looking up at the sky. Then she saw what he was looking at. A perfect, deeply vibrant rainbow had formed, its base directly in front of them at the top of the street, and its shimmering arc of colour rising above their heads. Jinpa was transfixed. He stood, gazing up, his arms out by his sides. And then Rose saw, in the sharp edge of roofline shadow on the street, what she had almost seen before, what she knew but couldn't place. The shadow of a human shape, there then gone. Someone was up on the roof.

"Jinpa!" He was ten paces ahead of her. She broke into a run and was halfway towards him when a single muffled crack echoed in the narrow street.

Jinpa fell face forward onto the ground.

Chapter 56

The sound was unmistakeable: a bullet fired through a silencer; an assassin's weapon. Rose sprang for cover, flush against the wall directly below the origin of the shot. Another crack echoed. She heard a scrape, a tile or stone being dislodged, above her. She sprinted up the street to the end, keeping close in. She tensed, leaped to cross the street taking it in three strides, then backed up against the wall round the corner out of range. She waited, breathing rapidly: no reaction. She crept forward to peer down the street. Now she could see along the length of the roofs. Against the sky down at the far end a form she recognised was standing, then crouching. She saw Fairchild's profile for an instant, then he was gone. In front of her in shadow on the road another form moved rapidly away from her, one hand elongated unnaturally in silhouette. The sniper, the person who had shot Jinpa, running along the rooftops after Fairchild, weapon still in hand.

She peered into the street. Jinpa lay unmoving on the ground. No one else had appeared. She approached and knelt next to him. Blood was pooling by his head. It was a good shot, a professional hit clean through the back of his skull. She was ready to stem the bleeding, shout for help, offer words of comfort, but it was too late for all that. He had died in that moment.

She needed to act quickly. She dug her hand into his satchel and found his ID papers but nothing else. She patted his clothing for pockets. Nothing. The bundle of photographs he had shown her in the cave was not there.

She looked up at the sound of voices. A cluster of people stood at the top of the street staring in horror. It was not what Jinpa would have wanted, but she could do no more for him, and this fight wasn't over. She left him there, lying in the middle of the street, and took off.

Chapter 57

Fairchild ran, stumbling over roof tiles. As soon as the shooter's gun had turned on him, he was in no doubt. Here was someone tasked to end two lives; Jinpa's and his. The second bullet had passed too close and if he stopped moving the next would kill him. But he was in no condition to outrun the sniper. He had to get off this roof.

At the end of the rooftops, a clutch of aerials and masts trailed cables down the side of the building, pinned to a long metal plate. Fairchild grabbed two of the cables and tugged them sharply. They gave way immediately, coming loose from their aerials and curling into the street below. He grabbed the plate itself and gave it a solid push. It came away from the wall by its top two screws, but the rest held. He shoved it again to separate it from the wall then swung round and levered himself onto it. It held for a few seconds, allowing him to let himself down several metres, before a length of it tore away from the wall, dropping him so abruptly he was almost thrown off. He gripped and hung, dangling. The plate snapped, sending him to the ground from four or five metres above. He landed on his back, metal and cables on top of him. A shockwave of pain immobilised him.

The plate buckled on top of him, once then twice. The sniper was shooting at him from the rooftop. This was not a strong enough shield. He pushed it aside, rolled to his feet and ran. A bullet buried itself in a wall, just missing his heel. He turned a corner and was amongst people in the busy street again. He weaved into the crowd and turned to look up. The sniper's retreating figure was silhouetted on the roof. He wouldn't shoot into a crowd. But once he got down from the roof he would be coming.

The street opened out into a marketplace. Fairchild dodged stalls and carts, moving as quickly as he could. He heard the screaming first. The sniper was sprinting towards him waving his gun. An effective way of clearing a crowd. He was some distance away but gaining fast. Beyond the marketplace the ground started to fall away towards the river. Fairchild dodged into a gateway off the square. Past a turn it led to a steep flight of steps down to the riverbank. He stopped and backed up against a wall. He wanted him this time. If he couldn't get away from the man, he had to stay and fight.

The sniper ran straight through the gateway without looking behind him. Fairchild took aim and fired. In that split second the sniper, having a clear view down to the shoreline, realised Fairchild wasn't in front of him, and turned. The bullet flew past his face. He spun round and raised his weapon. Fairchild's second shot caught the barrel of the sniper's gun as he took aim, which span through the air and clattered on the steps. Fairchild aimed again but the Chinese man ducked, evading the bullet and somehow launching himself directly at him. He landed a punch in Fairchild's wounded side, drawing an inferno of pain. A sharp chop on the wrist saw Fairchild's gun go the same way as the other. The Chinese man went for his neck. They grappled. Fairchild's leg missed a step and he landed heavily and fell, pulling the assassin down as well. They rolled down to the concrete slope leading steeply into the muddy water.

The sniper was on top as they hit the bank, and he rammed Fairchild's head into the ground. Fairchild felt an explosion, momentary blackness. Now the sniper was dragging him. With no warning his face was in the river. He coughed out a mouthful of foul water before going under again, the sniper pressing down on his chest and neck. The water closed over his face, invaded his nose, mouth, throat. His arms thrashed uselessly. He mustered strength to his lower body and thrust upwards. The pressure eased and he lunged for his attacker's neck and face. But it wasn't enough and the assassin swept his hands aside, clutched his throat and pushed his head firmly down. Fairchild fought, his eyes stinging, his lungs tightening, but the man had a grip like steel.

A judder rocked him. The grip weakened. He shot up above the surface coughing, gasping the air. In front of him the sniper sank limp, the back of his head a bloodied mess. At the water's edge stood Rose Clarke, holding a gun by her side, looking at him calmly. Behind her, men were running down the steps shouting. She glanced their way, stowed the gun and set off at a sprint down the riverbank.

Fairchild lay back, hooked the sniper's body by the shoulder and paddled into the main channel, away from the crowds on the riverside who could do nothing but watch. He let the water take them both downriver, seeing bridges passing overhead. Shivering, he could do no more than just enough to keep his mouth above water: the current did the rest. As the river swept into a bend, he let go of the assassin's body, letting it drift down towards the ghats, and struck out for the other side where no crowds were watching. There he pulled himself out of the stinking water and melted away into the city.

Chapter 58

He could still smell the river on him hours later. Washed, stitched, drugged up, in borrowed clothes, the rotten garbage smell was still in his nose, or maybe it was that the whole world stank like that. Two gin and tonics from the minibar hadn't helped. His foot resting on the glass table in front of the window, he had a view through off-white net curtains onto the stepped pavilions of Durbar Square below, but he wasn't looking at it. He swilled his drink and reflected, without generating any comfort. Jinpa was dead. His life's quest had failed. It was Fairchild who had endangered him in the first place, and Fairchild had been unable to protect him. Chu, applying the might of the Chinese state, had prevailed. It shouldn't be a surprise.

A double beep outside heralded the door opening. Walter walked in and stopped on seeing Fairchild. His look of mild surprise quickly evaporated.

"Do help yourself to a drink," he said.

"I understand you wanted to talk." Fairchild didn't move his foot off the table. Walter came over and leaned on the back of the other chair. He'd lost weight since Fairchild had last seen him. That mournful quality he'd always had in his face was emphasised even more now that his cheeks had sunk and the skin around his chin hung that much looser.

"You're looking old, Walter," he said.

"You don't look as though you're in the best of health either, if I might say so."

"I'm touched by your concern."

"We go back a long way, John," said Walter. "Time passes. You're not getting any younger yourself. Are you taking that into account?"

Fairchild removed his foot from the table and placed it on the floor. "I should stay out of trouble, should I? Be a good boy. Do as I'm told. Stop asking awkward questions."

"Try not to get shot or stabbed. Or both. A lot of people would consider that good advice."

"You seem to have an in-depth knowledge of my medical state."

Walter sat down. "Dr Parajuli examined you in the hospital at Dram. You don't recall? She's an excellent physician. You were in quite a bad way, I'm told."

"I suppose I should be flattered that you take such an interest in my welfare. Of course if you really cared, you'd tell me the truth and save me the trouble of having to find out for myself."

Walter sighed. "John, we've been over this so many times I don't know what you think I can say that's any different. I don't know what happened to your parents. I've said it to you a hundred times. I'm telling you everything, John, I really am." Walter's voice took on a rasping quality when he became impatient. It brought to Fairchild's mind so many different scenes: across a kitchen table; in a carpeted office overlooking the Thames; on a dusty airport runway. Walter was right. They went back a long way. Conversations like these had featured far too large in his life.

He placed his glass on the table. "So what do you want to say, then? Why send some woman halfway round the world after me?"

"Some woman? She saved your life, according to Parajuli. If it weren't for Rose Clarke, you'd be dead by the side of the road."

An image came into Fairchild's head of Rose by the riverside, gun in hand, looking straight at him over the water. The Chinese assassin had almost killed him. *You're not getting any younger yourself.* How much of that ugly fight had Rose observed?

"Lucky me," he said. Walter was watching him.

"You don't reply to my emails. What am I supposed to do if I want to speak to you?"

"How about nothing?" Fairchild heard his own grumpy adolescent self. Walter turned and got himself a miniature bottle of Scotch from the minibar. He sat down and cracked it open.

"I can't keep them at bay forever, you know," he said. "I'm not going to be here ad infinitum. As you said, I'm getting older. How will things be for you, John, when I'm no longer around?"

"Oh, I see. You're saving me again. From the others, the ones who really don't like me. You're the one who's on my side."

Walter took a swig of Scotch straight from the bottle. "I am more on your side," he said, "than Marcus Salisbury. You know who he is, don't you?"

"Of course I know who he is."

"He never liked your parents, was convinced of the worst about them. He's not the only one of that mind, is he? Of course he's decided he doesn't like you either. We know there are leaks, John. Damaging leaks. On strategically important operations. From high up. Salisbury has your name in the frame."

"He thinks I'm giving away British secrets?"

"Not giving away, John. Selling. He thinks you're selling them. It's what you do, isn't it? Extract information for money?"

"I see. And who does he think I'm getting this information from?"

"That's what he's sent me to find out."

Fairchild shifted his leg, which was hurting. "Sorry to disappoint, but it isn't me. You need to look elsewhere."

"Naturally, that's what I said. But he doesn't believe me. Come on, John, we both know you have people on the inside who feed you information from time to time. How did you know Rose Clarke's real name?"

"She told me."

"No she didn't. You told her."

"I wouldn't need to know that in the first place," he said petulantly, "if you hadn't sent her after me. I'm looking after my own interests, Walter. Watching my own back That's all. If you want me to be more of a friend of the Service, start treating me like one."

"You know, I think that could happen," said Walter. "But you need to make the first move. Come to London. I'll set you up to talk to Salisbury. We can persuade him. Others will speak for you. Not everyone hates you, you know that. Come home, John. It's about time."

He was starting to sound wheedling. Needy, almost. Fairchild hadn't been to London for nineteen years. The UK wasn't his home. The UK had taken his home, his family. He'd been on his own ever since.

"That's an overwhelming offer," he said. "Not everyone hates me. I'm on the verge of tears."

"You should think about it."

"We're not all like Rose Clarke, you know. Desperate enough to do anything you want to get back in. You must love having these people jumping to your tune again and again. Why she can't see right through it all, I really don't know."

Someone rapped sharply on the door.

"Perhaps you can ask her," said Walter.

Rose was at the door. At that news a piece dropped into place somewhere inside, with the click of something long in the making firmly and permanently completed. The final coming-together of what had been forming since that night in Hong Kong. A full realisation of what Rose

Clarke was to him: lithe, magnificent, exacting, furious like a storm. The thought of her consumed him. Yet something in him unravelled knowing she was outside the door, that those eyes would be looking at him, seeing who he was, knowing the things he'd done.

"Don't look so surprised," Walter was saying. "Most people do knock first. I suppose you think that's terribly conventional." He put down his almost-empty Scotch and got to his feet. He looked down at Fairchild for a moment. "You really do think you're better, don't you?"

It wasn't the worst thing Walter had ever said to him, not by a long chalk. But this time he sounded more contemptuous than Fairchild could remember. This time it hit him like a hammer. But he knew how to stop it showing. The old man's face was cold as he turned away from him to get the door.

Chapter 59

Walter smelled of whisky. He paused for a moment before letting her in. The expression on his face was dark, turbulent. He greeted her as if surfacing from a great depth. The room was a bog standard mid-market hotel room with a passable view of the historic main square. The window was open and a dirty net curtain was fanning slightly, caught in the air conditioning. On the table was an empty glass and several miniature bottles of spirits. Rose sat in the armchair.

"Enjoying some company?" she asked.

"Enjoy wasn't quite the word," said Walter. "Our mutual friend was here. It looks as though he didn't want to stay."

"Fairchild was here?"

"Just now. Sitting where you are." Walter's gaze turned to the open window. Rose got up and looked out. In the two storeys between the window and the ground, an elaborate ornamental balcony could have provided a means of dropping down, if you had enough time and didn't have a leg injury. She stood and scanned the crowds in the square below. Something caught her eye, almost out of sight on the far side of the square, but when she looked again she couldn't see what it was.

She turned back to Walter. "So you got your meeting, then."

"Yes, I suppose I did." Walter had picked up the Scotch bottle. "I can't say it went very well, I'm afraid."

"Well, I'm sorry to hear that." She paused. Walter slowly unscrewed the cap off the bottle and took a swig, making her prickle with impatience. It was as if he'd forgotten her career was on the line. "John is unwilling to cooperate at this time, it seems. He denies any involvement with selling secrets."

"Do you believe him?"

"He knows much more than he should, naturally. In that sense he's a security risk. But he wouldn't wilfully betray British agents. I do believe that."

"I see." Walter's faith was evident. Fairchild certainly had loyalty to his friends: his protectiveness towards Jinpa spoke to that. But he held a lot of anger. She'd been a victim of that in Beijing. Walter wasn't taking Fairchild's bitterness into account. "But Marcus Salisbury doesn't?"

"That's right. And John doesn't seem willing at this time to try and persuade him otherwise. He perhaps doesn't realise how difficult this might make things for him. In the past he has from time to time been given a free pass."

"Because of the way he lost his parents."

"Indeed. But that was a long time ago and the new generation isn't setting much store by that these days. There's a lot more going on now than Cold War leftovers. It will increasingly be the view that risk should be minimised, whatever that entails." He sat back in his chair. "The Kathmandu head of station told me earlier that someone shot a Tibetan monk in the street. A marksman, by the sound of it."

Rose confirmed the story and told him what happened to the Chinese sniper. Walter's eyebrows raised. "You killed him? Not Fairchild?"

"Oh yes. The other guy had the better of him. He didn't mention that, then?"

"No," said Walter, "he didn't. Did anybody see you?"

"Maybe. From a distance. I legged it, naturally. Chucked the gun in the river further down. Laid low for a while, cleaned myself up and came here."

Walter's eyes dropped to the table as he thought things through. "If you think you got away cleanly," he said, "perhaps you should stay on here for a while. Don't be in too much of a hurry to leave."

"What for? It's all over, isn't it? You got your meeting. Jinpa's dead. Fairchild won't hang around. Jinpa's the only reason he came here."

"I can't give up on him, Rose. He's not listening now, but I expect he's upset about this young friend of his. We must keep reaching out. We must try again, my dear."

Rose shook her head. "No, Walter. That wasn't the deal. You wanted a meeting with him. You've had the meeting. I've done what you asked. You said you could get me back in. You're going to, aren't you?"

Walter put his hands on his knees. He sat for a moment as if examining the backs of his hands. Eventually his eyes lifted again. "Do you have any indication at all, Rose, of what he's planning to do next? Where he might go now?"

"No! Of course I don't! Why would he tell me that?"

"And you really can't say what this Jinpa boy told him about his past?"

"I have absolutely no idea, Walter. Fairchild detests MI6. He doesn't trust any of us. I represent the organisation that ruined his life. I was sent to spy on him, for God's sake. Of course he's not going to tell me that stuff. This is really going nowhere. I just don't see what else you think I can do here."

She was aware that she'd raised her voice. Walter spoke soothingly. "Well, of course, things have been rather challenging…"

"Challenging? Trekking after him across the Himalayas? You think?"

"And you've done enormously well, Rose, and I thank you for that." Great. She'd won the egg and spoon race again. She made a tangible effort to calm down. "But there is a lot at stake here and it's clear our work is not done."

"He told you he's not passing on secrets. You believe him, you said. Go back to London and tell Salisbury that. They're looking in the wrong place."

"Sadly, it will take more than me to convince him, Rose. Fairchild needs to agree to be a part of this. To cooperate in some small way. If he is not, I fear for the consequences."

"For him?"

"Yes. For him."

A silence fell, during which memories flooded into Rose's head. She and Alastair excitedly comparing notes on some particularly gruelling training exercise. Landing in Algiers, the shock and strangeness of her first foray there. The dazed look on Tihana's face that last time they spoke. All of that had turned into this, an old man's attempts to right some perceived wrong done in the past. She'd got stuck in some kind of backwater: she'd been paddling like mad to get back but was making no headway. This wasn't her battle. It was hard, this kind of work, and she loved it, but it had to matter. She couldn't bring herself to put her life on the line for this any longer, or other people's.

"I'm sorry, Walter. I'm not doing this any more. This is all about things that happened a long time ago. I joined the Service to help protect my country from threats, threats in the here and now. I took on this job because that's how you sold it to me. I'm really not interested in running round the world as part of some internal vendetta."

She stood up. "I've done what you asked. I think you should honour our agreement. But if you're not going to, that's it, I'm afraid."

"Well, of course, if that's what you want," he said, "but I think it might be worth one more approach."

"Walter, I've just said. It's over. Are you going to give me my job back?"

Walter's eyes held a glint of steel. "Just give it one last try. See if you can find out what his plans are."

"And how do I do that exactly? I just ask him, I suppose. After I've tracked him down."

"You've tracked him down before."

"Look. You didn't get anywhere with him. Neither did I."

"Didn't you? He told you all about this friend of his. And he ultimately came to see me. He didn't have to do that, did he?"

"What are you trying to say, Walter?"

"As I said to you before, Rose, I've known him a long time." His voice was low and grainy. "I've learned to read his responses, although he thinks no one can. From time to time I can pick up on his attitudes. His feelings."

"His feelings?"

"You may have more influence on him than you think, my dear."

It took a second for Rose to comprehend what he was suggesting. "That's nonsense. I haven't influenced him at all. He does his own thing for his own purposes." Walter was way off the mark. Was he losing his grip on reality? Maybe that was what happened when you carried on doing this job for too long. If Walter knew what Fairchild had done to her in Beijing, he'd never entertain such an idea. Friendships notwithstanding, Fairchild was ultimately a mercenary motivated by self-interest, nothing more.

"Well, have it your own way. But I'm asking you to make one last approach. Before you leave Kathmandu. See what happens. If that yields nothing, fine. It's up to you, Rose."

Another silence filled the room, twice as long as the last. Rose shook her head again.

"No," she said. "I'm sorry, Walter. I think you're just trying to string me along. I won't take the bait. I'm out."

Walter stood still for a moment, like a statue. He took in a deep breath. "Well, you know where I am," he said, back to his normal tone. "There's something else you should see. Another piece of hot news from our local colleagues. Let's think. Yes, I expect it'll be on CNN by now."

He got up and moved surprisingly quickly across the room to pick up the remote control and flick through channels on the wall-mounted television. CNN was broadcasting a chaotic press conference, flashbulbs going off, questions being shouted. Behind a makeshift podium stood a number of shaven-headed monks in bright orange and yellow attire, including an older man in glasses with distinctive features and a wide smile. A famous smile.

"Is that the Dalai Lama?"

"It is indeed, my dear."

The Dalai Lama was speaking with some passion, words of hope and joy. Tears shone on his face. No wonder the cameras were snapping. She peered at the young man standing next to him, bulky and uncertain, his eyes down. The Dalai Lama had his hand on the younger monk's shoulder. Rose recognised him.

"That's Yonten. Jinpa's friend from the monastery. What's he doing there?"

"He's in Dharamsala. With the Dalai Lama. Who has just recognised him as the true Panchen Lama."

"But he's not. He's not the one. Jinpa was the one. Yonten was just his friend."

"Not according to the Dalai Lama, Rose. He is saying he has photographic proof."

"The photographs! Jinpa had them. He showed them to me in the cave. But they weren't on him when he was shot."

"No. Because this Yonten fellow took them with him to Dharamsala and is claiming the title himself. He must have abandoned your friend Jinpa en route."

"Jinpa said he'd gone. I thought he meant that he hadn't survived his injuries. This makes no sense." Rose felt light-headed. She stared at the screen, transfixed by the triumphant emotion in the Dalai Lama's face. "The Chinese are going to hate this," she said.

"Yes, I'm afraid they haven't responded terribly well. They're claiming he's a fake, of course. It's likely to become known that the person who shot Jinpa here in Nepal was sent by the Chinese authorities. That was all for nothing. So, you see, things have turned out all right for our Tibetan friends after all."

Rose felt colour rise in her face. She pictured the young man she walked with through the streets, his passion, his curiosity, his laugh. All his studying, his purpose, the sacrifices he had made, all of that was lost. "How can you say that? Jinpa was killed. He was betrayed by his own. How is that all right?"

Suddenly she had to get out of there. Walter now seemed transfixed by the press conference, remote in one hand, whisky bottle in the other. She barely even said anything as she turned and left the room. It occurred to her that this would probably be her last interaction with anyone from SIS. No bad thing, she told herself as she slammed the door and ran from the place. No bad thing at all.

Chapter 60

Rose was down by the ghats again, where she'd seen Jinpa that last time. There was no wind. Black smoke hovered and settled over the murky water, suspended in an overcast sky as the white-clad mourners tended to their pyres of wood and flesh and bone. This is where things end. This is how things end, how life and light and colour and hope are burned away to ashes, dregs of black and grey, while the smoke gradually clears to nothing.

She'd stayed in Kathmandu a few days after all, not on Walter's advice but because she didn't want to face the reality that this was all over. She'd just phoned Alastair. He didn't believe her, at least not to start with. You can't quit, he said. You don't quit. That's not you. Well I am, she said. I'm done, and I mean it. After the call she'd thrown the phone down and come here.

She was sitting on wide concrete steps leading down to the brown water. She wrapped her skirt around her legs and breathed in sandalwood. She felt a presence beside her and looked up. Fairchild stood, his eyes on the pyre in front of them. He eased himself down next to her without saying anything. He looked washed-out and faded.

"How did you know I was here?" she asked. His eyes rested on her for a moment, as grey as the sky, then they turned to the smoking ghat again. It didn't really matter. It was odd, how elusive Fairchild was when finding him mattered so much. Now that it didn't matter at all, he just showed up.

They both watched as the mourner gently stoked the burning logs. "Did you hear about Yonten?" she asked. He nodded. "I can't believe he'd do that. They all seemed so loyal."

"You think Yonten betrayed Jinpa?" His voice was slower and deeper than she remembered it.

"Don't you?"

Fairchild stared at the smoke for a few more seconds. "The Rinpoche was a clever man. It was his idea in the first place to switch the boys so that the Chinese took away the wrong one. He was the only one not to underestimate what the Chinese were capable of. He used to tell Jinpa that secrecy was the only weapon they had. I didn't realise that he felt the need to use it so effectively on those so close to him."

Rose stared at him. "The *Rinpoche* used Jinpa as a decoy? The Rinpoche knew all along that Yonten was the Panchen Lama?"

"The monastery takes in two boys from the same region of Tibet at the same time, the same age. There's nothing unusual about that. Who's to know which one was a significant reincarnate, and which one was just a boy from a nearby village? Jinpa told me that Yonten and he used to have lessons together, but Yonten didn't have the same interest in learning as he did. Maybe when the Rinpoche saw how the boys were developing, he took an opportunity to build in another layer of protection for the real Panchen Lama. Clearly favouring one of them, giving him special coaching and so on. If their inner circle had been compromised, the suspicions of the Chinese would have fallen on the wrong boy."

"But Jinpa was absolutely certain. He knew who he was."

"He had faith. That's what he'd always been told. The safest way was for the Rinpoche not to tell anybody, let people play out the roles he had given them. Until he absolutely had to tell."

Rose retraced events in her mind. "He must have told Yonten in the mountains, then. When he realised he was dying. It was the Rinpoche who told Yonten to leave with the photographs once they were over the border, and get to the Dalai Lama on his own. That must have been quite a shock for Yonten."

"Yonten would have passed through Kathmandu before Jinpa arrived, but nobody spotted him. Everyone was looking for two monks together."

She paused, looking up at the sky. "I'm glad Jinpa never knew. He died thinking that he'd succeeded."

"He did succeed." Fairchild was looking up as well. "He diverted the Chinese away from the real person. While he was being interviewed on television, Yonten could see himself clear all the way to Dharamsala. Jinpa was an excellent decoy." His voice held a note of bitterness.

Rose thought of her conversation with Jinpa in the cave. "All he wanted was to play out his role. And if you're right I suppose he did. He enabled Yonten to reach the Dalai Lama. That wouldn't have happened without him. It wasn't the role he thought he was playing, but he fulfilled it brilliantly. The Panchen Lama lives on."

Fairchild eyed her. "I'm surprised you take any of that talk seriously."

"I didn't say I believed it. But he did, and it inspired him. Is that a bad thing?"

He didn't answer. They both watched the smoke for a while.

"You should probably avoid China for a while," she said.

He shrugged. "Chu will be discredited. They'll paint her as a renegade operating without proper authority. That's how they can avoid taking responsibility for ordering a hit in a foreign country."

"You don't think she'll come after you again?"

"Maybe."

"And the Wong Kai?"

"I'll drop in on Darcy Tang and proffer my apologies. Perhaps there's something I can offer that will help to smooth things over."

"You think they're just going to let you walk in?"

"I think it's worth a try."

"Well, if I'd known how indifferent you were to your own survival, I might not have bothered saving your life. Twice. Three times, in fact."

She'd managed to generate amusement, something on his face resembling his expression when they'd first met in Hong Kong. "How do you figure that?"

"Getting you to the hospital in Dram. Stirring up your friend Zack to spring you from the prison in Chengdu. Shooting the sniper before he drowned you in the river. And that's not to mention that you'd never have made it to the cave in the mountains without me."

"After you'd murdered my guide and stabbed me in the leg, you mean."

"Well, maybe that one gets cancelled out, but the other three stand."

"And there's the Wong Kai."

"It doesn't sound like you're particularly worried about them."

"I guess I owe you."

"I wouldn't worry about it. I'm going home." The amusement left his face. "I'm out. I told Walter earlier. You were right before. They're not going to give me my job back. They're just stringing me along. I don't want to live like that. So I'll find something else to do with my time. Imagine that! You'll never have to set eyes on me again."

He blinked and looked away. It started to rain very gently. Neither of them moved. The grey of the concrete steps spotted and darkened. The pyre crackled and the smoke thickened.

"What will you do?" His voice sounded distant.

"I don't know. Something normal. It can't be that hard. Millions of people do it."

"Back in the UK?"

"I suppose so. It's as good a place as any to start."

They sat silently while the rain pattered. She pulled a scarf over her shoulders. "Don't you ever feel like giving up on all of this too, Fairchild? It can't be easy jumping from place to place all the time. You could settle somewhere, make a life for yourself instead of chasing ghosts round the world." His mouth twisted into a half smile. "Something funny? Don't tell me, that's exactly what Walter said. Well, he has a point."

He started to speak, then stopped, then started again. "I suppose Walter told you all about the night my parents disappeared?"

"A little."

"We'd been playing a card game. With forfeits. Riddles and puzzles, that kind of thing. I lost. I wasn't very good at losing. I had a tantrum and ran off. When I got back an hour later, they were gone. The first thing I did was search the flat for clues. I thought I was supposed to go out and look for them."

"You thought it was a game?"

"It was the kind of thing they did. They would turn even everyday things into a test, pushing me all the time. It's as if they were trying to prepare me for something."

"Like what?"

"They never got around to telling me that." He rubbed his face then shook his head as if clearing a memory. "Jinpa met a Russian. That's what he wanted to tell me. An old Buddhist monk called Dimitri who used to run with the mafia in Moscow. He knows what happened that night."

"So what did happen?"

Fairchild shook his head. "I'd have to go to Russia to find that out. Track him down, out east somewhere."

"It sounds like a very long shot."

"That's all I've got. It's the best lead I've had in years. Ever, in fact."

"So you'll go?"

"That's what I do. Maybe that's what I'm supposed to do, I don't know."

The rain had stopped already. Rose absorbed what Fairchild had said. He'd just told her exactly what he was going to do next, precisely the information Walter wanted from her. He had given her the means to go and ask for her job back. This didn't have to be over. If he were telling her the truth, she could still be back in. If Walter were to be believed. If she still wanted it.

He got up, struggling a little, his injuries still evident. "I wanted to say…" he said, and hesitated.

"Yes?"

"What I did in Beijing. That was a terrible thing that I did to you. I'm truly sorry."

Rose made an effort to mask her surprise. Some colour had invaded the pallor of Fairchild's face. "That's not something you do very often, is it?" she said.

"Spike people's drinks? No, it really isn't."

"I meant, apologise."

He was about to say something else, but at that instant the cloud suddenly cleared. Bright sunlight illuminated the riverbank and warmed her face. The river's surface rippled with a sudden wind. A gust swept over the pyre and blew the thick smoke directly into them. Particles swirled and invaded Rose's hair and scarf. Her eyes stung. She screwed them shut, waiting for the smoke to pass. When she opened them again, the pyre was almost burned through.

"Why did you tell me that?" she asked. "About your parents? About the Russian?"

There was no answer. Fairchild was no longer sitting next to her. She looked behind, up and down the river. No sign of him. It was a familiar feeling.

Beyond the smoke, in the sky the other side of the river, the faintest of rainbows appeared in the sky. The pyre was finally extinguished. The mourner was turning over some fragments of material, the orange and yellow of a traditional Tibetan monk's clothing. All that was left of Jinpa, all in the material world anyway. Maybe he was still here somewhere, up in the sky or in the eyes of a child in a faraway land. Who could prove otherwise?

She got up and began a slow, meandering walk up the river.

The Clarke and Fairchild Readers' Club

Members of the Clarke and Fairchild Readers' Club receive exclusive offers and updates. Claim a free copy of *Trade Winds*, a short story featuring John Fairchild and set in Manila. It takes place before Reborn, and before Fairchild and Clarke meet. Another short story, *Crusaders*, is set in Croatia and features Rose Clarke's fall from grace from the British intelligence service. These stories are not available on Amazon but are free for members to download. Members will also receive updates and offers directly from the author, and previews of new releases in the Clarke and Fairchild series. You can unsubscribe at any time. Visit www.tmparris.com to sign up!

Reviews are very important to independent authors. If you could take the time to review *Reborn* on Amazon, it would be much appreciated and provide valuable feedback to the author and other potential readers.

Author note

The Panchen Lama is a real person. In *Reborn* I have hypothesised the switch between young boys and the real persona's escape from captivity. *The Search for the Panchen Lama* by Isabel Hilton tells the full and real story of how he was identified, the role of the current Dalai Lama and his fate since. No one knows his current whereabouts although Amnesty International repeatedly asks the Chinese government for information about him and his family since they were seized back in 1995 when Gedhun Choekyi Nyima was just six years old. This makes him the world's youngest political prisoner, assuming he is still alive.

The journey across the Himalayan plateau and events on the Nangpa La glacier are inspired by *Murder in the Himalayas* by Jonathan Green, the story of how a thirteen-year-old nun was shot in the back and killed on the pass by Chinese border police. I have taken immense liberties with geography: in the book the arduous journey of the refugees took a full twelve days and makes Rose and Fairchild's suffering seem like a walk in the park.

You'll struggle to find Dram on a map as these days it's known by its Chinese name Zhangmu, which I find less evocative. Jinpa is unlikely to have been wandering the streets of Kathmandu as he did: real-life Tibetan refugees were confined to a compound. This might have been to keep them safe from errant Chinese security forces, but perhaps more likely so that the Nepali government could be sure that they passed through the country to India and didn't stay in Nepal and place further burden on this already impoverished country. I've gone for the slightly phonetic spelling of Tashilunpo, which might be more commonly rendered into Latin script as Tashilhunpo or Tashi Lhunpo.

Clarke and Fairchild will next meet in Russia, and in subsequent novels wherever there are interesting political stories to tell. Over the course of the series the mystery of Fairchild's parents will eventually be resolved. My inspiration for Rose is the Judi Dench interpretation of M in the later Bond films, and an imagining of what this M would have been like earlier in life when she was in the field. Some of the other characters will make appearances in later books: Zack, Alastair and Walter, in particular.

The Clarke and Fairchild series is written in British English.

About the author

My name's Tracey Parris and I live in Belper, a town near the Peak District National Park in the middle of the UK. I've been a market researcher and data geek, an English language teacher, a player of the flute, trumpet and Irish whistle (not at the same time), a marathon runner, a baker of fine cakes and a local councillor. I've been lucky enough to have travelled a lot, particularly in Asia and Europe, but I'm not done yet! I've been writing since 2011 and had a couple of short stories published online. The Clarke and Fairchild series, my first self-publishing venture, is a result of my fascination with international travel and the moral ambiguities of the world of politics. I had the idea for the character of John Fairchild in a moment of homesickness wandering the streets of Beijing, when I really, really wished someone was around who spoke the language!

See more about me on www.tmparris.com, or email me on hello@tmparris.com.

Printed in Poland
by Amazon Fulfillment
Poland Sp. z o.o., Wrocław
22 July 2021

28b8fe2d-4eb4-4c3e-92c0-05d2d1c33723R01